Make th

H. A. Robinson
x

CHASING *THE* Sunrise

H A ROBINSON

CONTENTS

Prologue	1
Chapter 1	3
Chapter 2	11
Chapter 3	23
Chapter 4	33
Chapter 5	45
Chapter 6	63
Chapter 7	77
Chapter 8	91
Chapter 9	105
Chapter 10	123
Chapter 11	133
Chapter 12	157
Chapter 13	177
Chapter 14	187
Chapter 15	207
Chapter 16	229
Chapter 17	239
Chapter 18	249
Chapter 19	261
Chapter 20	269
Chapter 21	279
Acknowledgments	287
About the Author	291

Copyright© CHASING THE SUNRISE 2018 H.A. Robinson All rights reserved.

Cover design by
Eleanor Lloyd-Jones, Schmidt's Author Services

Editing by
Eleanor Lloyd-Jones and Mike Ross

Formatted by
Tammy Clarke

No part of this book may be reproduced without written consent from the author, except that of small quotations used in critical reviews and promotions via blogs.

Chasing the Sunrise is a work of fiction. Names, characters, businesses, places, events and incidents are either the products of the author's imagination or used in a fictitious manner. Any resemblance to actual persons, living or dead, or actual events is purely coincidental.

For Suzie

Who loved when I didn't deserve it.

PROLOGUE

Childhood is simple.

You go through life thinking that one day, when you become that elusive thing called 'grown up', everything will somehow be the way it ought to be. You watch the adults around you going about their business, running their lives as though it's no big deal—as if being expected to take care of your own life, wholly without reference to anybody more senior, isn't the scariest thing in the world—and you think, sure, how hard can it be?

You see your parents with their mortgage and white picket fence, their two point four children and maybe even a dog if they're lucky, and think that it all just happens—that the world just waits for you to turn eighteen and then throws all that stuff at you. Like it's just that easy.

It never even occurs to you when you're a kid, using jumpers for goalposts and playing with toy cars, that the things your parents have might not be for you. You never think about the possibility of being different from other people. You just assume that boy meets girl, boy likes girl, boy falls in love with girl, boy asks girl to marry him, girl has babies, and they all live happily ever after behind their white picket fence, complete with dog, and maybe a rabbit or a goldfish.

I didn't know until I fell for my best friend that all that stuff wasn't going to be for me.

CHAPTER ONE

The third stair from the bottom had creaked for as long as I could remember. Then there were the old, rusted hinges on the front door that betrayed you the moment it swung open beyond forty-five degrees. The plush carpet in the hallway, however, effectively masked any heavy footsteps that might have slipped past my long since perfected ability to creep around without being heard.

Over the years, I'd made an art form out of sneaking from the house at all hours of the day and night. Sometimes, to avoid my dad's dignitary visitors, and sometimes merely to get out of the house where I had to leave myself at the door and slip into the skin of somebody I didn't recognise.

Inside the walls of the house, I was Thomas Williams: good, loyal son, a credit to his father, always respectful of the rules even at the expense of his own happiness.

Outside, there was an element of freedom.

When I woke painfully early each morning, the itching started right away: a slow bubbling beneath my skin that built and built until the need to tear myself free of everything that was 'me' couldn't be ignored anymore.

Sunrise had become my absolution, a rebirth of sorts. Each day was a new opportunity, a fresh start, another chance to get it right—a chance to somehow let go of yesterday's mistakes and let the dawn light catapult me into something better.

There was a moment each day, right before the first threads of gold hit the horizon when the world was still at its darkest and everything around me seemed to hold its breath, waiting, the air shimmering with anticipation of the hope the new day would bring.

And it was that hope that dragged me from my bed each morning and had me skipping over the creaky stair and slipping through the barely open front door to pull in my first gasping breaths of unstifled air of the day.

Today, first day nerves had me wound even tighter than usual. A vice had clamped itself so tightly around my throat that I wasn't sure how enough oxygen could possibly make it through. I was as ready as I could be. I'd even channeled my inner Elliot Peterson and done a bit of reading over the summer, albeit not as much as I probably ought to have done. However, no amount of reading could prepare me for the fact I'd be thrust back into constant contact with the very person I'd been avoiding like the plague all summer. It turned out, though, that the old adage of absence making the heart grow fonder had stood the test of time for a reason. And that reason came in the exact size and shape of my best friend, Luke Chang.

I'd hoped that keeping myself busy with some studying, gardening and swimming would give me some distance and keep my mind occupied enough to move on and get over the infatuation that had made me miserable for the entire final year of high school. In reality, though, while I did keep busy, my chosen activities weren't nearly mind-consuming enough to keep my thoughts away from the myriad of things I wanted to avoid. And so, I had spent hours at a time digging through textbooks or dirt while unwanted thoughts crashed and collided around my mind.

I didn't even like books that much. They were Abbi's thing, and she was God only knew where, doing God only knew what with the boy she'd once given up hope of ever seeing her the way she desperately needed him to. Perhaps their story ought to have given me hope, but I wasn't naive enough to believe that particular lightning would strike twice in the same place. Colwich was a small town, and one fairytale was all we were likely to get.

I was happy for them—I was—but, God, I missed them.

The summer had dragged on interminably with them gone while I battled to keep my family happy without losing myself along the way. I couldn't pretend to have been especially successful. Most days when I looked in the mirror, I wasn't even sure who the guy staring back at me was any more. I had been torn in different directions for so long now that I couldn't tell where I ended and everybody else began.

My dad wanted me to be part of his picture-perfect family, paragons of all that was good and pure, stalwarts of the town he set so much store by, and heir to his legacy of perfection.

Luke wanted me to be one of the lads, a best mate he could use as a wingman while picking up the latest in a long line of girls he could spend a single night with before moving on to the next.

Mr. Keane—my high school maths teacher—wanted me to study advanced maths and do 'great things' in the field, like I was his number robot, destined to spend my life solving equations and staring at screens.

Sometimes, it seemed as though the only person who wanted me to be completely and wholeheartedly myself was Abbi, and she wasn't here. I would never admit to her, or myself, how much I lived for the postcards that regularly dropped onto my doormat.

With the weight of everybody else's expectations curling my shoulders inwards, I silently slipped from the house as normal, hopping from stepping stone to stepping stone through the gravel of the driveway, then hoiking my bag up higher on my back the moment I hit the main road.

The air still held that early morning chill that would begin to break the moment the sun's rays split the sky in two. A few overachieving birds were already twittering away to one another, probably discussing the crazy guy who was sneaking around before the sun came up for yet another day.

By the time I reached my usual destination, the rest of the birds were in full chorus, the air pierced by their morning song as I crouched down at the water's edge and trailed my fingers through it.

This wasn't my place really. It was theirs—Abbi and Elliot's—but I didn't think they'd mind me keeping it warm for them. After all, so many pieces of my life were borrowed from anywhere and everywhere else now. Why not steal their special place, too? This was the place I felt closest to my friends, the only people who knew and accepted all of me, or as much as I'd ever shown to anybody else, anyway.

As the cool water chilled my skin, and the light began to crest across the far shore, I could almost hear the two of them laughing and joking, teasing each other in that way only they could get away with. They were the only people I knew who said 'I love you' with insults.

Turning my face to the growing morning light, I let my eyes fall closed—the sun painting the lids in bright pink just like the sky—and felt my usual surge of optimism. This was the day everything would change. It was a new start, a new college, new classmates and the possibility of a new me. An authentic me with no borrowed parts or painted masks to hide behind.

This was the day the rest of my life would begin and I wasn't going to waste it on impossible dreams.

After taking the longest shower ever and eating my Cheerios one hoop at a time, it was still too early for college, but I left anyway, unable to stomach the assessing expression on my dad's face as he talked about Delilah, the daughter of one of the town councillors, who would apparently be visiting with her mum that evening. I was, of course, expected to be nice. Like if he hadn't warned me, I would have crapped on their shoes or sworn in their faces. I didn't dislike his colleagues in the slightest. I just had no interest in being forced to socialise with them. I strongly suspected I'd have little or nothing in common with somebody named *Delilah,* but I would show up like a good little boy, make nice with the privileged strangers and then attempt to sleep for a few hours before doing it all again the next day.

It was the hope in Dad's eyes that broke me each time he talked about the latest girl he wanted me to make nice with—that unwavering belief that if he could just find the right one, he could 'fix' me. It was the way he looked between my brother and me wistfully, never voicing it but always quietly wishing I could have turned out more like him. He couldn't hide a single thing; it was all written plainly on his face. I was a straight A student who had never been in trouble a day in my life, but he would still have happily traded me in for my brother, who had been a C average student at best, complete with his caution for shoplifting, his apartment in the city, and his perfect girlfriend.

I walked to the college the long way round, taking the path along the river—my shoes scuffing up the dirt as I walked—simultaneously wanting to put off my first sighting of Luke, and wanting it over and done with so I could get on with the rest of the day.

I hoped it had been long enough since I'd seen him that I wouldn't react to him in the same way anymore. Maybe now I could see him with all his different girls hanging off him and remain somehow indifferent.

This was the hope the sunrise gave me every day.

It took precisely thirteen minutes and twenty-six seconds for that hope to die.

CHAPTER TWO

It didn't take me long to locate the coffee machine in the common room when I arrived over an hour before the day was due to begin. As far as I was concerned, coffee was the very essence of life. I'd discovered strong, Italian coffee the day I'd roamed into Nonna's home, and I hadn't looked back since. The stuff from this particular machine was a poor imitation in reality, but it still contained the required amount of caffeine to bring me back to life after so little sleep.

I was just about human enough to consider exploring the college when the bright red double doors burst open to a cacophony of sound that had my eyes swivelling from the life-giving nectar and meeting directly with those of my maybe-ex-maybe-not best friend, Luke.

God, those eyes...

They were such a dark shade of brown you almost couldn't make out where the iris met the pupil, and framed by his amazing honey coloured skin, the effect was mind-blowing—a sentiment obviously shared by the giggling girl under his casually draped arm. A giggling girl I was all too familiar with.

I wanted to hate him for being so damn perfect.

I wanted to hate him for going there with the vapid shrew who had hurt Abbi so badly and almost convinced Elliot to give up on his dream of being a doctor in favour of supplying her with her platinum hair dye and false nails a few years earlier.

I wanted to hate him for not even noticing that we'd barely spoken over the summer.

But hate, I suspected, wasn't the emotion that made my stomach flip over and my chest tighten whenever he was in the vicinity. It wasn't hate that made my head spin and my eyes refuse to look anywhere else in a room he occupied. And it definitely wasn't hate that kept me awake at night, thinking about the things that could have been if I hadn't fallen for somebody so utterly and completely unobtainable.

Luke Chang was perfect.

He was beautiful, funny, charismatic and intelligent. He was also straight. But try telling that to my heart.

Annika had apparently spent the summer working hard to become even more beautiful. She had the kind of tan that people paid stupid money for in salons, her hair had been bleached even brighter blonde by the sun, and if I'd been the kind of guy who noticed these things, I might even have said her boobs had got bigger. Out of loyalty to Abbi, I forced my eyes from Luke's for the shortest moment in order to cast a disparaging look of hate in her direction before turning back to him with accusation and disappointment battling their way free from my expression.

Of all the girls in town, he had to walk in groping that one.

Turning my gaze reluctantly back to my coffee, I blew on it, sending the steam erupting from the surface swirling around.

"He lives!" Luke called out, his voice sending my heart thundering in my chest and my hand tightening around the flimsy plastic cup enough to send scorching hot coffee spilling over the sides. "Thought you'd either died or left the country. What gives?"

He slid easily into the bench seat across from me and scooted across to make room for Annika, who joined him but never let her eyes roam anywhere near mine as I looked up at them both.

"Busy summer," I lied in a mumble, taking a sip of coffee just for something to occupy me as my stomach churned.

He kicked back in the seat, somehow making it look comfortable enough to lift his feet onto the table and cross them with his arms propping up his head. He had that way only supremely confident people had of making himself look at home anywhere. I half admired and half hated him for it.

"Doing what?"

What had I been doing? Moping... Swimming... A bit more moping. Gardening. Studying. I hadn't exactly made the best use of the long summer. I could have got a job, or travelled the world like my friends, but instead, I'd stayed in Colwich and spent the time hoping for and yet avoiding contact from the guy sitting opposite me now, questioning me accusingly as though he didn't have the ability to pick up a phone.

"Just the usual stuff," I finally threw out, hoping that would somehow assuage whatever curiosity he might have had. "You been up to much?"

God, could this conversation be any more awkward?

"Nah, not much really. Just chilling mostly."

Ouch.

That hurt more fiercely than a punch to the gut. He'd been doing nothing all summer and he hadn't once thought to check in or hang out.

I didn't have a leg to stand on, of course. I'd been just as negligent of our friendship, typing out a million messages then deleting them and staying away in the hope of shaking off this ridiculous crush. In my experience, proximity always, *always* provided a breeding ground for more and more feelings. Avoidance, however, didn't seem to be working either.

How had things become so awkward between us? Granted, we'd never exactly been the kinds of friends who spilled their hearts out to each other or talked about things much deeper than the latest series on Netflix, but we'd always been able to hang out or play football without this awkward, stilted conversation.

"Sounds good," I finally said, lost for what else I could possibly offer up and silently begging him to take the conversation forward somehow, because my usually verbose self clearly wasn't going to do it.

"Yeah, it was alright."

Apparently, neither was he.

We lapsed into a painfully dull silence, only broken by Annika's periodic huffing for God only knew what reason. She looked almost as uncomfortable as I felt, but I honestly wasn't even sure that Luke had noticed the weird atmosphere. He looked much as he always did: laid back and blissfully ignorant to the feelings of anybody around him.

"Done much swimming over the summer?" he finally asked, not sounding remotely interested in hearing the answer. Perhaps he felt the tension after all.

"Yeah, quite a bit. Keeps me out of trouble."

He snorted, slinging an arm over the back of the bench seat and curling his fingers around Annika's shoulder. "You seriously need to get laid, my friend. All that sexual tension isn't good for you."

I returned his grin with a flat smile of my own, not entertaining his assertion with a comment. The guy had girls queueing up around the block for him. There was no way he'd ever be able to understand the fact that I'd been pining after one person for so long I'd never even been kissed, let alone the fact that person was him.

"Hey, Anni, what about that friend of yours?" Luke questioned, a little too enthusiastically, sending alarm bells firing off in my head. A setup with one of Annika's vapid friends was not high up on my to-do list.

"What friend?" she replied in a sulky voice that made it clear she had zero interest in the conversation. Much like me.

"You know... the one with the hair."

Her eyes rolled dramatically into her head, and I realised just how much her whole sweet, good girl persona had been an act in the last year of high school. "Lots of my friends have hair, genius."

"You know the one I mean," he insisted. "She's like your cousin or something."

"Are you talking about Beatrix?" she cried out as though the name was poison on her lips.

He snapped his fingers. "That's the one. See? The one with the hair."

I had to admit I was intrigued about the hair, even if I had no interest in actually sleeping with this girl, or any other girl for that matter.

"She is *not* my friend, and we are *not* related. She's my mum's best friend's niece. She lives with her 'cause her mum offed herself or something. She's a total weirdo." She cut her eyes to me and they glinted with something distinctly unpleasant. "She'd be perfect for him."

If I cared in the slightest what she thought, I might have been offended by that. As it was, I let out a bark of a laugh that had her eyes narrowing on me impossibly tighter. "Annika, as always, your charm astounds me. Would you excuse me please? I have to make a call."

I couldn't get out of there fast enough. I could feel eyes on me as I forced myself not to run, walking with my head held high and stride as confident as it had ever been. Appearances were everything in this town. If you looked confident, people believed you were; if you acted like a decent human being on the surface, that was who you were, no matter how shady you might be behind the facade.

It appeared to the world as though I was one of the popular kids, always surrounded by people and never short of somebody to hang out with. Yet, as I stood against the wall outside, one foot propped against the burnt-red bricks, I stared at my phone and struggled to think of a single person I could call. What was the point in having a million friends if, when it came down to it, there wasn't a single one you could go to when it counted?

Scrolling down through my contacts, I saw names of people I never spoke to off the football pitch or out of the swimming pool. I saw the numbers of those I'd hit it off with for a single day, agreed to meet up with and then never heard from again. There was one person in there—just one—who I'd ever trusted with all of me, and I didn't even know which continent she was currently on.

I couldn't exactly stalk out of the room saying I needed to make a call and then go back in without even attempting to make one, could I? Shrugging and hoping for the best, I tapped on Abbi's name before I could second guess myself, and lifted the phone to my ear.

It seemed to take an age to connect—an age when all I could hear was the thudding of my heart in my ears and that same pained silence that had sat between Luke and I only moments before.

"Well if it isn't young Thomas. G'day, mate."

My heart and spirits lifted the moment I heard her voice crackling down the line to me. It had been months, broken up only by the occasional postcard and even more sporadic voice messages when they found some wifi. I dreaded to think how much this call would be costing me if she was where I thought she was, but in that moment, I didn't care. A friendly voice was a friendly voice, no matter where in the world I was hearing it from.

"Costa, I will give you anything you want, including assorted body parts, if you promise to never, ever do another accent again. Quite frankly, I'm offended on behalf of all Australians everywhere."

"Spoilsport," she grumbled good naturedly. "What can I do for you on this damn fine evening?"

"I don't need a reason to call my favourite person, now do I?" I questioned jovially, forcing more lightness into my tone than I really felt.

"Technically? No. But this is you: the guy who routinely forgets that he even owns a talky box, let alone actually using it from time to time. Have you opened *any* of the photos I sent you in Whatsapp yet?"

"What's-who now?" My face scrunched up in question, trying to remember the various apps she'd installed on my phone before flying away

"You're a dinosaur, Williams," she huffed, exasperated. "Now, tell me why you called. It's like... what? Eight-thirty in the morning there?"

"Just fancied a chat."

There was a beat of silence, during which I could practically hear her mind ticking over. Abbi was the only person I knew who overthought things more than I did. She was a champion at adding up two and two and getting fifty, and as close as we'd become, we still weren't really the kinds of friends who *just rang up for a chat*. She would send me ridiculous memes off the internet and nag me to join Instagram so I could follow along with their adventures, but we'd never really chatted on the phone unless there was a reason for the call.

"Is everything okay?" she eventually asked, slowly as though reluctant to ask. I couldn't really blame her. I wasn't one of those people who spilled their guts at the first opportunity. I much preferred to keep things close.

"College starts today," I mumbled, knowing that, for her, that would likely explain everything.

"Oh," she replied, drawing out the vowel sound in instant understanding. "And how's that going?"

I hesitated for a beat. Instinct told me to brazen it out and act like everything was grand, but this was Abbi, and if there was one person in my life who had proven they wanted all of me, including the not-so-fun parts, it was her. "I don't *really* need A levels, right?"

"You want to be a teacher, Tom. What do you think?"

"A career as a bin man doesn't sound so bad now I think on it."

"Uh huh. Sure. You can't peel an orange without gagging, but you could empty bins for a living. Dream on, pretty boy. Get your butt into that building and be the fabulous little diva I know you can be. I'm not above getting a plane across half the planet to kick your behind into gear, capisce?"

"Christ, when did you get so bossy, Costa?" I chuckled in spite of myself. This was why I'd phoned her. Abbi didn't do tea and sympathy. She did straight talk and arse kicking.

"Since I started travelling the world with a prankster who thinks it's funny to make jokes about drug trafficking on the way through airport security. Somebody has to be the grown up in this partnership." She attempted to sound exasperated, but love and affection bled into every single syllable when she talked about Elliot.

After her grandmother passed away, Abbi instantly jetted off to Italy with Elliot, leaving her fractured world behind her. There was a part of me that had worried about her going, sure she was trying to outrun all the things that hurt her rather than dealing with them. She and Elliot had been through so much. For a while, I'd even wondered whether their friendship would ever recover from their separation. I'd watched on as both of them were hurting, doing my best to pull them back together, but as the old saying went, you could lead a horse to water, but you couldn't force it to make up with its best friend when it was being stubborn and pig headed. It made me happier than I could say to know that they were back to their old selves, playing pranks and getting up to no good, spreading their unique brand of crazy all over the world.

"Sounds like a great time," I said with a laugh.

"Oh yes. Angering the TSA with inappropriate jokes is everybody's idea of a great time," Abbi quipped, and for the first time, I heard Elliot's voice in the background.

"You only *nearly* got arrested a little bit."

"And what did we learn?" she asked in her best school teacher voice.

"That people in airports don't have senses of humour?"

I heard the sound of a hand meeting flesh, painfully, if the grunt Elliot let out in response was anything to go by.

"And what *else* did we learn?"

"Jokes about drug trafficking are almost never funny," he grumbled.

"That's right," she confirmed. "And we'll be remembering that on our next flight, will we not?"

"Mmm," he hummed noncommittally.

"And if we don't remember that, what will happen?"

"A full body cavity search, and not the fun kind," he parroted, as though this conversation had been had many times before.

I couldn't help but laugh. This was the Abbi and Elliot I remembered fondly, always bickering good naturedly, but you knew they had one another's backs no matter what.

"You two give me hope for humanity," I said with a smile. "You will come home eventually, won't you?"

"You're kidding, right? The first day hasn't even started yet and you've already remembered you own a mobile long enough to phone me. You think I'd abandon you for two whole years in that place? Give me some credit. You'd never survive."

"No. I wouldn't. So hurry back. I'm man enough to admit that I miss the hell outta you, Costa. If you really have to, you can even bring Peterson back with you. If he makes it through customs without causing an international incident."

"It'll be a miracle if he makes it across Australia without falling victim to the didgeridoo he felt the need to buy despite the fact he can't make it do anything but fart noises."

"That would certainly speed the full body cavity search along," I said with a chortle.

"I like the way you think, young Thomas. Now, get your backside in that college and show everybody what you're made of. And for the love of God, check your damn Whatsapp occasionally."

"Roger that, boss. Thanks for the pep talk."

"All part of the service, buddy. Go get 'em."

CHAPTER THREE

Ever since I was a kid, numbers had somehow just made sense to me. I could never make words my friends—there were too many pitfalls, too many words that sounded the same but were spelled differently and too many rules that were constantly broken. Numbers stayed constant, unchanging. No matter what you did, the rules stayed the same. There was comfort in that when the world around you was constantly altering.

One day, I wanted to pass that love on to other kids. I'd wanted to be a teacher for as long as I could remember. I couldn't help wondering whether the woman standing at the front of the classroom looking like she'd accidentally drunk pure lemon juice had once harboured the same desire.

Her eyes scanned the room silently, taking in the small group of students shrivelling in their seats in front of her. I hadn't expected maths to be the most popular subject at A level. Most of the people I knew couldn't wait to drop it the moment high school was over, but I had expected a few more.

Nine.

There were nine of us, all spread out around the classroom, eyeing each other warily, each of us likely wondering the same things. What was the class going to be like? Would we be the smartest or the most stupid in the room? Would we end the year as friends after starting as total strangers? The teacher, on the other hand, looked as though the only question on her mind was which one of us she would tear apart first.

I'd chosen a seat around the middle of the room. Up front would have looked far too keen, and right at the back would have made me look like a trouble maker. In the middle, I was anonymous, an unknown quantity. There, I could form my own identity based on my abilities instead of preconceived notions based on outdated stereotypes. I'd picked my spot between two people I'd totally stereotyped and decided might be my kinds of people.

On the table in front was a girl sporting a bright pink t-shirt that read, 'There are ten types of people—those who understand binary, and those who don't.' Her long hair was so dark on top it was almost black, but underneath, it was dyed every colour of the rainbow. After snorting at her t-shirt, I had slotted into the table behind her, in front of the guy sitting at the back.

Beyond the fact that he had a mop of mousy brown curls and wore a black hoodie, I couldn't make out much more about him. His head was tilted down, his nose almost to the table, while long, slender fingers clutched a charcoal pencil that was rapidly skating over a sketch pad, a tinny beat emitting from the headphones stuffed in his ears. He didn't seem to have noticed the steam practically shooting out of the ears of the teacher, or indeed the fact that he was in a classroom at all. There was something kind of beautiful about his complete disregard for the world around him, as though he was completely lost in his creation.

Envy at how easily he switched off the world around him had my eyes locking with the hand that was bringing the tail of a dragon to vivid life before me. I was mesmerised, completely lost in the scene he was creating. Magic was happening right before my eyes, a fierce, fire-breathing dragon erupting from a page in the middle of a sterile, white maths classroom. It was so realistic that the smell of chalk dust and the sweat of thousands of teenagers somehow gave way to the burning embers of the village the dragon was terrorising. It was a black and white picture drawn by a teenage boy in a classroom, and yet somehow it had taken on life in my mind, and I was lost to it completely until a loud and stern coughing dragged me back to reality.

"Anybody who wishes to leave my classroom with an A level in two years time, I need your attention now. Anybody who would rather draw pictures and slack off for two years, I suggest you leave my classroom now."

My eyes snapped to the other dragon occupying the space before swivelling back to the guy behind me. He didn't appear to have heard her. His hand continued to sweep over the paper without a care in the world until I moved my hand to his table as subtly as I could, and knocked on the paper to get his attention.

His head whipped up so quickly I thought he was going to bang it on the wall behind him. Hazel eyes the shape of small almonds met mine, and I could almost see the scene he was creating growing smaller in the pupils as he stared at me with an intensely quizzical expression. His face was slender and pale, with a smattering of freckles over his cheeks and the bridge of his nose, which would have given him a boyish appearance if it hadn't been for the maturity beyond his years that burned back at me from his eyes.

Hiding my hand behind my body, I pointed in the direction of the teacher, who was now stomping around the room depositing textbooks thicker than the Oxford English Dictionary on every table. He glanced her way, his eyes widening in surprise and maybe a tiny bit of fear. His fingers instantly released the charcoal pencil, which rolled noisily across the tabletop before clattering to the floor at my feet.

I bent down to retrive it, smacking my head against the table on the way back up, and when I handed it back to him, his headphones were gone and he was watching the teacher nervously as she thrust a book across the table at him and shot him a contemptuous look as she moved on.

It was going to be a long two years with her in charge of my favourite subject. One look at the artist's face told me he felt the same way.

Every class that week began the same way. I'd slide into the same seat between the same two people, sitting sideways on my seat—not to be sociable but so that I could cast surreptitious glances over at Artist Boy's latest project. He never said a word, so deeply ensconced in his work, and I never attempted to initiate conversation. His standoff with the teacher, whose name, ironically, turned out to be Mrs. Bright, continued. Their relationship appeared to be based on hatred at first sight, though I had no idea why.

My other neighbour, on the other hand, had no such issues with opening her mouth. In fact, I'd never met anybody more loquacious in my life. By the end of the first week, I knew her name was Beatrix but if you called her that, you would swiftly and painfully regret it. I knew that touching her stash of Freddos was a capital offence, and that she had the biggest selection of geeky t-shirts I'd ever come across.

I knew nothing about silent guy.

Only that his surname was Cooper and that something about him rubbed Mrs. Bright up the wrong way.

Not a single lesson went by when I didn't hear 'Mr. Cooper' barked out in some form of disgust or anger. Half the time, he didn't even seem to be doing anything to rile her up. Unless you counted breathing. She just hated him, and it was starting to irritate me.

He never said anything, though, or spoke up for himself. He kept his head down, his shoulders curled inwards as though he were forming a wave for her words to roll off him. I couldn't work out whether his apparent indifference was real or simply a byproduct of the fact that the dislike was mutual.

I, on the other hand, wasn't even sure she knew my

name, and I was almost certain she didn't know Trix's. She simply referred to her as 'girl', since she was the only one in the class, and apparently thought that was acceptable. Since nobody in the classroom bothered to correct her, she continued to breathe fire over the class as effectively as silent guy's charcoal dragons.

Outside the maths classroom, things with Luke continued to be painful and awkward. We were surrounded by people every day in the common room, and I watched on as he worked his way through a whole new selection of girls, leading them on and teasing them in turn until they gave him what he wanted. I couldn't work out why they kept on coming back for more, and decided to focus more of my time on trying to work out their thought processes to avoid thinking about why I was still attracted to somebody who treated people so poorly.

One thing that hadn't changed, though, was Saturdays. Saturday was football day and had been for as long as I could remember. We'd been kicking a ball about in the local park since before they erected posts and we had to use jumpers for goals instead.

We didn't even arrange to meet up anymore. We'd just find our way there every week during term time without fail, meeting at no specific time. The other players varied week on week depending who we managed to rope in or who happened to be passing at the time, but Luke and I were constants.

Today, it was sluicing it down with rain, the kind that

was almost horizontal and stung your eyes with every step you took. Not ones to let a little water and a *lot* of mud slow us down, by noon we were slipping all over the place, our formerly clean clothes now dyed a charming shade of brown with lovely green slashes where we'd slid through the mud.

There weren't many of us this week. The driving rain may have had something to do with that. But the hardcore amongst us were having a whale of a time. I couldn't vouch for the quality of the football being played, but I still felt lighter than I had in weeks. The wind and rain soaked and chilled me right down to my bones, but I didn't care, because just for a little while, I felt like everything was normal. We laughed, talked smack, and generally acted as though the long summer of separation hadn't happened. While it might not have been everything I wanted, it *was* everything I'd missed, and I had to be grateful for that. Perhaps back at college things might not be so awkward now.

Physical exertion had always helped me to clear my mind when it got overcrowded, almost as though if my body were under physical strain, my mind was forced to shut off in order to send all the possible resources to my muscles to keep moving. I lived for that optimum moment when every cell in my body hurt and all I could focus on was forcing the next breath in through protesting lungs and pushing my arms and legs on impossibly further. Swimming was my favourite form of personal torture. I would cheerfully keep going for hours, enjoying the way my body sliced through the water as it cascaded over and against my skin.

But football was a close second, and today, everything hurt. It was bliss, the way my lungs cried out for relief as the raindrops battered against my cheeks like tiny pins, making my eyes sting and my nose run. I hadn't quite made it to that coveted point of blissful mental silence, but I was well on the way when Luke pulled up, raking a hand over his face and through his sodden hair. His usually perfect caramel cheeks were smeared with mud that had strands of hair sticking to his face.

"Think we should call it a day before somebody breaks their neck in this mud," he threw out between laboured breaths.

I stared at him with my hands on my hips, bent at the waist as my breathing slowed, losing that high I was just beginning to ride. "Not yet. Just a bit longer."

"Dude, you're about ninety percent mud at this point. Quit while you're... well, not ahead, but... still partly human at least."

"Nah, I'm still good. Let's go," I said with a chuckle, kicking the ball off the toes of my trainers into the air and then bouncing it off my knee. "Unless you're worried about losing..."

I was hoping to tap into Luke's well-developed and constantly engaged competitive side, but it seemed that the horizontal rain had drowned it, because he simply shrugged and turned on the spot. "Like that's ever gonna happen. Dream on, mate."

A momentary panic shot through me as the sight of him

preparing to leave, and standing there with water dripping down my face, I searched through my extensive arsenal of pointless facts for something—anything—to say to keep him around just a little bit longer. I wasn't proud of the desperation in my voice as I called out, "Did you know that playing in mud actually increases serotonin levels and makes you happier?"

He stopped in place, and for a moment, I silently congratulated myself on stalling him leaving, even if it was just for a few more seconds. And then he turned to look at me with one eyebrow quirked at me, the way he did when he was judging somebody who wasn't worthy of his time, and said, "I wonder about you sometimes, Tom. I really do."

I was starting to wonder about me, too.

I watched as he walked away without another word, my feet weighed to the ground by my heart, which had sunk right down into my soles. His words would have been enough to have it in freefall, but it was the look on his face that really sent it plunging without hope. It was a look that clearly said, 'I don't know who you are anymore.'

It hurt to admit that I wasn't sure I did either.

CHAPTER FOUR

I wasn't sure whether it was hope or desperation that continued to drag me out of bed each morning before it was light, knowing that another grey sky would block the sunrise from view. The rain had set in and decided to stick around, ensuring that each day remained as overcast and lifeless as the last. I trudged to college each day through the deluge, remaining wet through and uncomfortable all day, only drying off in time to make my way back home through the same. It felt as though I hadn't been dry in weeks, and I hated it.

I missed the daily renewal I somehow gained from watching the sun cresting the far shore of the lake each morning, the relief I felt when I saw those first rays hitting the horizon and glittering across the water towards me. Light brought hope, and hope was everything.

Nonetheless, each day, I found myself in the same spot, my body flinching back into my raincoat as the heavy drops battered at every millimetre of exposed skin. Today, the rain had been joined by its favourite companion: the howling autumn wind that had the water beneath the jetty swirling into a frenzy. It was beautiful in its own way, the power of nature over everything in its path. The trees bent to the will of the wind as I planted my feet beneath me and allowed it to assault my body. With my feet numb from the cold, it felt almost like flying. I lifted my arms at my sides, and they rode the air like the waves of the ocean, rising and falling with every gust as I leaned into the wind and soared. It wasn't sunrise, but it still felt like a renewal of sorts, cleansing it its own way.

I was lost in the moment, completely absorbed in the maelstrom around me, when a firm nudge against my leg threw me off balance and I had to scrabble to stay upright and not plunge into the whirlpool below.

'What the...?"

A wet nose tickled my fingers as they dropped like rocks to my sides, and I found myself staring into the eyes of the biggest Dalmation I'd ever seen.

"Where did you come from?" I murmured, dropping down to its side and tentatively petting its head.

I wasn't great with animals. Our house was a no pets, no mess kind of place, so this soggy wet fur ball licking my fingers had me a little rattled, especially since squinting into the horizontal rain showed no sign of an owner.

"Okay, buddy. You and I are going to make a deal. I'm going to be super gentle reaching for your tag, and you're going to promise not to bite me. Remember if you want me to ring your owner, I need fingers to dial the number. Do we have a deal?"

The dog's head tilted, wide eyes blinking at me in question as though it had no idea what I was saying.

"Just remember the part about dialling the number," I mumbled, cringing apprehensively as I slowly reached out for the tag dangling beneath its collar, a little too close to its huge looking teeth for my liking.

My fingers had just hit cool metal without so much as a twitch from the dog's jaw area when a muffled shout broke across the sounds of the wind and rain, and the animal beside me stiffened, its ears perking up in awareness. Rapidly withdrawing my hand, I stuffed it deep into my pocket, far far away from teeth of any kind, and I bounced back to my feet, my eyes searching through the haze of the rain for the source of the voice.

There was nothing at first, just the cacophony of the elements around me and the excited panting of the dog. I blinked away the water, and when I looked again, he was there, a familiar black hoodie his only protection from the rain, and a storm raging in his hazel eyes.

"You..." I murmured as recognition flared on meeting the turbulence in his gaze before he dropped down beside the dog, his fingers raking through its fur.

"He slipped the lead," he replied by way of explanation as he moved to clip it back to the dog's collar.

Four words. Just four and it was the most I'd ever heard him speak. Silent guy had a voice. It was raspy, just on the right side of hoarse, as though it wasn't used nearly often enough to give it that usual smooth flow, but it had spoken a whole four words to me.

"He's, uh... nice," I said, after trying and failing to think of anything better to break the painfully awkward silence.

He nodded, finally releasing me from the captivity of his oddly intense stare to assess the state of his dog, and I pulled in the first full breath since my eyes had met his. I'd never encountered anybody I was unable to drag into conversation before. Aside from maths, I wasn't that great at much, but chatting nonsense with total strangers was practically listable on my CV at this point. So why I stood there watching him tenderly checking his dog over, unable to find a single intelligent thing to say, was beyond me. Talking about the weather, while justifiable in the monsoon we were caught up in, seemed somehow too trivial for somebody like him. Talking about his drawings would have given away my snooping, and nowhere in my arsenal of random facts could I find anything that didn't make me sound like a total idiot.

Why I felt that mattered was something I pushed to the back of my mind for dangerous overthinking at a later time.

And so I stood there like an idiot, struck mute by being around somebody who used so few words to get through life. I watched as he pushed back to his feet, gripping the dog's leash tightly, nodded once more and then turned to walk away.

Rain washed over my face, running in rivulets down my nose as I stared after him until my tongue finally took matters into its own hands and called out after him. "Hey, do you have a name?"

He paused, his shoulders stiffening before his neck

twisted and his head turned to face me. "Everybody has a name."

Smiling wide enough to allow rainwater to flood into my mouth, I took a step forwards, dimly registering the fact that the air around us had turned several shades lighter. I'd missed the sunrise, too focused on the riddle of a boy in front of me.

"Is it a secret?"

I couldn't be sure—the rain was so heavy that my view of him was blurred—but I swore I saw a slight twitch of his lips before he shook his head, turned back to the road and walked away, calling over his shoulder, "Nope."

He might not have said much, but he had enigmatic down to a fine art.

※

Nine words.

He'd said nine words to me, yet somehow when I walked into maths first period, I half expected us to greet one another like old friends. Except when I walked into the classroom, his seat sat empty. Trix was there as usual, her stash of Freddos lined up along her desk already in anticipation of being mentally tortured by Mrs. Bright for an hour. The other six lads were in their usual places with stacks of screwed up paper littering their desks and the floor as they used the bin as a basketball hoop.

I just stood there, confusion wracking through me at his absence. He'd been fine only a few hours earlier, so where was he? Much as he and Mrs. Bright hated one another, he'd never struck me as the cutting class kind, but I guessed there was always a first time.

"Freddo for your thoughts, pretty boy," Trix chirped from her seat, surveying me with a vague look of amusement.

"Really?" I eyed her chocolate supply eagerly.

"Buddy, you've got more chance of Mrs. Bright spontaneously bursting out into show tunes and tap dancing in the middle of class, but tell me what you're thinking anyway. I'm nosy and I could do with a laugh."

"You're a cruel, unfeeling woman," I grumbled, finally vacating the doorway and sliding into the seat beside her, foregoing my usual place in the hope of scoring some morning chocolate.

"I don't know what you're talking about. I'm a delight." She grinned and swept her arm across her stash, pulling it towards her and away from my grabby hands. "So, are you going to tell me why you looked like you'd seen Donald Trump standing naked at the back of the room when you walked in or what?"

I blinked at her in disgust. "That's a visual I could have lived without, thanks."

"You are welcome, my friend." She grinned. "And stop avoiding the question."

"What question?"

"Trump. Naked. You, staring at the wall in horror... ringing any bells?"

"Oh, that. I was just wondering where artist boy is today. And by the way, I'm taking money out of your Freddo fund to pay for the years of intensive therapy it's going to take to get that hideous picture out of my mind."

Her grin quickly morphed into an evil looking smirk. "Wanna know what happened to the last person who tried to interfere with my habit? No. That's right. You don't. And I assume by 'artist boy' you mean Jake?"

Jake...

I turned the name over and over in my mind, trying to reconcile it with its owner. Jake was a happy name, the sort I associated with bouncy cocker spaniels and colourful kids on play parks. Not angry looking teenagers in black hoodies toting sketch pads filled with drawings of destructive dragons razing villages to the ground with their breath.

"Jake... right." I agreed with her, grateful to have at least finally put a name to the face.

"It's the third Tuesday of the month," she said with a shrug, as though that somehow explained everything.

"Yes, it is," I agreed, looking at her expectantly, waiting for the rest of her explanation.

It didn't come.

She just shrugged again before ripping a Freddo free from its packet and stuffing it into her mouth, the confectionary version of drawing a line under a conversation.

The words to object sat on the tip of my tongue, poised to throw more questions at her, when the door flew open again and Mrs. Bright stalked in, her arms full of books and a thunderous expression on her face.

"We'll discuss these woeful attempts at homework later on," she barked as she slammed the books down on her desk with a crash. "I suppose I ought to at least *try* to teach you something first. Though why I bother when you clearly don't listen to a word I say, I have no idea."

All the happiness in the room dried up instantly, faces falling and spirits drooping. The room that had been filled with fun only moments before was now as quiet and serious as a funeral parlour. I was a firm believer that there were no bad people, only sad ones. Everybody had reasons for behaving the way that they did. Every villain was the protagonist of their own story, and I always tried to remember that, to see people for who they were and not what they did. But even I had to admit it was getting harder by the day to see this woman as anything but a tyrant. I was almost glad silent guy—no, Jake, his name was Jake—wasn't there. Even on her best days, she seemed to take some sort of sadistic pleasure in tormenting him, so God only knew how this lesson would have gone for him had he been there.

We were working silently on the task Mrs. Bright had set, eight noses pressed almost flush against eight textbooks in a desperate attempt to avoid catching her attention. Ironically, the studious atmosphere I assumed she was intending to create was having the opposite effect on me. I couldn't concentrate in the stifled silence. It was too quiet, too oppressive. I felt as though I couldn't breathe, like the tension in the room was stealing all the oxygen clean away. I understood the subject matter perfectly well. The equations we'd been set to solve I could have done in my sleep, and yet staring at the complex combination of symbols, all I could see was a lost pair of hazel eyes, and all I could hear was the words third Tuesday of the month repeating over and over in my mind.

Lost to my thoughts but somehow keeping my pen scratching away at the page for the sake of pretence, I almost let out a surprised yelp when I felt a finger prodding my ribs.

Lifting my eyes as much as I dared, I met Trix's mischievous grin as she pushed a slip of paper under my arm before going back to her work as though she never looked up.

Peering down at it, I couldn't stifle the snort of laughter that burst from my lips unbidden.

Written in Trix's untidy scrawl were the words, 'Do you reckon this is why she perms her hair?' And next to the words was a very crudely drawn picture of the devil with a bush of curly hair attempting to cover his horns.

"Something funny about integration, Mr. Williams?" Mrs. Bright barked from her spot at the front of the room.

"Nothing whatsoever," I mumbled, dropping my head back down and swiftly covering the note with my arm. Something told me it wouldn't go down well if she found it.

"I didn't think so. Just because one reprobate has elected not to join us today doesn't mean you have to step directly into his shoes."

Making direct eye contact with her was where it all went wrong. Keeping my head down and agreeing with her would have been the sensible, self preserving thing to do, but shock had me acting before my brain was fully engaged with the situation.

Reprobate... She was talking about the guy who sat at the back of her class day in and day out, head down, quietly getting on with things and trying to keep on top of the hideous workload she insisted on piling onto us. He'd never so much as looked at her the wrong way as far as I'd seen, let alone disrupted her lessons or acted in any way like a reprobate would.

"I'm not sure I know what you mean," I said, locking my irritated gaze with her cold one.

"Well that's nothing new in this classroom, is it?"

Let it go, Tom. Let it go.

"Then maybe you should—"

My words cut off sharply when pain roared through my foot. Looking down, I saw Trix's bright pink Dr. Marten's boot still where she'd planted it. A subtle shake of her head had me quirking an eyebrow at her. She didn't exactly strike me as a pacifist but she clearly didn't want me antagonising this woman anymore than I already had.

I could feel the eyes of the entire class cutting into me as I drew in several deep breaths in an attempt to calm down. I wasn't an argumentative person by nature, but sometimes it felt like everything this woman did and said was targeted right at every last nerve I possessed.

"Maybe I should *what?*" she finally asked, standing up and resting her hands on her desk, leaning forwards over it as though moving the lasers in her eyes a little closer to their target.

An internal battle raged in my head as I refused to let my eyes drop from hers. Trix was right, though. Squaring off against a teacher in my first term at college was hardly a precedent I wanted to set.

"Nothing," I finally mumbled, letting my feelings on allowing the argument to drop filter into my tone.

"Hmm, I thought so. I don't tolerate childish temper tantrums in my classroom, Mr. Williams. Either get on with your work, or get out. Your choice."

The temptation to leave was strong, but the desire to get an education was stronger. Scowling, I looked away, feeling her acidic glare burning through the top of my head for an uncomfortably long time as I attempted to focus on the work.

CHAPTER FIVE

I couldn't feel my fingers.
Or my nose.
In fact, the only part of my body I could feel was the little toe on my right foot where pins and needles had started to set in from being crouched in the same position for so long.

The rain had finally stopped, leaving behind waterlogged ground, and Nonna's garden was a mess.

For the first month after Abbi left on her adventures with Elliot, the key she'd given me to Nonna's old cottage had burned a hole in my pocket. Selfishly, I'd mourned the loss of my place of sanctuary after Nonna's death, knowing full well Abbi wouldn't stick around long afterwards. Colwich had always been too small for her, but not for me. The town boundaries were my whole world, with everything and everybody I loved held neatly inside. But my home was stifling. Since the day I'd let slip to my dad how I felt about Luke in a moment of weakness, it hadn't felt like home anymore. Abbi and Nonna had offered me a place to go when being at home was too much, and although I knew logically nothing I could ever do would be enough to repay them, I'd taken to tending Nonna's garden for Abbi so it would still be the way she remembered it when she returned home.

The weather hadn't helped me to achieve that goal. Everything was under water, the usually neat lawn muddy and the flowerbeds in a state of chaos. But today, the sun had finally put in an appearance despite the cold that had my entire body numb, a fact that had buoyed my spirits since the first glints of light had touched the far side of the lake that morning.

Here, I could remember and forget all at once. The walls of the cottage were filled with memories, the bricks keeping a thousand secrets whispered in moments of weakness, of pain, of hopelessness between two friends who were hurting. In this house I'd allowed myself to be vulnerable and trusted Abbi to be okay with that. We'd bled together, she and I, and now she was thousands of miles away living her dream with the boy she loved while the boy I loved only occasionally remembered I existed.

The hard physical work of trying to fix the mess left behind by the storm kept my body occupied while my thoughts ran rampant—the good and the bad, the happy and the sad. I welcomed them all because without the bad, I would never experience the sublime as intensely. Life was made up of highs and lows, and just like a rollercoaster, you had to plummet downwards in order to climb back up. And as the garden slowly grew tidier, so did my thoughts, organising themselves into neat piles. I liked order, and thoughts were no different to anything else. They were neatly piled into three categories: things I could do something about now, things I could do something about later, and things I could do nothing about at all.

By the time the garden looked anything like it had before, every muscle in my body was aching but there was a strange sort of satisfaction in that. I surveyed my handiwork with a smile, leaning against the rake handle and jumping a foot in the air when an unfamiliar voice called out from behind me.

"So you're the secret garden fairy."

"I, umm... Excuse me?" I spun on the spot, my feet tangling clumsily with the rake and sending me plummeting painfully to the ground.

Well that was graceful...

"Good grief, child, are you alright?" A kind face moved into my eyeline as I stared up at the sky in a daze

"Jury's out," I groaned in response, blinking as the world slowly moved back into focus.

"I didn't mean to startle you." A hand, weathered by age, moved into my line of sight and I lifted my gaze up to the face that matched it.

Silver hair sat in perfect curls around the face of a kind old woman. Recognition flashed briefly in my mind but it was fleeting and left me just as clueless as before. I felt like I ought to know who she was, but my mind was blank.

"No, it was my fault," I mumbled, gripping her hand but not really putting any weight behind it as I pulled myself upright. I didn't want to be responsible for her falling down beside me and breaking her hip or something. "Sorry, I'm sure I know you but..." I tapped my temple with a single finger and she smiled in understanding.

"Lucy. I live next door. We met at Emilia's funeral. And you are Tom—the young man who kept Abigail going when the rest of the world didn't want to know."

I smiled indulgently, squeezing her hand once as her words sparked a memory of her somber face. "Actually, I think she kept *me* going."

Her hand gripped mine a little tighter as her lined face split into a soft smile. "Better to tread water together than drown alone I daresay."

"Yeah..." I swallowed down the lump that had risen in my throat and offered her a small smile. "Yes."

"And now she's off chasing those big dreams of hers and you're here looking after her grandmother's garden." Her voice lifted at the end a little, but it wasn't a question. Nonetheless, she looked at me expectantly, awaiting a response.

"Here I am," I agreed when it became clear she wasn't going to fill the gap my silence was leaving in the conversation.

"Well, you're doing a wonderful job. It's almost better than when Emilia was looking after it herself. I could never get my roses to bloom as beautifully as hers."

Lifting my eyes to take in her garden, I smiled in agreement. While Nonna's lawn was surrounded with flower beds that bloomed with flowers of every colour during the summer, hers was just a lawn with two sad looking rose bushes beside her front door. Looking at it, though, I could picture endless possibilities in the space. My mind turned over with images of how beautiful it could be when the summer arrived as I soundlessly moved towards it. My fingers raked over the bare branches of the rose bushes, seeing brightly coloured blooms where there were none.

"It could be just as beautiful. All it needs is a bit of tender loving care," I mumbled to myself, almost forgetting I wasn't alone.

"Alas, I'm afraid my days of crawling around on my hands and knees are long over," Lucy replied good naturedly, casting a doleful smile at her garden.

"You could dig out flower beds all along here," I went on, oblivious to anything but the images in my mind. "And then a little fountain water feature would look amazing just here." Crouching down at the corner where Lucy's garden met Nonna's, I dusted my fingers over the grass as it all came to life inside my mind. "And it needs sunflowers." At the sound of Lucy's chuckle, I glanced up at her sheepishly. "Every garden needs sunflowers. They brighten everything up."

"Mmm," she hummed. "They are beautiful."

"I could... I mean, only if you wanted, but..." I trailed off, feeling more than a little stupid. I didn't even know this person and I wanted her to give me free reign over her garden.

The garden at home had been landscaped years earlier, and my dad hired a professional gardening service to maintain it. Nonna's garden was already so beautiful, all it needed was maintenance. But this space was a blank canvas, a place where my imagination could run wild.

Surely it was too much to hope for that kind of freedom in a stranger's garden. She didn't know me from Adam, and yet the way she was looking at me, with a strange sort of affection and interest in her pale blue eyes, had hope swelling like a balloon in my chest.

"But..." she prompted.

My head dipped, my gaze shifting to my feet as they shuffled on the grass beneath them. "I could fix it up for you a bit, perhaps. Maybe. Probably not. You won't want—"

"You want to help an old lady make her garden more beautiful?" She sounded almost incredulous, as though she wouldn't be doing me a massive favour by giving me this chance.

"I, uh... Well, yes."

"I couldn't afford to pay you very much." She sighed sadly, her eyes moving wistfully over her lawn.

"I don't want your money. I just want your garden. Please. I have so many ideas."

I did. They were bursting into my brain fast and furious with every excited heartbeat. If she allowed me to do this, the space around me would be a haven bursting with colour by the time the summer came around. I could make it a paradise, I was certain I could.

She quirked a curious eyebrow at me as she moved a little closer and spoke again. "What about your studies?"

"I'm smart," I instantly threw back. "I can do both, honestly."

"Smart *and* talented, huh? That's an offer that's very hard to say no to."

"Then don't. I'll do a good job, I promise."

"Oh, no doubt of that. I've seen the work you've done on Emilia's garden. I thought for sure Abigail had hired a professional to look after it while she was away."

"So you have nothing to lose and heaven to gain," I prodded with a broad grin, sensing that this conversation was swinging in my favour. I could already feel excitement churning inside me at the thought of having so much freedom to create.

"It seems I do." Her face split into the most amazing smile I'd ever seen, and she reached out her hand to me once more, only this time she wasn't pulling me up in the literal sense but the figurative. Having something to focus on was going to save me from losing my mind this year. I just knew it was.

Eagerly, I took her weathered hand in mine and shook it a little too enthusiastically, already mentally cataloguing all the things I was going to need.

"That doesn't look nearly as much like torture as it ought to." I caught a flash of rainbow coloured hair before Trix's face swam into view, followed by a t-shirt that read 'I think, therefore we have nothing in common.'

I chuckled, my arms moving to cover up the paper in front of me that definitely wasn't what I was meant to be doing.

We had a free study period, which Mrs. Bright had *strongly* encouraged—and by encouraged, I meant threatened on pain of abject humiliation—us to use to catch up on the heinous ream of homework she'd set for the next day. I was starting to think that Trix was being too kind to her when she nicknamed her Satan. I mean, I'm sure even Lucifer had his reasons, but this woman was possessed. I was certain of it.

I'd elected to ignore her threats and spend some time letting my imagination run wild on designs for Lucy's garden.

"Maths is only torture when she teaches it," I replied with a grin, shifting my feet off the bench across the common room table from me to give her space to sit down.

She slid into the vacated spot to the sound of a snort coming from behind me. I whipped around as Trix lifted her eyes to the sound to see Jake bent over the brick-like maths textbook with sheets and sheets of balled up paper around him, stabbing uselessly at his calculator with increasing levels of frustration.

"Everything alright there, buddy?" Trix questioned, her tone cheerful in spite of the anger evident in Jake's posture.

"Peachy," he practically growled in response, not lifting his eyes from his work that I could tell was all wrong even from where I was sitting.

"You need some help there?" I questioned softly, twisting on the seat and stretching my legs out along it so I could face him.

His pen slammed to the tabletop as his free hand moved to massage his temples and a sigh huffed out between his downturned lips. Still, he didn't speak.

"Jake...?" Trix's voice softened, her tone coaxing, nothing like her usual confident chatter. And for the first time it occurred to me that maybe she knew him a little better than I'd realised.

His eyes darted up and locked on hers, widening slightly as though it was a shock to see her sitting there. There were so many emotions sitting right there in his gaze; there was anger, confusion, frustration and pleading, but there, sitting right in the centre of those stormy hazel eyes was just the tiniest glint of hope.

"Sorry," he muttered, dropping his gaze back to the textbook in front of him and gently plucking his pen back up, as though the apology were intended for the writing implement and not Trix.

I winced on her behalf when she jumped out of her seat and gracefully slid into the bench seat beside him, her hand moving to rest on top of his white knuckled grip on the pen, half expecting him to snap at her.

He didn't. He just shifted in his seat a little uncomfortably and lasered his eyes through the point of contact.

"Let me help," she whispered, squeezing his hand once before prising the pen free.

He kept his head determinedly pointed downwards, burning holes through the pages of the book with his gaze as he spoke. "I should be able to do it myself."

"Oh hush. No man is an island. Let me look." I wanted to laugh at how quickly she'd shifted from treating him like a cornered wild animal, dangerous and liable to bolt or attack, to snapping back to her usual no nonsense, straight to the point self. Their interaction was intriguing, like a strange dance that only they knew the steps to. In fact, I wasn't at all sure that Jake knew them either.

He didn't argue with her, just watched on half irritated, half incredulous as she scrubbed out his hard work and flicked back several pages in the textbook.

"If you had a decent teacher, you'd be nailing this stuff," she asserted after scanning the page.

"She hates me."

"She hates everyone."

Deciding that it would likely be counterproductive to argue with her about that, I kept my mouth shut and moved to sit opposite them. She *did* seem to hate everybody, but there was no doubt in my mind that she had a very special dislike for the boy sitting across from me. What I couldn't understand was why. He was the least disruptive person in the class. He never said a word or acted out in any way. As far as I could see, all he was guilty of was sketching in his pad before class and being absent on the third Tuesday of the month.

"Other people don't suck like I do," he muttered, self loathing lacing his tone as his shoulders curled in almost imperceptibly further.

"Pfft. Don't use Thomas here as any sort of model. He's a maths genius but he can barely spell his own name. It's literally the only thing he's any good at."

"Thanks, Trix," I mumbled drily. "Appreciate that."

"You're welcome, buddy. I don't call everybody a genius, so you can go ahead and be grateful."

"Noted." Rolling my eyes, I grabbed the textbook right out of her hands, ignoring her growl of protest, and began to read through. She was right. Mrs. Bright rarely bothered to actually teach anything. She subscribed to the school of 'reading the text in silence is enough', and I guess for some of us it was. But Jake was clearly struggling and had nobody to go to for help. Nobody who would give it freely without making snide comments or making him feel worthless, anyway.

We spent the hour with him, working through the chapter she'd set. Trix and I threw banter back and forth, and although he didn't join in, by the time we had to head back to class, I could have sworn Jake looked more relaxed and at ease than I'd ever seen him before.

What had been a seriously surreal day up to that point was rounded off with a good old dose of double maths. By now, I'd established a spot next to Trix instead of behind her, and I was even periodically honoured with one of her Freddos when she was feeling particularly generous. Up until today, Jake had stoically kept up his place at the back of the room in spite of the empty table between us my move to Trix's desk had freed up. My guess was he wanted to be as far from Mrs. Bright's vitriol as possible. So when he slouched his way into the room, his eyes as cautious as ever, and hesitated for a moment before slipping into the desk behind us, it took all my self control not to react beyond the smallest eyebrow lift in Trix's direction. Her lips twitched into a smile, but she didn't say anything to him.

I could hear his pencil scratching away at his sketch pad, though, the sound grating on every nerve that wanted to pivot in my seat and take a look at what he was drawing today. It was almost always dragons, but there was so much variety between each one, even in simple black and white, that each picture seemed to have a life all of its own.

Eyes down.

Focus on maths, Williams, I muttered to myself, twisting a pen between my fingers and waiting for the daily torture session to start.

I wasn't sure how it was possible, but I could have sworn that the soft sweep and grind of his pencil was somehow more lighthearted and less pained than usual, but maybe that was just wishful thinking from the parts of me that couldn't bear to see another human being hurting. And it was clear he was hurting. What I didn't know was why. And not knowing was driving me to distraction.

The temptation to turn around and look at today's dragon was growing into a permanent itch under my skin by the time Mrs. Bright walked in and dumped her enormous, heavy bag on her desk. I wasn't sure what it was she carted around with her in that thing, but I was starting to think it was filled with the bodies of all the students who had ever displeased her.

"I trust you all used your time wisely this morning as I requested," she said, sweeping around the desk to throw her thick black cardigan over the back of the chair.

Hand out expectantly, she moved around the room, collecting work from everybody before coming to rest in front of Jake's desk. "Your efforts," she sniffed, snatching his work from his hand and glancing at it contemptuously before stalking back to the front of the room.

Muscles bunched, I was poised and ready to dart out of my seat after her. Anger at her treatment of somebody who had never done a thing to her was a living beast inside me, roaring to break free and let loose. Couldn't she see this boy was already in pieces? He needed somebody to care, to take him by the hand and put some faith in him, not take his broken pieces and stamp all over them.

It was all there, just dying to burst out of me, but a warm hand closing around mine and squeezing just a little too tightly forced me to stop and take a breath. The small shake of Trix's head was almost imperceptible, but it somehow forced me back in my seat, though my body still vibrated with anger.

"You have to pick your battles," she mouthed silently to me the moment Mrs. Bright's back was turned.

I nodded stiffly in response, but my taut muscles and churning stomach refused to settle as she began to work her way through the marking, leaving us to once again teach ourselves from the prehistoric textbooks.

Unable to focus on the work while my body attempted to settle, I watched on, waiting for her to reach the bottom of the pile, waiting for her to realise her mistake, waiting for her to grovel and apologise for prejudging. His work was perfect, and I knew it. I didn't even realise that my leg was bouncing with anticipation until Trix's pen embedded itself in my flesh painfully.

Stifling a curse, I turned to glare at her, swiping her hand away along with the offending object.

"If you don't stop that, you're going to cause an earthquake in Japan," she hissed, one eye on the front of the room, the other flashing with warning. "Relax for heaven's sake. He can take care of himself."

I wasn't so sure about that, but I contented myself with a small glare that I then turned on Mrs. Bright, who was oblivious to the entire exchange, lost in the puddle of red ink she was spilling over somebody's work with just a little bit too much relish.

I monitored every movement of her face—every twitch of her jaw, every tilt of her lips and every lift of her eyebrows—waiting for the moment she'd be forced to acknowledge that she was wrong, but her expression remained completely impassive.

It seemed to take a lifetime for her to look up, but when she did, my hope died. She wasn't contrite; she was furious.

"Jacob, a word please," she called out, breaking the tense silence and setting my teeth on edge.

There was a moment when her words hung in the air, rippling on my frayed nerves, and I could almost feel the confusion coming from behind me. He didn't move for the longest time, as though it was taking him several minutes to decipher her words.

He did finally rise from his seat, black hood pulled up over his hair and his chin dipped inside the neckline, as though he were trying to leave as little of his body as possible exposed to the acid shooting from her eyes. His steps were slow but deliberate as he approached her, leaving a safe distance between his body—taut with an unnamable emotion—and her desk, where she was sitting with her eyes burning holes through his protective hoodie. The rest of the class were uninterested, focusing on their work, but I couldn't have looked away if somebody had offered to pay me.

"Would you care to explain this to me?" she questioned, wafting his work at him accusingly.

He didn't speak—when did he ever?—but instead reached out a hand towards the work that was rapidly becoming crumpled beyond recognition in her fierce grip. She didn't allow him to take it, though, instead yanking it away and flattening it out on her desk.

"From whom did you steal this?"

My jaw dropped in perfect time with his as my fingers curled around the edge of my desk, ready to push me to my feet to intervene.

"I...I'm sorry?" His voice was impossibly quiet, but there was a dangerous edge to it, a tone that said he was getting ready to blow.

"I should think so. I expected you to hand in your own work, not four pages of somebody else's."

There was a sharp intake of breath, and I wasn't sure whether it came from him or me, but by the time our lungs were full, I was on my feet, heart thundering in my ears.

"But—"

"There is no way this is your own work. So I'll ask you again, from whom did you steal it?"

It was almost audible when the narrow thread tethering him to reason snapped in two, and his hands slapped down on her desk, his face only inches from hers as he hissed, "I'm *not* a thief," through gritted teeth.

Unflustered, not a hair out of place or a hint of fear on her face, she sneered back at him. "You will step back from this desk this instant or I will be forced to call the authorities."

For a moment, nobody moved. The entire classroom held its breath at the silent stalemate the two were locked in. My fists were clenched so tightly that my nails cut into the soft flesh of my hands as I stood poised, waiting, watching, hoping...

The only sounds in the room were the rhythmic ticking of the clock on the wall above Mrs. Bright's desk, and the heavy, pained sounds of Jake's breaths as he dragged them deeply into his lungs. With every breath, his shoulders fell just a little more, until he finally pushed himself off her desk and made for the door.

His hand was curled around the handle, ready to drag it open and make his escape, when she spoke again. She just had to have the last word. "The apple didn't fall far from that particular tree, did it?"

I only had a moment, a split second to see the agony creasing his features before the door slammed open and he was gone, leaving a stunned silence in his wake.

My gaze lingered on the empty doorway for only a moment before turning on the woman who had caused this mess in the first place. Daggers so real I could almost see them were shooting from my eyes in her direction as she brushed off her hands as though shaking off a mere inconvenience, only pouring petrol over the fire inside me. All rational thought left me and I lost the ability to control the words that spat from my mouth.

"What the *hell* is wrong with you?" I seethed, keeping my fists glued to the table to avoid moving from my position and giving her an excuse to threaten me, too.

"Sit down, Mr. Williams," she replied with a long-suffering sigh, all nonchalance and disinterest as she continued to sort the papers on her desk without casting me so much as a glance.

The part of me that had always respected authority slammed right down into the seat without a moment's thought, but my body remained upright, rigid, taut with tension and anger that refused to die down.

"He did nothing—*nothing*—to deserve that. Do you dislike him that much, or do you actually enjoy making people miserable for sport?"

By the time the words had finished spilling from my mouth, I had my own books shoved into my gaping bag and I'd grabbed his from where he'd left it under the table in his haste to get out.

"He behaved exactly how I would expect him to. He's a thug, young man, and you would do well to expend your efforts on somebody more worthy of your time."

This time, with my hand on the door handle and both bags swinging from my arm, *I* would have the last word.

"You don't get to throw a lit match onto a pile of straw and then act surprised when it burns. *You* caused this. Nobody else."

Slamming the door closed so hard behind me that the sound echoed and reverberated right down the long corridor, I followed the noise with my eyes in search of Jake.

He was nowhere to be seen, and I had almost no frame of reference for where he might be. I'd sat in a classroom with him, close enough to smell his cologne and see the beautiful pictures he drew, for weeks on end, and I knew almost nothing about him.

CHAPTER SIX

Choosing a direction at random, I turned and walked, peering through the glass in the classroom doors in the hunt for the elusive boy I desperately needed to find. He was nowhere, and despair began to tinge the corners of my molten anger and simmer it to a gentle boil.

I barely knew him, and I couldn't even begin to pretend to know how it felt to be treated so appallingly by somebody he ought to have been able to trust, but I did know a tiny bit about rejection and how heavily it could weigh on your soul.

I'd watched Abbi suffering silently with the knowledge that she was unwanted by her parents for years, never truly understanding how utterly horrifying it could be to wake up each morning knowing that no matter what you did, you'd never be enough, until the day I finally poured my heart out to my father.

After wrestling an internal battle for almost a year—

longer, if I really wanted to be honest with myself—feeling like a stranger in my own skin, all of my childish plans for the future had slowly fizzled away as my heart had refused to listen to reason and insisted that its magnetic north was somebody I could never have. The pain of what could never be had slowly eaten away at me until my distraction caused me to spill expensive red wine all over my father's even more expensive antique dining table, and he'd finally lost patience with me.

I'd watched on aghast as the words spilled out of my soul without stopping, and eyes that had only ever looked at me with love and pride slowly frosted over. He wasn't a bad person, my father; he just didn't understand. How could he? He'd lived his life the way everybody expected him to—married in his twenties, two-point-four children, nice house in the decent part of town, and a job in local government to boot. Up until that day, he'd supported every one of my dreams, giving me the leg-ups I needed to achieve them where he could, but falling for another boy, the one I'd spent my childhood playing football and watching Star Wars until all hours of the morning with was just one dream too far.

Ice had taken up residence in his usually warm eyes that day, and it had never thawed.

Lost in melancholy thoughts, I found myself breaking through the double doors at the end of the corridor into the rainy school yard that bordered the playing fields. On the far side of the field, about as far from where I was standing as it was possible to be without leaving the grounds, I could see a distant, black-clad figure edging through a small gap in the hedge surrounding the field.

Sighing and lamenting the fact I'd left my coat in the common room before maths, I shrugged a little deeper into my sweater and started towards him. The rain lashed at my face as I broke into a jog at the border of the field, the ground squelching beneath my trainers.

"Jake!" I called to his retreating back as I broke through the gap I'd seen him go through. "Christ, are you practicing for the Olympics or something? Slow down."

Not responding, or even showing any sign that he'd heard me, he kept up his punishing pace as I fought against the elements in an attempt to catch up with him.

"Seriously?" I panted. "You're gonna make me chase you?"

That got his attention. He rounded on me, but where I'd expected to see anger, there was only dejection and misery. "I'm not making you do anything. Please, leave me alone."

The sadness in his eyes tore holes right through my soul as he watched me approaching him with a painful wariness. "Just wait, please. I just want to..." I trailed off, words turning to ash in my mouth as I tried and failed to think of anything to say that didn't sound trite at best and downright condescending at worst.

"Want to what? What do you want from me, Tom?" Shoulders slumped, he allowed his chin to drop to his chest, eyes screwed tightly shut. "You want me to thank you for the fact that she was right in there? It was all your work. So yeah. Thank you. Can I go now?"

He went silent, refusing to look at me, apparently waiting for some sort of dismissal that he wouldn't receive from me.

"You and I both know that what she said was total bullshit. What I don't understand is why you're blaming the fact that she's a repugnant human being on me." I allowed a bite of irritation that I didn't truly feel to sneak into my voice as my arms crossed over my chest and one eyebrow tilted up accusingly.

"I..." His tongue snaked out of his mouth and caressed his lips as his head dipped further. "You think she's..."

"Positively the worst teacher I've ever had and quite possibly one of the worst human beings I've ever met."

His shoulders sagged as some of the tension seemed to drain out of his body and his head finally lifted, though his eyes remained anywhere but on me.

"Oh..."

"Yeah. Oh." I chuckled and moved towards him, holding my breath for fear of somehow scaring him away again. "I rescued your bag. You're welcome."

Nudging his shoulder with mine, I held his bag out to him and swore I saw his lips twitching upwards the tiniest bit. "So where were you running to in such a hurry?"

One slouching shoulder lifted in a half hearted shrug. "Not really sure. Just... anywhere but there, I guess."

"Understandable." I nodded and smiled as he plucked his bag from my outstretched hand. "Want some company? I tend to find if I'm left unsupervised for too long, I get up to no good, and I feel like maybe I've already got myself into enough trouble today."

His forehead creased for a moment and his eyes considered me carefully, as though weighing me up and trying to figure something out. "I don't think I've ever met anybody like you before."

Sniffing with a grin, I nudged his elbow as I started to walk in the direction he'd been heading. "I like to think I'm one of a kind. Come on then. Keep up. We have somewhere to be."

"We do?" His face scrunched up adorably in confusion, but he moved off and fell into step beside me.

"Yup. It'll be fun, I promise." Explaining nothing further, I walked with purpose across the fields in the general direction of my home. "We just have to stop off somewhere first."

By the time we made it to Lucy's house, the sun had almost completely set, and the air was heavy with yet more rain, but she had a great security light and the drizzle just made the ground easier to work. I was in my element, digging out the flowerbeds I'd envisioned for the garden, the tension from the maths lesson slowly draining away and leaving me relaxed and happy in a way that only gardening could.

Jake had barely spoken since we'd left the college grounds, following me almost blindly to collect my tools from my parent's garden shed and then on to Lucy's without once questioning where we were going or why. I wasn't sure whether to be flattered or concerned with how easily he'd come along for the ride, but I suspected he was simply relieved to be away from that classroom with its stifling atmosphere of dislike.

When we arrived, I'd handed him a spade, marked out the area and told him to go nuts. I had to admit he was a grafter. Rain water glistened in his hair, dripping down his forehead and over his nose as he thrust the spade into the earth over and over with a surprising amount of aggression for somebody who so rarely seemed to show any emotion at all.

"So, did you accidentally run over her cat? Electrocute her goldfish? Pour fairy liquid in her water feature? What?" I questioned, my lighthearted tone belying my genuine curiosity.

He jabbed the spade into the ground once more, his slender jaw set and determined. Leaving it in the ground, he leaned an elbow on the handle and used his free hand to brush a sodden curl away from his eye. "Huh?"

Grinning, I set my own spade next to his and matched his pose. "Just wondering what you could possibly have done to make Mrs. Bright dislike you so much. It was the water feature, wasn't it? My friends Abbi and Elliot got into the garden centre once, and... Anyway, I digress. What did you do?"

His eyes narrowed infinitesimally before dropping to his feet. "*I* didn't do anything."

"Then why does she—?"

"Maybe she doesn't hate me. Maybe I really am just that bad at maths. I mean, judging from the evidence, there's every possibility I'm kidding myself thinking somebody like me could ever actually achieve something." There was a hint of anger lodged in his throat, syphoning its way into his words, but he controlled it so carefully with every syllable that it would have been easy to miss if I hadn't been watching and listening so intently.

"Somebody like you," I repeated, one eyebrow cocked in his direction.

"Yes," he replied dismissively before yanking the spade out of the ground once more and going back to work with even more gusto than before.

"Are you always so cryptic?" I asked, undeterred by his obvious evasion.

"Are you always this nosy?" he threw back.

"Touché." I chuckled. "And yes, I am. But we're not talking about me."

He sighed heavily and glanced at me briefly before concentrating back on the task. "Why do we have to talk about anybody? Why can't we just hang out, pretend to be mates?"

"We are mates."

"No, we're not. You don't know anything about me, and all I know about you is that you get up freakishly early in the morning and you're irritatingly good with numbers."

"See," I laughed and prodded his thigh with the handle of my spade, "this is where we'd do that talking thing you're so resistant to. I'm an open book. Ask me anything."

"Okay," he said with the tiniest flicker of a smile that somehow ignited hope inside me that I could forge a friendship with this guy. "Why did you come after me?"

"That's easy." I shrugged. "Because in my experience,

the people who push you away the hardest are the ones most in need of somebody to push back."

He didn't respond, just levelled me with a stare that seemed designed to bring me to my knees. There was so much hidden behind the shutters in his eyes that had always been kept so tightly locked before. Now, though, there was a small crack, and chinks of light were starting to stream through, leaking long hidden emotions out along with it. There was pain there—so much pain—but also intense longing. But longing for what? For me to shut up and leave him be? Or for somebody to listen and be there no matter how hard he pushed? I'd never seen anybody more in need of somebody to lean on.

"My turn," I eventually asserted when his gaze grew uncomfortable. "And don't look so scared. I'm harmless. Mostly."

I grinned widely, hoping to earn myself even the smallest lift of his lips in return.

Nothing.

His glare turned challenging as he spoke again. "I never agreed to a game of twenty questions."

"And yet, here we are playing it. Now hush, I need to think of a good one."

He didn't reply but muttered to himself, something that sounded a lot like 'dog with a bone', and wiped a mud covered hand over his face, brushing away the raindrops but leaving a lovely smear of dirt right across his cheeks.

Snapping my fingers gleefully, I danced around my spade to face him again as he turned back to his work. "I thought of a good one."

"That's nice for you. I'm not answering it, but you knock yourself out anyway."

"It's a good one, honestly. You'll like it."

"I doubt that." He was guarded now, wary, his eyes darting from me to the churned up earth and back again.

"Honestly, you have no trust whatsoever. I'm wounded. You cut me to the quick."

A huff, then silence.

"Now remember, the rules clearly say you have to answer truthfully or you're subject to a forfeit, and I think of the *best* forfeits."

More silence, accompanied this time by a roll of his eyes. This was good. Eye rolling meant sarcasm and familiarity, not hostility and distrust. I was definitely getting somewhere.

"Okay, so tell me—and remember, this is very important, life changing even—do you prefer Coke or Pepsi?"

He blinked once, twice, three times, and then my heart stalled in my chest as his face collapsed in on itself and he let out the most heartrendingly beautiful burst of laughter I'd ever heard.

"Seriously? That's your oh so important question?"

"Seriously." I nodded. "This is vitally important so make sure you answer carefully. The entire future of our friendship depends on this answer. No pressure or anything."

"So if I told you I didn't drink either…?"

"Dead to me," I confirmed with a grin.

"Wow. Harsh. Okay." He looked thoughtful for a moment before stating confidently, "Pepsi."

I stared at him seriously for a long moment before breaking into a grin. "Good answer. Your turn."

"Okay, as it happens I do have a question. Why are we here, in the driving rain, digging up this garden? Is it even yours? God, do you even have permission to be here? Are we trespassing right now?"

"You know, your total lack of faith in me is starting to hurt, buddy."

He shrugged and motioned for me to go on.

"I have permission. If you're looking for a rule breaker, you want my friend Abbi who owns the cottage next door. I'm more of a permission than forgiveness kind of guy. The lady who owns the garden can't look after it so she said I could go nuts."

"So, this is your job?"

"Not exactly. It's more of a hobby."

"A hobby," he repeated. "You do this for *fun*?"

I nodded.

"In the rain?"

"Skin's waterproof. Ish."

"And this is enjoyable for you?"

"Of course," I confirmed with a laugh. "What's not to enjoy?"

"I believe I already mentioned the rain."

"Rain is good. It helps the flowers grow."

"And the mud."

"Won't hurt you." I laughed. "And that was at least eight questions so that definitely makes it my turn."

"Let joy be unconfined," he quipped dryly.

I hummed quietly to myself as I thought, tapping my teeth with my fingernail as he watched me, cautious again.

"Do you really think you're bad at maths?" I finally asked, head tilted in curiosity. It pained me to see the lack of confidence he was plagued by, and the part of me that Luke called my 'bleeding heart' desperately wanted him to see his worth.

"You don't have to be a genius to know that. You only have to look at my results."

"That's not—" My objections to his reply were cut short when The Imperial March from Star Wars suddenly blared loudly from my bag, letting me know somebody was phoning me.

I stared at it for a moment in surprise. Much to Abbi's irritation, I rarely remembered to use my phone, or even switch it on. The only person who never seemed to remember that was…

Eyes widening, my chest contracted with a combination of excitement and nerves as I darted forwards and fumbled over the zip with cold, wet fingers. They did eventually close around the chirruping phone, lifting it free only for it to slip out of my grip and land face down in the mud at my feet. Cursing, I bent to retrieve it while Jake laughed from behind me. I was growing to love that sound.

The cursed object finally safely in my hand, I swiped madly at the screen as the rain dripped down, making everything more difficult.

"Hello? Hello?" I blurted out when I finally managed to connect the call.

"Where are you, dude?" Luke's voice demanded, letting a swarm of butterflies loose to batter my insides.

"I'm..." The butterflies dropped like a stone to the pit of my stomach when I realised that he knew nothing about the garden or Lucy or even the friendship I was trying to cultivate with Jake. He knew nothing about my life since starting college, and I knew nothing about his. Still... he was calling me and that had to count for something, right? "I'm just doing some gardening work for a friend. What's up?"

"Get your butt round here, pretty boy. You have a date tonight."

"I... what?"

"You. Have. A. Date. It's all organised. All you have to do is get here so we can make you look hot and then turn up and try to be charming." He snickered as though that was going to be a challenge for me. He probably had a point. He was the charming one who somehow made girl's clothes fall off just by smiling at them. I was the one who had a head full of useless facts and tried to make people laugh with rubbish jokes.

"Do I get a say in this?" I questioned, torn between amusement at his audacity and nausea at the fact he was setting me up with somebody else.

"Nope. Are you on your way yet? We don't have much time."

"But, I—"

"See you in a few."

The line went dead.

He hung up on me.

Staring at my phone in disbelief for a moment, I shook

my head as though it would somehow drain that conversation from my brain. It didn't work.

"Everything okay?"

I turned on the spot to see Jake watching me with concern in his face.

"Yeah, I, uh... I have to go. Apparently."

His face fell, disappointment clouding his expression that sent guilt tearing through me. Leaving him after the day he'd had felt all wrong, but God, I wanted to see Luke.

"Oh, right."

"Sorry, that was my best mate, Luke. He needs me to, uh... go."

"Luke... Your best mate is Luke. Luke Chang?"

"You know him?" I had to admit I was surprised. They didn't exactly move in the same circles.

"I'm familiar with his work," he muttered, dipping his spade into the ground hard and moving to pick up his bag from the ground. "Well have a good night. Thanks for rescuing this." He thrust his thumb over his shoulder to point to his bag before abruptly walking away, leaving me staring after him in confusion.

"Something I said?"

CHAPTER SEVEN

Getting the gardening tools back home on my own proved trickier than I'd expected. By the time they were all back in their places in my mum's perfectly organised shed, the rain had finally penetrated right down to my bones and my arms felt a little like I imagined Sisyphus' felt after a couple of centuries of pushing that boulder up the hill.

I'd received two texts from Luke already, saying simply, 'Waiting', and I hated the way my heart squeezed painfully every time I saw his name flash up on the screen.

My hands finally free, I wiped them off on my already filthy jeans to reply with, 'Patience is character building. I need a shower.'

I was just about over the threshold into the ice palace I called home when the screen lit up once more with the words, 'No time. Shower here.'

Use Luke's shower.

Use Luke's shower while he was in the next room...

I had enough experience of this unrequited crush of mine to know that proximity could be both a blessing and the worst kind of curse. When my heart could sense him nearby, it careered out of control, trying to beat its way free of my chest cavity and into his. But hearts couldn't be freed. They were captives, subject to our whims and bad decisions. And everything inside me, apart from my battered heart, was telling me that going there tonight was the worst decision I could possibly make.

My heart, though, had never listened. The reckless organ that kept the rest of my body going seemed determined to send me spiralling down a path that would leave me shattered into pieces that could never be put back together.

"Are you even listening to me, Thomas?"

The sharp voice cut through my agonised attempt at decision making and landed me right back in the doorway to the kitchen where my clothes were dripping filthy rainwater onto the tiled floor as my dad stood in front of me wearing an aggravated expression.

"Sorry," I muttered as my heart dropped into my stomach. I'd hoped to get in and out without seeing him. My dad had been my hero my entire life—a stalwart of the family and a constant advocate for hard work paying off—so the sad disappointment that lingered on the edges of his expression every time he looked at me now left me feeling depleted.

His stiffly formal shoulders dropped a little as he grazed his eyes over my sodden form and he let out a low sigh, cupping the back of his neck with his hand. "What happened to you?"

"It's raining," I replied obviously.

"I may need glasses, but even I'd figured out that much. But why are you covered in mud and soaked through? You'll catch your death." He held a hand up, indicating for me to stay put, and disappeared into the utility room, returning a moment later with a soft blue towel that he handed to me with a hint of a smile.

Nodding my thanks, I started to scrub at my dripping hair, oddly grateful for the fatherly concern in his tone. "I was working in a garden. I sort of have a project."

"A project." One eyebrow lifted under his perfectly styled silver hair. "Is this *project* going to interfere with your studies?"

"Have I ever let anything interfere with getting the grades I wanted before?"

He nodded, my answer apparently enough for him, and he turned on his heel, ready to leave. "Well, I'll leave you to get to work then."

"Actually..." I let the word hover in the air, stalling him on the threshold of freedom from this stiflingly awkward conversation. "I kind of, sort of, have a date thing tonight."

He stiffened, his spine suddenly ramrod straight, and I could practically see the unease rippling from him in waves.

"Blind date, courtesy of Luke," I added, knowing that my words had taken his nerves and strummed them like the strings of a guitar.

He couldn't stop himself from replying to that. His

voice was hoarse with tension as he asked, "You told Luke... about your..."

He didn't finish. It seemed saying the word was just a step too far for him, but I waited anyway, a dormant part of me hoping he'd find a way to make peace with who I was. His lips slammed shut into a flat line, though, as the small amount of colour he had drained visibly from his face.

Would it be so bad if I had?

The words were sitting there on the tip of my tongue, fighting to break free from my lips, but I wasn't that guy. One bout of defiance in a single day was about all I was capable of. Instead, I ducked my head and let him off the hook.

"It's with a girl, Dad."

"A..." Surprisingly, the first emotion to hit his features was confusion, but elation quickly followed, an almost manic smile spreading over the face that had been radiating disappointment only seconds earlier. "Well, I suppose that one night won't do any harm. You're a bright boy. I'm sure you'll catch up. Do you need a lift anywhere? Who is she? Do I know her parents? You have cash?"

I enjoyed a fleeting moment of wellbeing, basking in his interest before the bittersweet tang of what might have been burned my skin like acid.

Could I do it? Could I force myself to conform, to squeeze myself into the mold that others wanted me to fit, sacrificing my chance to love freely and without restraint?

"I have what I need. Thanks, Dad," I choked out through a throat that was trying hard to stopper the words and hold them inside.

Half an hour later, I was crunching my way down the gravel driveway to Luke's enormous house, silently talking myself out of running in the opposite direction. My steps slowed more and more the closer to the imposing house I got. Intending to take a moment to collect myself when I reached the door, I allowed my body to fall back against it gently to pull in a deep breath and prepare myself for the agony that was bound to be on the other side. Only, when I fell back, the door failed to catch me because it was no longer sitting in its frame.

A strangled cry echoed from my lips as I continued to fall backwards, my backside hitting the floor with a painful thud, and I found myself flat on my back on the Chang's mosaic tiled hallway floor, staring up at the boy I couldn't stop thinking about while he stared back with amusement.

"You always did know how to make an entrance," he quipped, offering me a hand with a smug grin. "Where you been? You've been ages."

Grabbing his hand, I toyed for a moment with the thought of yanking on it and pulling him down beside me, or even *accidentally* on top of me, but common sense or just sheer cowardice stopped me and I allowed him to pull me to my feet instead, not meeting his gaze.

Avoiding his eyes was essential if I wanted to pull this off without giving myself away as the fraud I apparently was. "I had to go home first. Contrary to popular belief I'm not an actual labrador and I don't mindlessly come when I'm called."

"Sure you don't," he replied good naturedly. "Come on, Rover. Let's get you ready."

He stalked off upstairs, leaving me behind to cast my eyes over my chosen outfit and mumble to myself, "I am ready."

When I finally made it up the stairs after him and rounded the hallway into his vast bedroom, I hadn't banked on seeing Annika sprawled out on his bed as though she'd always belonged there.

It was my duty as Abbi's friend to hate her with the raging fire of a thousand hells, but now, I was starting to really dislike her off my own back. Logically, I knew that me and Luke was never going to happen, but that didn't mean I would ever be okay with him being with *her* of all people—the vapid shrew who had hurt Abbi so badly and jeopardised Elliot's future in medicine because of her own selfish whims.

I did my best to be friendly, though, an attempt to leave my animosity at the door for Luke's sake if not for hers.

"Annika," I said with a stiff nod.

She rolled lazily onto her side and looked me up and down with an expression of mild disinterest. "You won't need to do much, Lukie Bear. She's not exactly revving up for the catwalk anytime soon herself."

I snorted. I couldn't help it. The soppy way she said *Lukie Bear* was just too much for me. It was just so... un-him. He could ham up the Prince Charming act on the surface when he needed to, but in reality he was probably the least romantic person in Colwich.

"Were you expecting a night with Melanie Jacobson? She has standards, you know," she told me, totally misreading my reaction to her words.

"Trust me, *Anni Bear,* if the date was with her, there'd be a Tom shaped hole in Lukie Bear's door that I'm positive he wouldn't thank me for."

Her face soured as the realisation of the real reason for my snort dawned on her, and she rolled back onto her front, her legs kicking up behind her as she turned her attention back to her phone.

Luke emerged from his ridiculous walk-in wardrobe with handfuls of his own clothes, which he dumped on the bed before turning to size me up once again.

"Christ, I feel like I'm on one of those god-awful TV makeover programmes," I grumbled. "I'm dressed. It's bad enough I'm even doing this thing but you are *not* dressing me as well. I'm going as I am or not at all."

He huffed, but didn't argue with me, and I finally let my eyes meet his. Where my knees had been, suddenly, there was only jelly, and I wobbled precariously at the look of intense scrutiny and maybe slight approval that lingered there.

"Yeah, okay, you don't look too bad," he muttered, almost to himself.

Not too bad.

The jelly turned to acid and I dropped down onto the bed with a thump, earning myself an unnecessary huff from Annika.

Not. Too. Bad.

Like I was some ugly duckling who needed their preening in order to scrub up into something worth looking at. I wasn't vain by any stretch of the imagination, but coming from the guy who was not only the main attraction in my dreams but also, supposedly, my best friend, that hurt.

"Do I get to know who it is I'm meeting?" I questioned dully, trying and failing to inject some enthusiasm into my voice.

"That would kinda defeat the object, buddy," Luke replied, apparently oblivious to the sharp downturn in my mood. "It's a *blind* date."

"Right. Great." I tried to ignore the way my knees protested as I pushed back to my feet. "Well I suppose I better..."

Grinning, Luke grabbed a piece of paper off his desk and thrust it at me. "Pick her up from here. You have a reservation at Chopstix at seven. Apparently she loves Chinese food."

"Well at least I know she's sane," I quipped, scanning the address before stuffing it in my pocket with a shaking hand, mentally preparing myself for a night of trying to force a square peg into a round hole.

The street where the mystery girl lived was quiet when I reached it only a few minutes later. It was a long, narrow road lined on both sides with tall, terraced houses. Cars were parked thickly on either side, leaving only a narrow bit of road for passing traffic, of which there seemed to be plenty. Horns blared as impatient drivers tried to force their way through, leaving the road all but gridlocked, and me grateful that I was too young to drive.

It looked as though the mystery girl's house was at the

opposite end of the street, so I made my way through the driving rain, dodging puddles and skipping out of the way of the waves sent into the air by the passing cars, only looking a little bit like a drowned rat by the time I stood on the doorstep, staring at a blue door with a brass knocker, talking myself into using it.

Man up, Tom. She's a girl not a dragon.

My silent internal chastisement didn't soothe a single one of my rattling nerves or settle the hive of bees buzzing around in my stomach, but nonetheless, my hand lifted and slapped the knocker sharply twice.

Nobody answered for the longest time, but there was no doubt that somebody was home. The conversation seeped through the wooden door as though it wasn't there at all, draining my confidence away with every muffled word.

"Your date is here," a female voice shouted loudly, as footsteps echoed past the door, but didn't pause to open it.

"Oh joy. Reckon if we don't answer the door he'll think we're out?" The second voice triggered a flash of familiarity in my mind but wasn't loud enough for me to place it.

"He might be hot."

"Sure, Annika would set me up with a hot guy instead of keeping him for herself. The best I can hope for is that he's not an active member of the Nazi party."

"He might be a decent human being then," the first voice attempted.

"In this town? Please. I'll be lucky if I don't finish the night chopped into tiny pieces and fed to the ducks at the lake."

I moved to knock again, but froze, my hand in the air allowing rainwater to find its way down my sleeve as the conversation continued.

"I'm not sure ducks like human flesh."

"Anybody who has ever tried feeding them Hovis might disagree with you there. One of them almost took my hand off once. I was three. Those things are savage. If I was going to kill somebody, I'd absolutely, one hundred percent, use the ducks to dispose of the evidence."

Well that was reassuring...

Clearing my throat, I knocked again loudly, calling out, "Hey, if I promise not to chop you up to feed the waterfowl, do you think I could come in? It's pissing it down out here."

Silence poured through the door, thick and embarrassed, and I couldn't help the grin that overtook my face. They clearly hadn't known I could hear them.

Still, the door didn't open.

"Would it help if I told you that blood makes me queasy?"

"Wait a minute," the second voice called out suddenly. "I know that voice."

The door flew open, and for a moment, all I could see was a chaos of brightly coloured hair before it was flung back to reveal a very familiar face.

"Oh. My. God," Trix cried, her hand flying to her mouth as she tried and failed to stifle a laugh. "It's *you!*"

"Not doing my self esteem any good right now, Trix, I'm not going to lie," I quipped, attempting to sound serious, but my relief at seeing a familiar face where I'd expected the kind of hostility Annika exuded broke through and forced my expression into a smile.

"I daresay your fragile ego will survive. Now get in here before your hair goes curly, pretty boy. I am *so* relieved it's you."

"Because of the not a serial killer thing?"

"Because of the not a total numpty thing."

"You say the nicest things," I said, with a nudge to her shoulder.

"I know, right? I'm a diamond. Shall we go then? Where are you taking me, Prince Charming?"

"Did you know there's actually a national chopsticks day?" I questioned, snapping the wooden implements between my fingers as Trix sat staring at hers, trying to work out how to use them.

"Why is that even a thing? Why are *these* even a thing?" she grumbled, eventually giving up and inserting the sticks in her mouth like woolly mammoth teeth, earning herself disparaging looks from several other diners.

"I dunno." I shrugged. "But if all else fails, apparently they make great drumsticks."

Allowing the sticks to fall from her mouth, she quirked an eyebrow at me with a small smirk curling up her lips. "Isn't that, like, really offensive to somebody somewhere?"

"Probably," I conceded. "But pretty much everything is. I mean, I'm a white middle class male so even my existence is offensive."

She snorted loudly, and a ladylike looking woman on the next table bristled, straightening her skirt along her legs as though her perfection could make up for the reprobate beside her.

"Well, true, but you know you have the gay thing going for you, so there's that."

I blinked. Stared. Blinked again.

She went on like she'd said nothing of any consequence, spearing a piece of chicken with a single chopstick and proudly stuffing it into her mouth.

"I'm sorry, what?"

She grinned around her chicken, mumbling with her mouth full, "Trix knows. Trix always knows."

"But... how?"

I'd known her for only a couple of months and she'd somehow picked up on what my best friend of over a decade had missed. How was that even possible?

"Oh, please, Thomasina. You're not that subtle. Anyone with a pair of eyes can see the lost puppy dog eyes you give to that knobhead Luke whenever he's in the vicinity."

"But..." My forehead creased as my mind flicked back over every interaction with him while she was present. Was I really that obvious? Why was I here, on a date with an admittedly way cooler girl than I was expecting, if it was so blatant that Y chromosomes were my thing?

"You're right," she agreed, as though I'd made some sort of statement. "He does have a great butt. I'll give you that one. The fact that he has the personality of an octopus is totally irrelevant."

I moved to protest, my lips flapping around in an attempt to find words to defend him, but she went on talking as though I weren't even there.

"Although, you never actually hear people saying bad things about octopuses. Or is it octopi? Whatever. They're probably pretty decent actually. Wasps, though. They're the real knobheads of the animal kingdom. He's definitely a wasp."

Struck temporarily mute, all I could do was stare at her as she went on, detailing all the ways in which she wished wasps would be removed from the planet, not actually saying it but alluding to the fact she basically wanted the same to happen to Luke.

Luke. The guy everybody either liked or wanted to be. He owned the common room, had half the female population either hanging off him or wishing they were, and here in front of me was, apparently, the exception who proved the rule.

Shifting awkwardly in my seat, I racked my brains for something to say to ease the weird tension that had taken up residence in my stomach. "Did you know octopuses die after giving birth?"

She stared at me, open mouthed in what I chose to believe was an awed silence at my superior octopus knowledge but was, more realistically, probably disgust or mere confusion.

Eventually, when her jaw found its way closed again, she licked her lips before saying, "We'll discuss why the hell you know that later. Does it bother you that I noticed?"

Did it?

"I... I'm not sure," I finally croaked out when it became clear that the possibility of changing the subject was off the table. "Nobody's ever just... noticed before."

"They can't have been looking very hard, then. At the risk of crushing any Hollywood aspirations you might be harbouring, I gotta tell you you're a terrible actor."

"Thanks," I replied drily. "I'll scrub movie star off my list of possible careers then."

I searched through my mind for a joke to tell to take my mind off how much her words had inadvertently stung.

They can't have been looking very hard...

Abbi joked constantly about what a social butterfly I was compared to her, yet she so much as frowned and Elliot could tell what was wrong. Apparently she had a collection of frowns, and he was able to identify every single one of them. He knew absolutely everything about her, including the things she fought so hard to hide. And as much as I tried to be content with what I had and the life I lived, knowing there were so many who had impossibly difficult lives, I couldn't help the longing that shot through me at the thought of being so completely accepted by somebody, loved no matter what.

"What did the ocean say to the other ocean?" I asked, my voice flat despite the enthusiasm I tried hard to inject into it.

"Umm..." If she was surprised by the change in subject, she didn't show it. "No idea?"

"Nothing. They just waved at each other."

She snorted. "You might want to rule out a career in stand up comedy, too, buddy."

CHAPTER EIGHT

"So, how'd it go?"

"Good morning to you, too," I mumbled into my coffee, blowing on it softly and watching the steam rising from the surface dance and twist around my breath.

"Yeah, yeah, whatever," he replied good naturedly, grinning as he jumped onto the back of the bench seat opposite and crossed his legs on the tabletop. "Tell me everything."

"That might take a while," I mumbled with a dry smile.

"Ugh, nobody likes a smart arse, Thomas. You know what I mean. How was the date? Did you two get along? Are you seeing her again?"

"Well, given that I have maths second period, I guess I'll be seeing her in about an hour and a half."

His face creased into a confused frown that marred his impeccable features, a line appearing in the honey coloured skin between his dark brows. "I don't follow."

"It's only really a *blind* date if you haven't sat next to them in lessons every single day for two months, dude. This was really more of a partially sighted date."

"Ugh, figures she'd study maths," he huffed out with an eye roll. "Nika said she was a total geek."

One eyebrow quirked at him as I sat back and folded my arms, attempting to stop the slight twitch at the corner of my mouth. "Is that so?"

"You know what I mean. God, I'd forgotten how facetious you are in the morning."

I blinked and stared at him in abject disbelief. *I* was the morning person. He was the one who wouldn't allow people to speak to him until he was at least a third of the way through his second coffee of the day.

"Do I?" I asked, a little ice entering my voice.

"Do you what?"

It was clear from his tone that this conversation wasn't going at all the way he'd hoped, and since it wasn't giving him the information he was after, he was rapidly losing interest in it.

"Know what you mean?"

"Of course you do. I mean, it's different for you, isn't it?"

"Different... how?"

He shrugged, growing more exasperated by the second, though I wasn't sure I understood why. "Well you're a guy, aren't you?"

"Christ, Luke, in one sentence you just managed to achieve the impossible and make Westborough Baptist Church sound positively progressive. What the hell difference does that make? Trix gets better grades than nearly every 'guy' in that class."

"Defending her honour, are we? You've got it bad, lover boy," he went on, unperturbed by my simmering anger on Trix's behalf.

I wanted to scream at him, to shake him and force all his words back inside of him, to force him to look at me until he could see me—the real me, not the one he'd somehow convinced himself existed. He wanted a wingman, a brother in arms who would help him to work his way through the remaining female population of the town. He didn't want me—the guy who only knew how to pine after what he couldn't have, who looked at him and saw not the chance to pull more girls but the haunting shadows of what might have been if things had been different.

"I need to get to physics," I forced out through a throat that wanted to close up completely.

"Mate, it's not even half eight yet. You have ages."

"Yeah, well I have some coursework I need to finish off first," I lied.

"You haven't even told me how the date went yet. How was she?"

I sighed, sweeping my phone and headphones into my open bag and throwing it onto my back before standing from the table. "Great. Perfect. She's everything I've ever wanted."

I swept out of the common room like I had one of Jake's dragons at my heels, trying hard not to think about how every conversation I had with my best friend seemed to leave me feeling worse about myself.

It's amazing how when you're looking forward to something, time slows to a crawl, the hands of the clock almost working backwards in an attempt to keep you from that elusive moment of happiness when the time arrives. But when it's something you're dreading, suddenly everything seems to go by in a blur. A lesson that would usually feel like a life sentence can suddenly race by in the blink of an eye.

And so it was with physics. I wasn't sure whether it was an actual law of the subject or just bad luck, but that day, the lesson seemed to race by at lightspeed, all while my stomach churned at the thought of walking back into the classroom I'd left so abruptly the previous day.

I had no regrets, none whatsoever.

Mrs. Bright had been bang out of order treating Jake that way, and I wouldn't have been able to live with myself if I hadn't at least tried to defend him. It wasn't like he seemed especially keen to stand up for himself, though why that was was still a mystery to me.

By the time the bell rang, signalling the end of my short grace period, the churning in my stomach had turned to an all out war, leaving me almost doubled up in pain as I shuffled my way slowly to the dreaded classroom. Rebellion had never been something I was good at. I'd watched on amused for years as Elliot had challenged authority at every turn, and always wished, with a tiny part of me I kept hidden, that I could be more like him. I was more of a do as you're told kind of guy—a toe the line and don't ripple the water student. But injustice was like an itch I couldn't scratch, sitting there right under my skin, driving me to distraction until I was forced into action.

But where had it got me?

Afraid to walk into the one classroom in which I actually excelled.

Still, at least Jake knew I had his back now.

After several deep breaths, I finally grabbed the handle and pushed my way through the door and into the room, expecting a look that would turn me to ashes, but Mrs. Bright wasn't there. In her place was a man I didn't recognise—young, fresh faced, and with more kindness in his expression than any of us ever expected to see from anybody sitting behind that desk.

It was probably pretty rude of me to stand there staring at him, mouth hanging open like a guppy, but discovering that my hour of nerve fuelled anxiety had been for nothing had rendered me momentarily mute and paralysed.

"Can I help you?" the unknown man asked as I mastered the use of my eyelids while the rest of my body remained stubbornly frozen in place.

"Don't worry," Trix's voice called out as the sound of chair legs scraping along the floor rang through the room, closely followed by a hand closing around my arm. "He was expecting crazy old witch, not fresh young hottie. He'll regain the use of his body soon."

He looked a little bemused as she steered me to my seat and pushed me unceremoniously into it with a thump, but not remotely angry, which was a refreshing change in this room. It wasn't until the door opened again that I managed to drag my eyes away from Mr. New. Jake edged into the room, keeping his head down and eyes glued to the floor. His headphones were tightly in his ears, and his usual sketch book was tucked under his arm, his armour well and truly in place.

My body came back to life at the sight of him, the apprehension clearly splashed across his face giving me back the use of my muscles. I offered up a smile in his direction, hoping to catch his eye and let him know this lesson, at least, was going to be okay. But he didn't look up, not even when he made his way right to the back of the classroom, sending my heart plummeting into my shoes.

I'd expected hostility from Mrs. Bright, probably aimed at both of us, but I'd foolishly thought that we could at least put up a united front together. It seemed, though, from the way he'd put as much space as possible between not just himself and the front of the room but also himself and me, that he was throwing up walls right around himself. And I was very much on the outside again.

"Well that's weird," Trix muttered in my ear as she bent to retrieve her books from her bag. "I thought you guys had bonded."

"So did I..." Brow furrowed, I twisted in my seat to watch as Jake settled in his old place, pulling sketching pencils from the pouch of his hoodie before leaning over his blank white page with purpose. Though I wasn't sure that purpose was creativity so much as just to block out the rest of the room. I was still toying with the idea of forcibly breaching his walls and plonking myself down in the seat beside him when Mr. New cleared his throat and called the room to order.

"Hi, guys. I'm afraid you're stuck with me for a couple of days while your usual teacher is..." He trailed off, shifting through some sheets of paper on the desk.

"In prison?" Trix finished for him hopefully.

I snorted, but Mr. New didn't react at all, still hunting for some elusive sheet amongst the many in front of him.

"Off sick, he finally finished, brandishing a thin booklet in the air in triumph. "I'm not really a maths teacher so I'm relying on you to help me out with what you need from these lessons."

I could still hear the tinny bass beats from Jake's headphones behind me, and when I turned to look at him, he was lost in his sketch, probably not even realising the lesson had started.

"Actually learning something would be helpful," one of the lads from the other side of the room called out, earning himself a laugh from the rest of the class, minus one, and a confused but polite smile from the teacher.

"Okay," he said, lengthening the word awkwardly, like he didn't quite know how to proceed after that statement. "Well, Mrs. Bright has left me with this workbook she'd like to you complete before she returns, hopefully later in the week. I'll hand these out and you can start to work through them. If you have any questions, I'll do my best to help you as much as my biology teacher brain will allow."

"I wouldn't mind learning some biology with him," Trix muttered softly as he turned to begin handing out the workbooks.

"Mmm," I hummed distractedly, my eyes moving once again to Jake, who appeared no closer to engaging at all with the lesson. I wasn't even sure he'd noticed that Mrs. Bright wasn't there. He was totally lost in his creation, his lips moving soundlessly to whatever music he was listening to while his slender hands moved deftly over the page. It was like poetry, the way he fell so far inside his own head when he worked. I could have watched him all day, but I quickly averted my eyes when Mr. New dropped down beside his table and plucked an earphone from his right ear. My eyes widened when Jake jumped almost a foot in the air in surprise, dropping his pencil. It went skittering across the floor as the whole class went silent, all eyes on Jake, who shrank into his hoodie looking beyond uncomfortable.

My foot tapped nervously against the floor, waiting for Mr. New to begin admonishing Jake for not paying attention, but it never came. He gestured to the dragon slowly taking shape on the sketch pad as Jake watched him cautiously, and a wide smile overtook his admittedly quite beautiful face. "Wish I could draw like that. You studying art A level?"

It took a moment before Jake's head began to nod almost imperceptibly, his eyebrows rising as his expectations, which had obviously matched mine, were not met.

"You have a lot of talent. Keep it up, lad—just not during class, yeah?"

"Yes, Sir. Sorry," Jake said quickly, folding his sketchpad back up and reaching for the workbook he'd been handed with trepidation on his face.

Everybody finally settled down to work, the usual

pained silence lingering in the room despite the absence of its usual cause. Habits, it seemed, were hard to break. The work wasn't too hard. Most of it had been covered in some form or another in lessons, though the frustrated sighs and huffs emitting from the table behind me suggested Jake wasn't quite so comfortable with it.

My entire body vibrated with the need to turn around and offer to help, but the cool way he'd refused to meet my gaze kept my eyes firmly on my own work instead. Several times, when the despondent sounds escalated, I was sure he'd raise his hand and ask for help, but he went stubbornly on alone.

Alone.

When I really thought about it, alone seemed to be how he spent a lot of his time. Was he just an introvert, or was some sort of pain at the root of his withdrawal?

When his sighing turned to more of an agonised groan, I moved instinctively to help him, pushing from my seat at the same time as the teacher whose name I still had no idea of. When I met his eye, I paused, ready to plonk back into my seat and let him deal with it, but a short incline of his head in Jake's direction told me to keep moving.

Jake's back grew ramrod straight when I slid into the chair beside him and elbowed his arm away from where it was covering his work. Torn between sadness and irritation that my proximity seemed to cause that tension in him, I elected to ignore it and use maths as a bridge over the gap that seemed to have widened between us.

"Which bit are you having problems with?" I questioned just as Mr. Probably-too-hot-to-be-a-teacher ducked down beside the table, too.

"I'm fine," he lied vehemently, convincing precisely nobody.

"Uh huh." I nodded with a roll of my eyes. "And I like to dress up as a ballerina at weekends and dance to Tchaikovsky. Hand it over, buddy. No man is an island."

"This man is," he grumbled, trying and failing to block my attempts to steal his work. "An island with a *lot* of ocean around it. Shark infested ocean. And jellyfish. Lots of jellyfish."

"Good job I have thick skin then, huh?" I grinned and tapped him on the head with his workbook. "Which bit are you struggling with? You might as well save all three of us time by not lying because at this point I'm basically a dog with a bone."

"My god you're annoying," he groused, as I laid his work out flat on the table and started to look it over.

He hadn't got very far at all. There was more work scribbled out than visible, and his frustration was clear in every deep indent of the pen on the page.

"I shall take that as a compliment," I said with a chuckle, grabbing his wrist so I could wrestle his pen free of the tight grip of his fingers.

"It wasn't meant as one."

"I know. Now hush, I'm doing sums." Mr. Definitely-too-young-to-be-a-teacher watched on amused as I tried to make sense of what was left on the page while Jake sulked beside me. He could sulk all he wanted. He wouldn't ask for help so he was going to get it whether he wanted it or not. Some people only needed gentle coaxing to accept kindness; others needed cannons up their backsides, and I suspected Jake was the latter. Well, I was a cannonball and he was going to take my help even if it killed both of us, which I suspected it might.

"Listen, you don't need to—"

I shot him a look that had his mouth snapping closed instantly while his eyes widened, probably in surprise that he'd actually done as he was told for once. Abbi called it my 'future teacher face' and it had never yet failed me.

Slowly, we worked through the workbook together, side by side, while Mr. How-did-he-get-his-hair-to-fall-like-that watched on with interest. He chipped in some help where he could, and between us, we made it to the end of the lesson without any of us losing patience or body parts, which felt like a minor miracle.

"You ever thought about a career in teaching?" Jake and I both looked up from packing our bags at Mr. God-his-smile-was-dreamy's words, and I couldn't help but smile.

"Actually, as it happens," I replied sheepishly.

"Good. You have a gift for helping people to understand things. Hell, I'm terrible with numbers and even I understood what you've been doing for the last hour. *That* is a talent, kiddo. Don't waste it. And you..." He turned to face Jake who glanced down at his feet rather than meet his eyes, evidently expecting some sort of admonishment. "I expect to have a piece of your artwork hanging on my wall one day."

He didn't look up, but the corners of Jake's mouth definitely twitched in a small, shy but pleased smile. How often did people say positive things to him? From the surprise that creased his brow and the minuscule lift of his permanently hunched shoulders, I guessed not that often.

I almost fell off my chair in surprise when, as Mr. Definitely-my-new-favourite-teacher turned to leave, Jake coughed lightly before asking, "Hey, Sir, do you have a name?"

Grinning, I nudged his foot with mine and teased, "Everybody has a name, Jacob."

"Washford. Mr. Washford," the teacher replied before sauntering off and leaving the room.

The moment he was gone, Trix rounded on us with a manic glint in her eye. "You two have all the luck, spending the entire lesson with that magnificent specimen."

Jake let out what I thought might be a laugh, but the sound was so unfamiliar coming from him that I couldn't be sure. He made to leave, slinging his bag onto his back and plucking his sketch pad from the table. I grabbed his arm halfway up to reinsert his earphones.

"Hey, you know if you need help with this stuff, we could make this a thing. Let's face it, none of us are gonna be learning anything from Mrs. Bright any time soon."

"That's okay. I'm—"

"I swear to god, if you tell me you're fine, I'm going to beat you over the head with this workbook until I draw blood. You hear me?"

"Christ, are you always so violent?"

"Only when it's deserved. So meet me in the library after last period and we'll finish off those questions, okay?"

"But..."

"Okay?" I interrupted.

"You don't ha—"

"Jacob, this book is getting perilously close to caving your skull in. Let's not do the 'I don't want to be an inconvenience' dance, yeah? You'd be helping me as much as I'd be helping you. Tell me no if you hate me or whatever, but if you want the help, let me give it. Please."

"I..." His feet shuffled beneath him as his eyes looked anywhere but at me. For a moment, I was sure he was going to say no. He looked as though he was torn between falling at my feet or punching me square in the face, but eventually he gave a small nod that made my heart soar with happiness.

CHAPTER NINE

The word library was a little grand for the tiny room where I'd arranged to meet Jake. It was a long shot to think you'd find the book you were looking for in there, with the space almost entirely taken up with tables, and just three bookcases along one wall holding a random variety of books nobody had ever heard of, along with a single, battered copy of The Hunger Games.

The title was apt. I was starving. So much so that my own elbow was starting to look appetising. I'd worked through lunch to complete my own workbook after spending the lesson helping Jake with his, and now my stomach felt like it was trying to force its way free of my body in search of food. I was in serious danger of crossing that fine line between hungry and hangry, and as the seconds ticked by on the obnoxiously loud clock hanging right above my head, my patience was rapidly wearing thin.

He was late.

And not popped to the toilet on the way to meet me

late. The kind of late where I was starting to feel like an idiot for waiting, but I wanted to believe that he would turn up. I wasn't even sure why it mattered. It was him who needed the help after all. I could go home and relax. Or even better, go to Lucy's and do more on the garden, after a pit stop for some serious refuelling, definitely including donuts. Yet here I was, sitting around like a mug, waiting for somebody who clearly didn't want my help.

Mild irritation scratched at my skin until it had swelled into a living, breathing anger inside my chest. Realistically, I had no right to be so mad. I'd pretty much coerced Jake into agreeing to meet, yet somehow I'd expected him to show up and be grateful for the help. Maybe he'd even smile at me, and we'd laugh over some stupid mistake we made, and by the time we left, we'd be friends. Real friends.

That dream was dying now, as rapidly as my patience, and suddenly there was only one place I wanted to be. I packed up in record time, stuffing everything into my bag haphazardly and ignoring the sound of ripping in my haste. Whatever it was would have to be sacrificed to the Gods of my anger and hunger. Stopping at the vending machine on the way out of the building, I bought as many Snickers bars as the change in my pocket would allow and stuffed them into my mouth one after the other on the way to the town leisure centre.

It wasn't long before I was standing on what had always felt like the edge of the world, my toes curled around the familiar tiles, ready to plunge headfirst into the abyss that always calmed my mind.

The cold water cascaded over my head and shoulders

as I dove in, and I allowed my body to slice through the water until my lungs cried out for oxygen and my eyes stung. As my head broke through the surface, I could already feel the odd tension draining away, my focus only on the next stroke and the next.

Was it foolish of me to have hoped?

I wasn't even sure what it was that drew me to Jake. He was quiet and reserved, bordering on painfully so—not my usual choice of friend at all. And yet there was something about him that called to me, like a lost part of my soul recognised the same thing in his and craved a connection I couldn't work out how to forge.

Lap after lap, I pushed my body until everything hurt except my mind, which was blessedly clear. The anger was gone, along with the hurt I wouldn't admit to feeling over Jake's no-show. It was what it was. I would be there for him if he needed me, but in the meantime I couldn't afford to give him that amount of power over my emotions again.

The blissful indifference lasted as long as it took to drag my aching body from the water and shower the day off myself. By the time I made it home, my mind was churning once again, and I wasn't at all prepared for the instant assault of my parents the moment I walked through the door.

"How was your night?" my mum asked hopefully, perched on a stool at the breakfast bar in the kitchen, peeling the most oddly shaped potato I'd ever seen in my life. "You were home late. Does that mean you had a good time?"

Turning to shut the door behind me, I fumbled with

the handle for a little longer than necessary just to hold the Spanish inquisition at bay for as long as possible. When it was well and truly shut and I couldn't put it off any longer, I turned around to face them, the hope in their eyes forcing every bit of oxygen from my lungs in a whoosh.

"It was... Yeah... I guess we had a good time," I offered up, feeling arrows of hurt shooting through my soul at the way their eyes lit up. Like maybe I wasn't defective after all. Like maybe I could be the son they wanted me to be. Like the moment I'd taken all their plans for my future and stuffed them through an imaginary shredder had never happened.

"And she's a nice girl, is she? You must invite her around for dinner."

"What's her name? Would I know her parents?" my dad interjected, leaning his hip against the counter and looking more animated about my life than I'd seen him in almost a year.

Would you be saying all this if I'd told you I had a date with a boy?

The question burned the tip of my tongue, and I bit down on it sharply to keep the words from tumbling free and ruining everything. The bitter tang of copper told me I'd bitten down a little too hard but questions had been asked that I needed to give answers to.

"Trix," I pushed out through my constricted throat. "Her name is Beatrix."

"Beatrix what?" my dad pushed.

"I... I'm not sure." How could I possibly have sat next to

her in maths everyday for weeks and never picked up on her surname? Some friend I was.

"And is she pretty?"

Was she? I was hardly the authority on female appearances. She looked nice to me but I wasn't trying to get into her underwear.

"Uh, yeah, I guess so?" Lacking any sort of conviction, my words came out as more of a question than a statement, and I knew I'd made a mistake long before my mum let me know it.

"Good grief, Thomas, I hope you didn't show her the same level of disinterest," my mum cried out in horror.

"All girls like to be told they're beautiful, son." Dad clapped his hand down hard on my shoulder, making my knees buckle dangerously beneath me. "Your mother needs to hear it at least three times every day."

I didn't tell them that Trix wasn't like other girls, that she would likely take being described as a genius over beautiful any day. I didn't tell them that unlike them, she didn't look at me as somebody who needed to be fixed. That while I felt absolutely no romantic feelings towards her whatsoever, I was starting to feel more true friendship with her than I'd ever felt with anybody other than Abbi.

"Invite her for dinner this Sunday. Your brother will be home. It'll be a lovely occasion."

My heart, already a long term resident in my shoes, felt like it sank another ten feet through the floor.

A family dinner. With the prodigal son. And a girl my parents were already envisioning a happily ever after with that would never happen. *Could* never happen.

My tongue felt like it had been raking over sandpaper for hours when I finally managed to move it enough to reply that I would ask her.

Everything felt wrong, like the world was topsy turvy. The fake me I couldn't stand seemed to be so much easier to love than the real me who was hidden inside and screaming to get out.

By morning, the ache of inadequacy had festered into a burning pain deep inside my chest that wouldn't shift no matter what I did, and the call of the sunrise was stronger than ever. I had no idea what I needed, or even what I wanted, but I felt certain that the sunlight would heal over the cracks of what was broken inside me as it spilled over the land, bringing the hope of a new day with it.

The wood of the jetty was cold beneath my thighs as my feet dangled just short of the water, and tangled thoughts tied themselves in knots inside my mind.

My parents, the ones whose dreams I'd crushed.

Luke, the best friend who wanted a wingman I didn't know how to be.

Trix, the girl who saw right through my daily performances to the terrified boy inside.

Jake, the boy who... Who what?

Everybody in my life had their role, compartmentalised into boxes just like the ones I forced myself into each day. But Jake... He didn't have a box. I didn't know where to put him in my mixed up mind. All I knew was... he mattered.

I wanted to know him, beyond the guarded day to day persona he put out there. And even scarier than that, I wanted him to know me. I wanted him to see past the character I played for the ones who saw me as the popular kid, to the loneliness that tore me to ribbons inside every single day. I wanted him to realise that maybe he and I weren't as different as he seemed to think we were. That just because my walls weren't out there for all the world to see, complete with moat and drawbridge, didn't mean they weren't there.

Was there anybody in Colwich who wasn't hiding their true selves behind masks and costumes?

My father, the career politician pretending to be the perfect family man while hiding the fact he was ashamed of his son behind gleaming white smiles and loving photo opportunities.

Luke, the womaniser who pretended to care about girls just long enough to get what he wanted from them before throwing them away like yesterday's newspaper.

Jake, the emotionally closed off robot who had, just for a moment, allowed me to see the vulnerability he fought so hard to hide, giving me access to a world of pain he fought so hard to keep hidden.

And me, the biggest fraud of all, hiding behind dumb jokes and hastily memorised fun facts in the hope that nobody would see just how much I didn't fit in in any of the circles I moved in.

How could you trust what you saw when everybody around you was playing a role?

The sky was clear as it morphed slowly from the familiar inky blue through purples and pinks, until I felt the first of the early morning warmth tickle my toes and begin to recharge my soul. Another day, another chance to find that elusive peace I craved.

I stuck around far longer than usual, the sun well and truly risen before I shrugged my bag back onto my shoulders to head to Lucy's for an hour in her garden before college. Perhaps I was unconsciously hoping to see a familiar Dalmation and his owner, but neither appeared. And what would I have said to him even if he had? There was a part of me that was still hurt and angry that he hadn't bothered to show up the previous day or to let me know he wouldn't be there, and nothing good would come of me voicing that.

That assertion was put firmly to the test when I walked into the common room two hours later, freshly showered after taking out my frustrations on Lucy's unforgiving turf, to see him hunched alone in one of the booths, bent over what looked like the very workbook I'd been intending to help him with.

My foot bounced rapidly against the tiled floor as I waited not so patiently in front of the drinks machine for my coffee. There were only a few early birds scattered around the large room, most feverishly working to complete overdue coursework or chatting quietly in small groups. Only Jake was alone. Jake and I.

A vindictiveness I didn't usually possess almost had me seeking out company elsewhere until the sad slope of his shoulders and the defeated way his pen hovered over the page without ever dropping to make a mark tugged on the hopeless organ in my chest and dragged me to sit opposite him.

I didn't speak, because if I did, what would I say? Still, it was clear from the stiffening of his shoulders the moment he registered my presence. He didn't look up, though, his eyes remaining determinedly focused on the work that he wasn't progressing with at all until they practically cut holes in the paper with their intensity.

If I didn't speak, how long would the silence last before he found it unbearable?

I suspected he would outlast me by quite a way. He was the king of painful silences, after all.

Still, if my friendship with Abbi had taught me anything it was that stubbornness wasn't just a character trait but a way of life. So I channeled her, with a small, determined smile before reaching out and snatching the workbook away from him. He didn't let out so much as a token protest. He didn't even look up, just kept his head down, letting it drop onto his arms as I began to look over the work.

"How long have you been sat here doing this?" I questioned softly, my eyes lifting to take in his defeated exhaustion.

"Hour," he mumbled in reply.

"You've written out the next question... in an hour."

"I'm a slow writer," he replied drily, but the tired tone of his voice belied the chirpy way he tried to answer.

"I'll say. You know you could have had an extra hour in bed this morning if you'd been in the library at three forty yesterday." It was a cheap shot, but I couldn't resist. I did feel a twinge of guilt at the pained sigh that emitted from him in response.

"I'm sorry," he said, so softly I could almost have imagined it.

"If you didn't want the help, you could've—"

"I *need* the help."

"Then why didn't y—"

I swallowed down the rest of my words with a loud, painful gulp the moment he lifted his head from its resting place on his arms. "Jake..." I whispered, scanning over the broken skin on his bottom lip, the puffy swelling under his left eye, and the bruising where his eyebrow was meant to be. "What happened?"

"I had an altercation with a door. The door won."

"A door?" I questioned sceptically.

He shrugged. "Why not?"

"Jake..." He was smiling but there was no amusement in his eyes. All I could see was misery with a hint of anger.

He sighed, exasperated. "Tom."

"There was no door, was there?"

"What's that got to do with you?" The icy hard edge to his voice startled me, and when he met my concerned gaze, I could have sworn I saw a flash of betrayal there that I had no way of understanding.

Ignoring the barb of his words that tried to slice into me, I reached out without thinking, my finger gently tracing the line of the split in his lip as my brows drew in tightly in concern. "Somebody did this to you."

I half expected him to jerk away or bat my fingers clear of his face, but he did neither. It was almost like he'd been frozen in place, his breath held, the only part of him that moved his eyes as they tracked my every move.

"Does it hurt?" My fingers drifted up to the bruise

marring his eyebrow, dusting lightly over it as I watched for the slightest flinch of pain.

His eyes fell closed as his tongue darted out to caress the spot my fingers had left vacant, and just for a moment, an expression of peace glanced across his face before a loud, familiar voice cut through the moment and Jake jumped away from me with a start.

"Thomas!" Luke called out as he practically danced into the room, sending my heart into its usual Luke-induced jig. "I need to talk to you, buddy."

He leapt over the back of the bench opposite and took up position behind Jake, his legs on either side of him and his hands resting on his shoulders.

"Party, dude," he said cheerfully, leaning forwards, apparently oblivious to the way that Jake was crushed against the table in front of him.

"I'm sorry, what?" I asked, attempting to drag the table closer to me to give Jake the ability to breathe. How had I never noticed before that the damn things were nailed down?

"Halloween. Party. Mine. Bring your girl."

Jake's eyes finally lifted from their staring contest with the table at that, shooting unvoiced questions my way that I couldn't decipher.

"My... girl," I repeated, screwing my face up in confusion.

"Yeah, you know. Whatshername. The one with the hair... You said you hit it off, so second date is a winner. Could be *the night*."

That familiar nauseated feeling I was beginning to

associate with rejection took over my body as I attempted to force a cheery smile onto my face. It didn't look as though Jake was faring much better. His hands were balled into white knuckled fists against the wood of the table, and his face wore the expression of somebody who was intensely uncomfortable.

"Party. Sure. Right. We'll be there." I nodded with fake enthusiasm. "I think you need to..." I waved my hands in Jake's direction. "So he can, you know, breathe?"

Luke looked down in surprise, as though he'd only just realised Jake was even there, despite the fact he'd been resting his hands on his shoulders for the past few minutes.

"Oh right, yeah. Sorry, man." He didn't sound remotely sorry as he ruffled Jake's hair patronisingly before jumping off the bench with a bound and sauntering off to the group I felt less and less a part of on the other side of the large room.

"Are you okay?" I questioned. "Sorry about that. Luke is..." I trailed off. How the hell did I explain Luke to somebody who didn't know him?

"An arsehole?" Jake suggested, the vehemence in his voice surprising me.

"No. No, he's not. He just... He can be a bit oblivious sometimes. He does his own thing, you know? Like he's in his happy Luke world doing his thing and sometimes he forgets that other people don't live there, I guess."

"You just described an arsehole. Anybody who goes through life doing exactly what they want entirely without reference to the feelings of others is an arsehole. You always seem determined to see the best in people, but sometimes there just isn't any good to see." There was fire in his eyes now, burning so bright and strong it almost took my breath away. I'd never seen him so incensed about anything. Not even Mrs. Bright's treatment of him. Why was he so happy to sit back and allow that to happen every day, yet one run in with Luke's occasional carelessness had him spitting fire. It didn't make sense.

"That's not true," I protested calmly. "He's just..."

"Just what? Thoughtless? Careless with other people's feelings? Stop putting him on that pedestal, Tom. He doesn't deserve it."

"You just don't know him like I do," I insisted, attempting to draw a line under the conversation by grabbing his pen from the table and turning back to the workbook. "Let's get this done. We don't have much time."

"Don't bother," he said, his voice a little irritable now. "There's no point anyway."

"Yes there is. Don't you want to pass?"

"Sure," he spat. "I want to pass this paper so I can go right ahead and fail the next one."

"Or you could stop being stubborn and accept some help."

"You spent the entire lesson explaining this stuff to me and I got it. I did. I thought I'd be able to do it, then I got home and opened the workbook to find it had gone back to looking like it was written in a foreign language I'd never studied."

"Yeah, well head injuries will do that to you," I said drily, indicating the swelling above his eye with a small smile.

"Being *stupid* will do that to you," he threw back, the fire receding from his eyes and leaving behind hopelessly burned cinders of despair.

"You're not—"

"You're wasting your time with me. Focus on your own work. I'll go ahead and do what everybody expects of me."

"Which is what exactly?"

"Abject. Failure." Anger laced with dejection practically screamed at me from his quietly spoken words, and my chest contracted painfully, sensing a sort of kindred spirit.

I was weighed down by the burden of other people's dreams for me. He was hurting from a lack of them. Other people's expectations were killing us both.

"So prove them wrong," I choked out through the lump that had risen in my throat. "Prove them all wrong."

"How can I prove them wrong when I know they're right?"

God, I wanted to shake him, to make him see that his worth wasn't dependent on the opinions of others, or even his abilities in the classroom. Grades weren't everything and neither was trying to impress people who had no intention of ever being impressed.

"If you don't believe in yourself, how can you ever expect anybody else to?" I questioned softly, my hand twitching, the urge to reach out and clasp his tightly curled hand almost overpowering.

"I don't," he mumbled. "Expect nothing, and you'll never be disappointed."

"That's a kind of depressing way to go through life."

He shrugged. "Low expectations are a way of life for some of us. We can't all be brilliant like you."

"Brilliant," I spluttered. "I'm not bad with numbers, but I'm far from brilliant. Do you have any idea what I'd give to be able to draw the way you do?"

He snorted bitterly. "Pretty pictures don't get people onto veterinary science courses at university."

"I guess we all crave the talents we don't have. I look at people who can draw, who can create, and I ache because I'll never have that ability. One of my best friends, Abbi, can weave words into pictures that transport you to places you've never been. I've always envied her that. Yet she can barely add two and two without a calculator. Everybody has their skillset, the thing that sets them apart, but that doesn't mean that we can't do well in other ways, too. You're more than just a pencil and a sketchpad, and we *can* get you a decent A level in maths."

His head shook slowly from side to side, sadness ringing from his eyes, his posture, his everything. "It's too hard, Tom. I should have listened to the ones who said I'd never make it. They all knew I'd stuff up eventually, and they were right. I got the grades in my GCSE's because I worked like hell for them, but hard work isn't enough any more. You have to have something to back it up, and I have nothing. I'm stupid. Useless."

Like one of his dragons, a beast roared to life inside me at his words, obliterating my sadness for him and replacing it with a determination fuelled by anger. "I don't know who 'they' are, but whoever they are, they had no right to make you feel that way. You are far from stupid, and if I ever hear you describe yourself as useless again, you'll be sporting a twin for that shiner, you hear me?"

A little taken aback at my vehemence, he stared at me for the longest time. All I could hear was the racing of my heart in my ears, and all I could see was his stunned face through the red mist that had descended over me.

Finally, he nodded slowly, his eyes never leaving mine as he spoke again. "I don't think I've ever met anybody like you before."

"What? A pain in the bum with no boundaries?" I grinned, hoping to ease the tension lingering over his shoulders where he seemed to so often carry it.

"Somebody who always looks for the good in everybody, who will go out of their way to help people whether they deserve it or not. I don't think you realise how rare that is."

Heat suffused my face as I chewed on the inside of my cheek in an attempt to suppress the smile that was begging to break free. He was talking to me, not just grunting odd words or hiding behind a sketch pad. He was actually being candid for the first time since I'd met him, letting me see into some of the wounds that had caused his silence and trusting me not to pour salt into them. For some, this would still be considered evasive, but with him, the words he was gifting me with meant everything because they were usually so scarce.

The fact that he was offering compliments didn't hurt either...

"I believe in people. I believe that in spite of the horrific things we do to each other, there is goodness in every single human soul. In some, it's right there at the surface for all the world to see. In others, it's a little harder to find, buried beneath the scar tissue of years of hurt or pain, but it's there all the same. You just have to be willing to look for it."

Bright green eyes bored into mine with an intense expression, as though sizing up my words and trying to find some sort of untruth in them. "You think there can be redemption for everybody?"

"Everybody," I agreed. "People aren't born evil. Everybody is capable of making a bad decision that will change their life in an instant. But every morning the sun rises and brings with it a new day and a new chance to make things right."

"And what if the world has already decided who and what that person is? Written them off as worthless because of their past mistakes?"

I cocked my head at him, one eyebrow raised and my mind racing to figure out where these questions were coming from. "The world can be cruel. I'm not denying that. There will always be those who want to see the worst in everybody, who will use those split second choices against us for the rest of our lives. But if you look deep enough, you'll probably find that those people are hurting, too. All you can do is power through and try to prove to the world, one day at a time, that those decisions you made don't define you. Every sunrise is a new chance to do better."

A small twitch at the corner of his lips drew my gaze just as his face split into an admittedly small, but nonetheless beautiful smile that reminded me of sunflowers.

"You're wrong, you know," he said softly. "You said you're no good with words, but you are. You really are."

I returned his sunflower smile with one of my own, finally giving in to the urge to squeeze his hand, not caring that the common room was now teeming with people because of the bubble we'd somehow found ourselves encased in. "And you're wrong, too. You're far from useless."

CHAPTER TEN

"So, I'm thinking about inviting Jake to Luke's party," I said nonchalantly, shifting blocks in a mindless game on my phone while my legs swung in the air behind me.

"Oh?" Trix replied, her finger slamming against the buttons on her game controller as a seriously creepy looking zombie died on the screen of her ridiculously large TV. "How come?"

"I dunno." I shrugged. "I think he might be lonely."

"And going to a party full of the idiots he avoids every day in college is going to fix that?" she deadpanned, pausing her game and swinging around in her chair to face me.

"It might be a start."

She sighed, planting her controller on the desk beside her and jumping up to face plant onto the bed beside me. "You know he's not like you, right? He's not a social butterfly who can adapt to fit every situation he finds himself in."

"Aww, Trixibelle, you think I'm a social butterfly?" I crooned, rolling over on her bed to face her.

"Dude, you've practically made trying to fit in an art form."

"Trying?" I pouted.

"With varying success." She nodded, pulling down her t-shirt where it had ridden up in her leap, to reveal the slogan, 'I went outside once. The graphics weren't that great.'

"I don't know whether to be hurt or flattered by that."

She hummed thoughtfully while reaching into her bedside table drawer and pulling out a handful of Freddos. "Hmm, a little from column a, a little from column b."

"Well that's reassuring."

"Hey, don't get me wrong." She held her hands up, a Freddo held in each. "You're extremely good at what you do. I'm just not sure I understand why you do it."

"Do what?"

"Isn't it exhausting?"

"This conversation is starting to be..."

"Sometimes I feel tired just watching you, but then being nice to people isn't really my thing, so..."

"Yeah," I agreed with a laugh. "I've noticed."

"Harsh but fair." She nodded in agreement with a smile plastered across her face. "So Jake, huh? Does this mean you're over that weird crush you have on your—quote,un-quote—best friend?"

"Jake and I are just friends," I asserted with a roll of my

eyes. "At least I think we are. Kinda... I don't know. He's kinda complicated but I think we're doing the friends thing now. I mean, he sat with us again in maths yesterday so there's that."

"'Kinda complicated' may be the biggest understatement I've ever heard in my life, Thomasina. The guy makes Edward Rochester look chilled out."

"Who?" I scratched my nose in confusion.

"Christ, Thomas, don't you read?"

"Not really," I admitted with a shrug. "I did read the York Notes for 'To Kill A Mockingbird' last year. Does that count?"

She sighed heavily, her eyes drifting to her precious bookshelves stuffed to bursting with reading material. "Okay, so Jake is Boo Radley."

"His dad keeps him locked in the house?"

"No," she huffed.

"He stabs people with scissors?"

"It's a good job you're pretty and good with numbers, dude. Seriously. Could you have missed the point of that entire book any more?"

"Aww, Trixibelle, you think I'm pretty?"

"Okay, your head..." She lifted her hand to head height. "The point." She waved the other hand right over the top before crashing it into the back of my head painfully. "Boo was misunderstood by everybody and defined by the very worst moments of his life, the worst choices he made. That's Jake. Except it's not his own choices he's paying for."

I blinked and stared at her in silence for a moment, trying to make some sense of what she'd said. The words

Mrs. Bright had spat at Jake in anger floated into my mind, sending questions skittering through me like skittles falling through the tube in Ker-Plunk.

The apple didn't fall far from that particular tree, did it?

"What happened?" I questioned softly.

She shook her head sadly. "Not my story to tell. But do me a favour?"

"Of course. Anything."

She scratched her nose and eyed me awkwardly for a moment, shifting her body into a more comfortable position and leaving me hanging for way too long.

"Traditionally, favours are easier to do when you know what they are," I prompted impatiently when I was starting to worry she wasn't going to say anymore.

"I know, I know," she grumbled. "I was just thinking."

"Did it hurt?"

"Ha-bloody-ha. You're so sharp you'll cut yourself one of these days."

"Good job I have groovy Spider-Man plasters to patch myself up with then." I grinned. "So what's the favour?"

She hesitated.

"Just spit it out, Beatrix, for heaven's sake."

"Fine," she sighed out. "But promise me you won't go mad."

"All evidence points to that ship having sailed, but I'll do my best."

"'Well, it's just that I'm kind of a people watcher, and I can't help but notice this thing you do where you... sort of classify people."

I blinked in confusion, and stared at her, hoping she'd go on and give me more to work with.

"Go on..." I hedged, curious and a little scared to hear more.

"I guess you're a bit like the sorting hat in Harry Potter," she offered, and I wasn't remotely surprised that she used one of her geeky fandoms to explain. "You take the things that people show you and you put them into... well not houses, obviously. But... boxes perhaps."

"So, I'm a hat who puts people in boxes... Should I be offended?"

"You make it sound so sinister." She chuckled and patted my hand with hers. "It's not like that. I just... It's like you're scared to just be completely yourself with anybody, so you have to sort of... figure people out so you know which Tom you can be with them."

My eyes widened, my brows lifting as my stomach rolled at her observations. "Okay, so less serial killer and more total fraud?"

"No," she quickly protested. "It's not like that. I don't think you're even aware you're doing it. Listen, forget I said anything."

A strangled sound emerged from my throat in response as I tried to make sense of what she'd told me. I wanted to deny it, to list off all the ways in which she was wrong, but I had no ammunition because the uncomfortable truth was that she was right.

"And the favour?" I forced out, my voice small and unsure now. I'd always been the observer, not the observed.

It was unnerving to have somebody in my life who could see through every single one of my survival strategies.

"Just... give him time before you box him up, okay? He's not the guy he makes out he is anymore than you are. He deserves for somebody to see him—truly see him—for the person he can be not the person everybody thinks he is."

"Everybody except you?"

She smiled but the light never hit her eyes as she said softly, "I told you, I'm a people watcher, same as you."

I nodded. "And you? What box have I put you in?"

She grinned, dusting off her already immaculate clothing and snapping her fingers like a diva. "I am, of course, in the fun, slightly quirky but awesome friend box, which I'm totally okay with."

"And the modest box. Don't forget that one," I quipped.

"Yes that one, too." I stiffened when her expression flattened to serious in an instant. "But you've also shoved me headlong into the maybe she'll help me convince my family and friends that I'm straight box, and I'm not doing that, Tom. I'm sorry. I just won't. You're perfect as you are. You don't need to pretend to be somebody you're not, and anybody who thinks you do isn't somebody you should be seeking the approval of."

Oxygen seemed to go from plentiful to scare in the blink of an eye as I stared down at the blinking game on my phone, suddenly fascinated by the coloured blocks in the mindlessly simple game. "My mum asked me to invite you to a family dinner on Sunday," I admitted with a sad smile I hid along with the rest of my face.

"She a good cook?"

I peeked up at her with one eye. "Her roast potatoes are to die for."

"Absolutely no using the word 'girlfriend'."

My head shot up at that, my eyes locking with hers, filled with hope. "You mean...?"

"And no full naming me. You call me Beatrix and I'll tell your mummy about how you yelled at Mrs. Bright and walked out of class. Hardly behaviour befitting the mayor's son now, is it?"

I snorted with genuine laughter for the first time since the conversation had erred into serious territory. "I hate to disappoint you, *Beatrix,* but the only reason he didn't kick me out when I told him I was gay was because it was election season and he didn't want to tarnish his family guy image. Me walking out of class would be a minor infraction in comparison to that."

She looked unsure for a moment, caught somewhere between outrage on my behalf and the desire to laugh at the careless way I talked about it as though it didn't matter. I silently hoped for laughter.

In the end she opted for neither, and in her usual Trix way, avoided the issue at hand by saying, "Fine. Call me Beatrix and I'll choke you with a parsnip."

She was back.

I was sandwiched between the graphite dragon behind me and the living, breathing embodiment of the beast in front of me. Waves of nerves were rushing at me from behind while the scratching of Jake's pencil grew more and more frantic the longer Mrs. Bright sat in silence at the front of the room, shifting books around her messy desk. She cast the occasional glance our way, daggers shooting from her eyes at both of us, but she didn't say a word. Was she starving us out? Waiting for our discomfort to escalate to the point where we couldn't contain it anymore? There was no way she had nothing to say for herself. The question was whether she would directly confront what had happened the last time we'd all been in a room together, or whether she'd opt for the more passive aggressive option. Either way, I was braced and ready, but I wasn't sure Jake was.

Keeping my eyes focused forwards, watching carefully for the moment she would choose to strike, I blindy reached behind me for his frantically sketching hand and clasped it in mine. He stilled, the pencil dropping from between his fingers as my hand squeezed his once. A soft sigh was my only reward for now, but it was enough when I felt some of the tension leaving his tightly fisted hand and his chair scraped slightly against the floor as he shifted in his seat.

And that was the moment she decided to look up and clear her throat to start the lesson.

Nothing.

No barbs.

No thinly veiled threats or insults.

No outright bullying.

She taught the lesson.

Hell, some of us probably even learned something.

She left Jake and I completely alone. Didn't even pick

on us for answers. It was almost as though the will to be a gargoyle had completely drained out of her.

I didn't understand it, but I wasn't one to look a gift horse in the mouth. So, as the lesson went on, I slowly relaxed into the work we'd been set, allowing my usual pleasure at the logic of the problems to fill me up in a way it hadn't during Mrs. Bright's reign of terror.

A small knot of tension returned to my stomach as I packed up my books at the end of the lesson, half expecting her to wait for us to relax before sinking in her venomous teeth.

It wasn't until I was solidly out of the classroom door that I allowed myself to believe she wasn't going to attack in any way. I froze just beyond the door, blinking in confusion. Never once, in the almost two months she'd been teaching us, had she ever turned up the opportunity to make at least passing comments about the mathematical talent or lack thereof in the room.

Lost in my confusion, I didn't come back to reality until a solid form cannoned right into my back, sending me sprawling forwards into the wall with a yelp.

"Christ, Thomas, you're like one of those people who pootle along at sixty miles per hour in the middle lane of the motorway," Trix grumbled, grabbing hold of my arm to keep me from toppling over.

Jake followed her out of the room, looking just as perplexed as me, and stopped to look at us curiously.

"Sorry," I muttered. "But you've got to admit that was weird as hell."

"What was?" Trix asked.

"Think he means the passable, possibly even enjoyable lesson we just sat through," Jake offered.

"You noticed that too?" Starting to move along the corridor, I dragged them along with me, linking my arms through theirs.

Jake seemed startled by the contact at first, but he put up no protest and quickly relaxed into step with me on route to the common room.

"Do you think she had a personality transplant while she was off sick?" he asked with an unfamiliar lighthearted laugh that made my stomach flip flop with hope.

I'd always been surrounded by friends, but these two felt different. Trix had already seen what I fought so hard to hide, and... well... I'd already shared more of my soul with Jake in one conversation than I had with the others in years of so called friendship. Just for a moment, with one misfit on either side of me, apparently both happy to be there, I was filled to the brim with an overwhelming feeling of wellbeing.

I should have known it couldn't last.

Happiness was such an abstract concept—elusive, and easily lost, like sand falling through your fingers no matter how hard you tried to cling onto it. You were left with tiny grains, fragments of what you had, but the heart of things was almost always lost forever, floating off on the wind while you watched on helplessly.

CHAPTER ELEVEN

"You did what?" I sputtered as Jake had a similar reaction beside me.

"Oh come on," Trix drawled with a grin, plonking herself down sideways, taking up the whole bench seat on one side of the only free table in the common room, leaving Jake and I to awkwardly slide in beside one another. "You can't be that surprised. I mean, she was so far over the line that I doubt it was even visible to her any more. Neither of you were going to report it because, well..." She wafted her hands in our direction as though that explained everything. "So I did it for you."

"So not a personality transplant then?" Jake questioned with an amused chuckle.

"Wait. Wait," I demanded. "You spent last night philosophising over my character flaws for literally hours, and you never once felt like mentioning this?"

"And miss out on the chance to watch you both crap your pants in class today? Pfft. No. That was *gold*."

"You know those video games you play with the soulless demons in?" I questioned.

"Yup," she replied, popping the p enthusiastically.

"You realise they're not meant to be instructional, right?"

She simply beamed silently to herself as she lay back in the booth, her rainbow hair fanning out around her like a brightly coloured halo.

"Thank you, Trix," Jake said out of nowhere, his voice about as solid and confident as I'd ever heard it.

"For what?"

"For going to bat for me. For us." He didn't say any more than that, but we both heard what he didn't say—that not many people in his life would go out of their way to stand up for him. Was there anybody else? We were the only people I'd ever seen him spend any time with, and we'd basically had to force ourselves on him to get him to accept our company.

"Anytime, my friend. Anytime," she replied, and her tone told him in no uncertain terms that when she said anytime, she really meant it.

I fought with myself over whether to invite Jake to Luke's party, but something just kept the words lingering on my tongue, holding me back from letting them slip out. Perhaps it was the memory of the look on his face when I told him I was leaving Lucy's garden to meet Luke. Or the way he'd shrunk away from him in the common room. Or maybe it was just the way he seemed content to keep himself to himself. Whatever it was, the words took up root on my tongue for the rest of the afternoon when we spent a free period together working through some of our maths coursework.

The time we spent together was punctuated by laughter instead of that stilted awkwardness that had characterised our early encounters. When he relaxed enough to let the weight on his shoulders fall to the ground for a little while, he was funny and engaging, and I found that the time passed by strangely quickly.

Questions buzzed around my mind that I couldn't bring myself to ask for fear that I'd lose this fun, relaxed version of the guy who had always been so uptight before. It felt like the answers to the questions would somehow fill in the gaps in the puzzle that was this enigmatic guy. Whose mistakes did Trix think he was paying for? Why did he spend so much time alone? Where did he go on the third Tuesday of every month? And why dragons? Always, always dragons.

Maybe the time would come when I could ask him those things without fear of scaring him off, but for now I was content to just feel like I could finally truly call him a friend.

※

Flyers for Luke's party were everywhere. He didn't know how to do things by halves so the entire college seemed to have been invited, if not directly then by the bright orange leaflets that could be found on every single surface in the place. Twice, I opened up my bag to find handfuls had been stuffed inside when I wasn't paying attention.

It was Friday, the day before the party, and I still hadn't worked out a way to invite Jake along. He had to have known about it by then. Unless they walked around with their eyes completely closed all the time, nobody could possibly have remained unaware of it. Orange wasn't exactly a subtle colour, was it? Still, after I'd finished with party prep at Luke's I'd offered to spend the evening helping Jake with some coursework for maths, so there was still time.

My hands were covered in disgusting pumpkin innards as I tried my hardest not to make a mess of the job Luke had entrusted to me. Pumpkin carving was easy, he'd said. Just follow the stencil and it would be fine.

Well... what was meant to be a Scream mask looked more like a lopsided fried egg after my lame attempts at artistry, but I persisted, hoping this particular pumpkin would be housed somewhere inconspicuous. Beside me, Luke was busy stirring all sorts of liquids into a huge cocktail cauldron, stopping to do a taste test periodically and slowly getting more and more tipsy as he went.

"Here, try this," he said, offering me a solo cup of the disturbingly coloured punch. "That pumpkin looks like a four-year-old carved it, dude."

"I know," I sighed. "I think I can definitely scrub sculptor off my list of talents." I accepted the cup from him and took a small sip, sputtering at the burn as I coughed and sent the liquid up through my nose.

"Blimey, Luke, are you trying to kill everybody?"

"Too strong?"

"Mate, my liver just shrivelled up and died from a sip.

Maybe add a touch more of the stuff without a percentage volume on the side, yeah?"

He grinned. "Spoilsport."

He busied himself trying to make the concoction less toxic while I tried to fix the mess that was my pumpkin with limited success. Conversation between the two of us had never been hard in the past. We'd always had an easy sort of banter, nothing deep—Luke wasn't really a deep and meaningful conversation kind of guy—but I'd never felt so hopelessly lost for ways to initiate interaction before. We'd talked about the decorations, the weather, and some Netflix series he was obsessed with that we both knew I'd never actually sit and watch, and once those topics had been well and truly exhausted, we'd drifted into an uncomfortable silence that I hated with every part of myself, knowing it was the result of the inappropriate feelings I was harbouring for him. There was nothing like unrequited love to put a stopper in the easy flow of any conversation.

He went on as usual, apparently completely unconcerned about the wall that had grown and grown between us. Had he even noticed, or was it all me?

"We haven't done this for ages," I said softly into the quiet.

"What's that?" He was preoccupied now with stringing spider streamers across the ceilings and spraying cobwebs from a can across every available surface.

"Hung out, you know. We never do it anymore." I stopped short of admitting to missing it because that sort of vulnerability tended to bring Luke out in hives.

"We play football every Saturday." He shrugged,

clearly not missing the times we'd hung out almost every day after school, acting the fool late into the night.

It wasn't hard to put my finger on when everything had changed. The moment I'd snapped into self awareness and realised that the way I was feeling for him wasn't just the attachment of good friends, it had inadvertently put a strain on every one of our conversations. It was the elephant in the room, this big secret that I was keeping locked away inside for fear of losing what we had, and yet somehow it was destroying us from the inside out anyway. Holding back so much of myself was tearing me apart and making every relationship I had feel fake. Making *me* feel fake.

Since the moment the one person who had known every part of me and still wanted me around had stepped onto a plane to her own adventures, I'd felt adrift. I was at sea, treading water pointlessly on and on, because I had no compass to tell me which way to turn. There was nobody I could go to for guidance because I didn't know a single other person who had been in my situation. Abbi was great for a pep talk, and she knew all about feeling isolated and alone, but through all her trials and the pain she'd suffered, she'd never once appeared to be afraid to be just exactly who she was. Her attitude was 'do you and to hell with anybody who didn't like it'. It was a nice philosophy in theory, but my fear of suffering the same rejection I had with my dad over and over again paralysed me every time I so much as thought about showing all of me to the people who mattered.

"Yeah, I guess," I agreed reluctantly, wiping more

pumpkin goop off my hands with kitchen towel. "But this is different."

His only response was a quiet, noncommittal grunt that stopped me instantly from trying to take that conversation any further. Having exhausted all topics I could think of to talk about, I dropped into silence that he seemed more than happy to go along with.

After my god awful pumpkin, I graduated onto less creative tasks like setting out what felt like about a billion red plastic cups on the kitchen counter and attempting to rationalise the mess in the room Luke called his 'man cave'. I wasn't sure how it was possible for such a huge house to be so untidy but Luke was a master of mess so that particular job took up the rest of the afternoon, and by the time I was done, I was exhausted and ready to wash away the awkwardness of the day in a scalding hot shower.

It wasn't until I turned the corner onto my road and spotted Jake loitering uncertainly by the gate to our driveway that I remembered that the shower would have to wait.

"God, am I late? I'm so sorry," I called out, hurrying to his side as he fingered the gate nervously.

"You live *here*?" he questioned, disbelief colouring his tone.

"Well, yeah. You've been here before," I replied, confused. "To get the tools, remember?"

"Oh, I remember. I just didn't realise the mansion next to the shed was your house."

I snorted. "It's not a mansion. It's just... home. Actually, I generally call it the ice palace."

I wasn't ignorant to the charmed life I lived. There seemed to be two types of people in Colwich—the haves and the have nots—with very little in between. I would cheerfully have traded the large home I'd grown up in, along with everything of value inside, for a taste of the happiness and freedom of spirit I'd had only just over a year ago when I'd still thought I'd grow up, get married and have babies one day. Houses were just bricks and mortar, walls to keep the things you wanted on the inside and the ones you didn't on the outside. It was only some residual sentimentality on my dad's part that meant I was still allowed on the inside.

"The ice palace?"

I nodded, pushing the gate open and ushering him through. "You'd understand if you lived here."

He looked mildly curious but didn't pry. He did, however, stare up at the house as we approached as though torn between awe and fear that it was going to swallow him whole or something.

"It's just bricks, Jake. It doesn't bite," I joked, grabbing him by the elbow when he stalled at the door and dragging him inside.

"It might," he mumbled in response, almost too quietly for me to hear.

"Want a drink?" I ignored his nerves, figuring he'd relax more quickly if I stopped drawing attention to his awkwardness.

He paused for a moment in the doorway before stepping to the counter and placing his hands flat on the top.

He levelled me with a playful smile I hadn't expected and said, "Got any Coke?"

"Wash your mouth out." I grinned, swinging the fridge open and pulling out a bottle of Pepsi. "Make yourself useful," I ordered, gesturing to the cupboard where the glasses were kept.

He dutifully obeyed, pulling two tumblers out and sliding them along the counter to me.

"That's dangerous, you know, reminding me of our unfinished game. You might prompt me to start asking more questions you don't want to answer."

"Oh yeah. If you ask me to choose between M&M's and Smarties I'm going to have to call this evening off."

"Life is filled with difficult choices, Jake. Which is it to be?"

"Maths," he said decisively. "I choose maths."

I gasped in mock surprise and covered my heart with my hands. "I never thought this moment would come. I'm so proud right now."

"Yeah? Well don't get those hopes up too high. I'm still going to be the worst student you've ever had."

I laughed. "Buddy, you're the *only* student I've ever had."

"Case in point then. You can try to try to get me up to speed on this course and it's never going to happen. I can't do it. End of."

I huffed a sigh and handed him a glass of Pepsi before squaring my eyes with his. "Every time you use the word 'can't' a puppy dies."

"Yeah?" He snorted. "I don't believe in fairies either."

"Dragons, though? You believe in those," I suggested, head cocked to the side and watching him with interest.

His eyes widened as he took a sip of his drink, swallowing loudly before placing the glass back on the counter with a shaky hand. "Dragons," he croaked, pausing to clear his throat before continuing. "Dragons are the embodiment of what I've learned about humans over the years."

"What? They're scaly and breathe fire?" I quipped with a small chuckle to hide how genuinely curious I was to hear what he meant.

"More that they look beautiful and majestic on the surface, but get too close and you will more than likely get burned."

I paused for a moment, watching him tangle his fingers together awkwardly just for something to do then lift his glass once more to his lips where it shook and clanked against his teeth.

"Jake…"

"But yeah, also they're just cool and I like to draw them."

"Who did this to you?" I persisted.

"So are we doing maths or not? I need to prove you right," he went on as though I hadn't even spoken.

I stared at him in disappointment for several seconds before nodding resignedly with a sigh and leading him up to my bedroom to work.

My desk was tiny so we lay sprawled out over my bed with our books and pens scattered around us, and Spotify playing softly in the background. I didn't push anymore. He'd made it very clear he wasn't interested in answering difficult questions of the non-calculus variety. I tried hard to get into the mindset of somebody to whom this kind of work didn't come naturally and worked through it right from the beginning.

He was good at building walls and protecting himself from the pain of sharing his emotions with others, but when it came to hiding confusion or frustration at not understanding the work, he was truly woeful. His breathing changed to heavy, pained huffs, his eyes glazed over with confusion, and his fingers tugged at the ends of his sleeves; he was an open book, which worked in my favour. When I saw the signs, I would slow down and re-explain things without him even needing to know I knew he was struggling. I'd quickly learned that he wouldn't tell me but battle on regardless. Presumably, asking for help was one of his dragon issues and he wouldn't do it for fear of somehow getting burned.

And so I learned to read him, read his silent, unconscious clues that all was not well with him, and either he was oblivious to my tactics or he quietly allowed me to get on with it. Either way, it worked for us, and before either of us knew it, the evening had turned into night, and the work was done. I even thought maybe he understood better what he was doing.

There was a moment after we both put our pens down when neither of us quite knew what to do with ourselves. As much fun as we'd had bantering back and forth, this wasn't technically a social visit, and I half thought he'd want to leave right away. It was pretty late after all. Instead, he let out a long, weary sigh before rolling over onto his back, his eyes closed and his hand over his forehead.

His closed eyes gave me a moment to truly study a face I felt like I knew well and yet when I really looked, I realised I barely knew it at all. His skin was pale, the bridge of his nose scattered with freckles, and his jawline was sharp and defined. But I'd seen all that before. What I'd missed was the way his lips turned up at the corners when he was relaxed, and the dark, bruise-like shadows marring the spaces beneath eyelashes I daresay Annika would have killed for. His hair was a tumbling mess of curls atop his head that only became more disarrayed when his hands shifted and his fingers raked through them as a yawn erupted from his chest.

Even as relaxed as I'd ever seen him, the line of tension that sat between his eyes never left, and I had to suppress the urge to reach out and smooth over it with my fingers.

"Thanks for helping me," he said through another yawn as his body curled backwards in a stretch. "I suppose I should—"

"Hey, do you have a curfew?" I interjected, a plan forming in my mind that I was almost certain he wouldn't go for.

He snorted. "Hardly."

"Excellent. Get up then. I have an idea."

He groaned. "Why do those words fill me with fear?"

"Because you're sensible." Wrapping his hand up in mine, I tugged him upright and gave him time to come around to the idea of some fun while I grabbed a backpack and stuffed everything we'd need inside.

"Uh, Tom, you do realise it's closed, right?" Jake questioned, his voice quavering with uncertainty as I beamed up at the building in front of us.

"The big closed sign is a dead giveaway, isn't it?" My head twisted on my shoulders to offer him a grin.

"And yet here we stand?"

"Well, young Jacob, I have a friend called Elliot who once taught me that rules are really just enforced suggestions. And it's far easier to get forgiveness than permission."

One pale brown eyebrow lifted as his head tilted in my direction. "And if we get arrested?"

Walking over to the tree I'd used to scale the wall at night for years, I gripped onto a branch with one hand, dangling from it and grinning back at him. "What's life without a little adventure, right?"

The tree was in the perfect position to make breaking and entering a little too easy to call this a real adventure, but unlike Elliot and Abbi, I wasn't a career rule breaker. This was about my limit. I strongly suspected the pool management knew I did it and turned a blind eye. It tended to be a summertime pursuit, but what was a little frostbite between sort of, almost friends?

"Coming in?" I called out, balancing on top of the wall for a moment before jumping down onto the concrete below.

The water of the public outdoor swimming pool was an inky petrol blue with moonlight rippling over the surface, inviting me in. I watched it, mesmerized, aching to plunge under the surface, certain that Jake would feel the same strange healing from the embrace of the water.

Counting inside my head, I had almost given up on him joining me when I heard the telltale sounds of unmistakable tree climbing. There was the creak of a branch, the scuffing of shoes against the bark, the rasp of hands around the branches and then a moment of silence as he stood silhouetted against the moon at the top of the wall.

"The water looks lovely," I coaxed.

"It looks cold," he countered, eyeing the ground below him cautiously. "And that concrete looks bone crunchingly hard."

Bending double, I tapped my shins and looked up at him grinning. "No bones broken here. C'mon, live a little. Bend your knees and you'll be fine. Make the jump."

Eyes tightly shut, he did as I said and dropped lightly to the ground without breaking anything, then stood and looked around curiously.

"I've never seen this place empty before."

"I prefer it like this," I said softly, ducking to trace my fingers over the softly lapping surface of the water. "It's peaceful."

Kicking his Converse off, he dropped down beside me and dangled his toes in the water, wincing slightly at the initial shock of the cold. "I didn't have you down as a fan of peaceful."

Smiling serenely, I tugged my hoodie over my head. The cold air hit me instantly and my smile widened. The way it bit into every inch of exposed skin lit me up from the inside and made me feel alive. My spirits soared as I divested myself of the rest of my clothes, completely unconcerned to stand in front of Jake in my boxers. Something told me he wasn't the kind of guy who would judge.

"There's probably lots of things you don't know about me," I said, pulling the towels from my bag ready for when we got out. "That's the fun part of that conversation thing we've talked about."

Before he had chance to reply, I turned, curled my toes around the edge of the poolside, and plunged in headfirst before I could think better of it. Gliding smoothly through the water, I ate up the moonlight with every stroke, the splashing I created drowning out my chance of hearing whether or not he'd joined me.

When I made it back to where I'd started, panting with exertion and adrenaline coursing through me, he was standing with the water up to his chin, his hands moving lazily through the water as he watched me with interest.

"You never mentioned you were part fish," he accused through chattering teeth.

"I told you," I said with a grin, cutting my hand in the water and sending a cascade over his head. "There's lots you don't know about me."

"Is there anything you can't do?" he grumbled, his hands wringing over his face to clear the chlorine from his eyes.

"Well, my singing has been known to clear entire rooms, I have the attention span of a gnat, and ask me to draw one of those dragons of yours and you'll see just how bad I am with a sketch pad."

"You say you have a bad attention span, but I've seen your single minded focus when you have a maths book or a garden in front of you." Stretching his hands out in front of him, he took a deep, bracing breath before plunging himself under the water and crying out at the cold.

We fell into a rhythm, swimming side by side, and although he'd accused me of being part fish, he was definitely not one hundred percent human himself.

"Can I ask you a question?" I asked after we'd powered through enough lengths of the pool to bring life back into our extremities and paused, treading water in the deep end.

"History very much suggests that you can," he huffed out with an amused sigh.

"Good point." I grinned and deliberately splashed him again with a pass of my hands. "But you're not allowed to say no right away. You have to at least let me finish and think about it before refusing."

"Okay," he replied, drawing out every vowel sound in a totally unconvincing way as he sent a retaliatory wave of water back in my direction.

"I mean it. No saying no right off the bat."

"Fine," he grumbled, beginning to shiver again. "Are we having fun yet?"

I laughed. "*I'm* asking the question, not you. And yes, you are. Look at you. You're having the time of your life. So..." I hesitated. "There's this party tomorrow night, for Halloween, you know."

"No," he asserted instantly, despite his promise.

"Stop breaking the rules," I protested.

"Says the guy who broke into the swimming pool after hours..."

"That's totally different." I wafted a hand at him dismissively, sending droplets of water spraying through the air.

"Sure it is." I could practically hear his eyes rolling as he spoke. "So, this party then. What else do I need to know before I'm allowed to refuse to go?"

"Shut up. You're not refusing. It's gonna be awesome."

"Tom, you think maths is awesome. I'm not being rude or anything but it doesn't really seem like your standards are that high."

"You know, I think I preferred you when you were silent and brooding," I said then, laughing, I ducked under the water, swimming down and grabbing his flailing ankle and tugging him down. Bubbles erupted around us as he slipped under the surface, along with a gurgling sound that was either him cursing my name through the water, or laughing along with me. Either way, I was laughing like a deranged banshee when I breached the surface once more and gasped for air while brushing my hair away from my eyes. He soon followed, bursting into the air with a loud splash, his entire torso lifting clear of the water for a moment that seemed to linger and shimmer in time before he dropped back down again.

I stared.

I couldn't help it.

I stared as I tried to think of something to say that didn't in any way reference the long, silver scar that was cut permanently across his chest and down his stomach to just above his navel. I thought it was a trick of the light at first. Moonlight could be deceiving after all. But there was no way what I was seeing was caused by drops of water and moonlight.

First the mess somebody made of his face, and now this...

For a moment, he didn't seem to realise the change in my mood. He was still laughing as he swam towards me with determination, splashing as much as he possibly could as he came. It wasn't until he stood and found himself almost nose to nose with me that he realised I wasn't laughing any more.

"Did I kick you in the face or something?" he asked, clearly worried as he studied my crestfallen expression.

"No," I replied softly. "Did somebody do that to you?"

I could see questions sitting on his lips, waiting to be voiced as they moved silently in confusion.

"Who messed your face up, Jake? And don't lie to me and tell me it was a door or you fell down the stairs. I'm not stupid."

"Have fun, you said. Live a little." He turned and began to swim away from me with long, angry strokes until I reached out and grabbed at his shoulder.

He stopped abruptly and turned on the spot so quickly he sent water flying through the air, soaking us both all over again.

"You never mentioned it was a trap, did you?"

"Wait," I pleaded. "Not everybody who wants to spend time with you has some sort of agenda, Jake. Some of us just give a damn. It really can be that simple."

"I trusted you," he spat out. "Just for one stupid moment, I really thought you were different from the others."

"You still *can* trust me," I protested feebly against the tirade of anger spewing from his lips. "I'm not—"

"What was it? A dare? A bet? Find out the freak boy's secrets and then spread them around for even more popularity than you already have? Or did you just fancy finding out what the inside of a prison was like?"

For a moment, I was too busy trying to find the words to defend myself to make any sort of sense of what he was saying. It hurt more than I cared to admit to myself that this was how he saw me.

And then I tuned in to the words he had spoken and my entire body froze, confusion dousing my body as I fixed him in my gaze. His breaths were fast—too fast—fuelled by his impassioned words and the anger and pain that were all too clear on his face. The part of me that couldn't bear to see any living being hurting itched to reach out and somehow soothe the misery from his brow and the tension from his painfully taut jaw and shoulders. I wanted to make it okay. I wanted to be there by his side and let him bleed every single thing that hurt out onto my shoulders instead of letting him carry that burden alone anymore. And then I wanted to sit with him while the first rays of sunlight baptised him in the hope that only a new dawn could bring.

But all I could do was gape at him in stunned silence while the words he'd spoken sank in agonisingly slowly.

Prison.

What the hell did he mean by that?

My tongue was useless, turned to ice inside my mouth as the seconds ticked over into minutes without either of us making a sound. All I could hear was the soft lapping of the water against the poolside and the rushing of my heart in my ears as he returned my confused stare with a challenging one of his own. A stare filled with a hundred moments he was afraid to share. A thousand nights spent awake for fear of the memories that would assault him the moment he closed his eyes. A million dreams that single word 'prison' had shattered.

I half expected him to leave, to run in an attempt to outstrip my questions and his demons, but he remained right there. Perhaps he was just as paralysed as I was by what had slipped from his lips. Had he meant to say those words or had they tumbled free in a moment of rare, unprecedented candidness?

"Say something," he growled when the tension in the air grew so thick it seemed like we'd both choke on it.

"I..." The word fell out on a puff of air that hovered in tiny cloud of fog over the pool, while I negotiated with my tongue over producing something more coherent. "I don't understand what you mean."

What else was there to say?

I had no knowledge of his past or even his present. All I knew was I wanted to be a part of his future, but the explosions burning up all the hope that had been in his eyes were rapidly dwindling my expectations for even that.

"Don't lie to me. I'm not stupid." He spat my own

words back at me with a sardonic bite, no humour whatsoever in his eyes.

"I'm not," I whispered in response.

"You expect me to believe that? That you haven't sat with your *buddies*, laughing over newspaper clippings and plotting how much you can mess with me? Those newspaper clippings are my life. *This* is my goddamned life. I have to live with what happened that night every single day, and I am *so* damn sick of being fodder for the jokes of unimaginative people with nothing better to do than dredge up the past."

In a blink, bewilderment became fury, and fury became crushing pain.

"If you think I'm the kind of person who takes pleasure in the misfortune of others, why are you even here?"

His body practically vibrated with the need to withdraw, to get away from this confrontation that was everything he usually worked so hard to avoid, and yet he stood firm, unmoving, his chin held high in defiance.

"Tell me," I barked when his determined silence began to grate on the few nerves I still had left.

"Because just for a little while, I thought you were different from the others," he admitted, his shoulders sagging in a defeated slump as all the fight seemed to leave him in a rush. "I thought maybe there was one person in this godforsaken town who didn't hold that night against me."

"What night?" I demanded through gritted teeth. "I have no idea what you're even talking about."

"Don't lie to me," he hollered shrilly, his agonised tone

sending ripples of desperation across the water.

"Jake..." I pushed softly, taking several steps forward in the water before reaching out and placing my palm flat over his chest where I could feel his heart racing as fast as mine beneath the jagged scar I was certain was only the tip of the iceberg that encased his pain. We were both practically blue with the cold, but neither of us seemed to have any inclination to get out of the frigid water to warm up. "Whoever it was who took your trust and shattered it, it's not me. I'm not on some screwed up mission to hurt you more than you have been already. That's not me, okay?"

"There's no way," he croaked, the crack in his voice sending splinters into my heart where they settled and caused an ache I had no chance of soothing. His eyes dropped to the point of contact between my skin and his, glazed and unsure but begging me not to take the organ beneath my hand and grind it to dust while he watched on helplessly. "No way you live in this town and don't know..."

I sighed softly, my thumb moving lightly over his skin that was pebbled with goosebumps from the cold. "What happened? You can say it. It's just me and the moon listening here, and neither one of us is going to tell."

His hand shifted to cover mine, shaky but firm, and his head dropped low on his shoulders, his chin skimming his chest.

"There was an accident. My dad was driving." He paused as the words got stuck somewhere in his chest, reluctant to see the light of day after being locked up inside there for too long. "He shouldn't have been driving," he added darkly.

"And you were in the car?" I asked, keeping my voice low for fear of shattering a moment that felt so sacred.

"He's not a bad person. He's not," he insisted vehemently. "You told me, you said everybody can be redeemed. That has to go for him, too, because he never meant to hurt anybody."

"It goes for everybody, Jake. Everybody."

Twisting my hand beneath his palm, I curled my fingers around his and squeezed gently. His grip was slack for the longest time, and my breath latched in my throat, waiting... hoping. And then slowly, his fingers began to curl into mine. Before long, his tentative movement had turned into a death grip, and I fought hard not to wince at the strength of it.

Warmth spread through me in spite of the overwhelming cold. He was falling apart and somehow finding the strength to trust me to be there and hold him together.

"The prison..." I murmured, almost to myself, starting to piece together the jigsaw pieces that made up this complicated boy clinging onto me as though his life depended on it.

He nodded, all the breath and fight leaving his body in a single whoosh. "He got fourteen years, and a family have to work out how to live without their kid."

The hand not closeted in his leapt to my mouth as a horrified gasp escaped my lips. "Oh God..."

"Yeah," he let out on a sigh. "She was nine. *Nine*. The obituary said she wanted to be a ballerina when she grew up, and she still believed unicorns were real. She was walking home from ballet class, all white tights and pink tulle, practicing pirouettes on her way over the pedestrian crossing. She sure as hell didn't expect a man with four cans of John Smiths in his system to drive right at her. She would have been fourteen now." He paused for a moment, weighing his words as though unsure whether to say the rest. Apparently, he decided that nothing he added could make the story any worse, so he finally went on, "Mrs. Bright was her godmother."

He ducked, his shoulders disappearing beneath the glistening surface of the water, and I suspected his knees had given out. Clutching his hand tightly, I pulled him closer and wrapped my arm around his shoulder, guiding him gently towards the edge of the pool. I needed to get him out of the water, fear that a combination of the freezing cold and the shock of the turn the conversation had taken would throw him headlong into hypothermia urging me forwards.

His movements were mechanical and stiff as he managed to pull himself clear of the water then stood there shivering wildly but doing nothing to shield himself from the cold. Moving quickly, I wrapped him up tight in one of the large towels I'd brought with me before grabbing my own and then pulling the blankets I'd packed underneath free, too. And we sat, backs against the wall, slowly warming up and allowing the night to catch up with us.

I'd always wondered what it was that made Mrs. Bright victimise him so much more than the rest of the class, and now I knew. She was grieving, angry, and punishing him for actions he'd had no control over, events that had taken place when he was still a child himself.

CHAPTER TWELVE

The town was filled with the last of the hardcore Friday night revellers as we walked slowly towards nowhere. I had no inclination to go home yet, and I suspected he didn't either. He was silent beside me, stewing over the past I'd inadvertently forced him to dredge up.

He'd been in the passenger seat of the car when his father extinguished a human life—the life of a child no less —had sat and watched on helplessly as a one and a half tonne car stole away the hopes and dreams of somebody only just beginning her life.

How did you even begin to live with that?

In one night, I'd gone from wanting to lift the weight from Jake's shoulders to knowing that was a burden nobody could ever take away from him. Those memories would never go away no matter how much he ran from them. Perhaps there were some things the sunrise couldn't fix.

Perhaps some hurts ran too deep to magically heal over each morning.

But I'd told him, I'd said that the absolution of the first morning rays was for everybody, and right now he needed the sunrise. One bad decision from his dad was all it had taken to change Jake's world, to tip it upside down irrevocably and leave him reeling.

Guilt.

That was the unreadable emotion I'd seen in his eyes so many times that I'd mistaken for hurt. He felt responsible on some level for the mistakes his father had made.

It seemed odd to be surrounded by people enjoying their Friday night, most of them drunk enough to do some impressive damage to their livers. Laughter and obnoxious merriment rang out all around us as we trudged on, hands buried in pockets searching for warmth, and minds lost inside the bubble of the conversation we'd had.

Without thought, as we left the town centre, I steered our subdued walk in the direction of the only place I could think of to go. Jake needed the sunrise, so I would share it with him.

I wasn't sure whether to be concerned about how easily he allowed himself to be led there, or how little protest he gave when I sat down on the end of Abbi and Elliot's jetty and dragged him down beside me. I pulled one of the blankets free of the bag once again and wrapped us both in its warmth before relaxing into the anticipation of the moment that healed me every single morning.

Could it somehow do the same for him?

Speech felt wrong somehow, so we sat side by side in

the hushed stillness that only comes once a day and waited. He never questioned what we were doing there or why. He simply sat and stared at the horizon, turbulent thoughts racing across his expression as clear as day.

I had no idea how long we sat there. It could have been minutes. It could have been hours. All I knew was that by the time the first sunbeams tickled the horizon, a little of the turmoil had drained away from Jake's face, leaving him looking utterly drained. When he finally let out a long, agonised yawn, I shifted where we sat, tugging on the blanket to pack it away.

"Come on. You need to sleep," I ordered gently, touching his arm coaxingly.

"Not yet," he protested weakly. "I'm not ready to go home yet."

I smiled lightly, pulling a little harder and feeling him give way and begin to stand. "Yawning is your body's way of giving you the twenty percent battery warning, Jake. And you're going to need plenty of energy for the party."

He groaned. "Tom..."

"No arguments. I promised you fun tonight and failed to deliver. This time will be different."

"Mate, I appreciate the sentiment, but half the people at that party—hell, probably all of them—will know about the accident. I don't think I'm going to be welcome there."

Irritated, not with him but at every single person who had ever made him feel unwanted because of something he had no control over, I turned and gripped his shoulders, shaking them slightly and watching his head wobble a little comically on his shoulders. "That's ridiculous," I insisted.

"Were you the one behind the wheel of that car? Did you force those beers down your dad's throat and then put him in the driver's seat?"

"No, but I sure as hell didn't stop him."

"Jake, you were what...?" I did a quick calculation in my head based on the information I'd been given. "Eleven? Twelve?"

"Eleven," he confirmed.

"How many eleven year olds do you know who can control what their fully grown fathers do?"

He didn't respond but dipped his head, hopefully absorbing my words and taking them to heart.

"You have to forgive yourself. What happened was tragic and awful, but it wasn't your fault. Surely you can see that."

Lifting his arms, he forcefully pushed my hands from his shoulders and twisted away. "What I see, Tom, is the way people in this town look at me. I hear the way conversations stop when I walk into a room. I have to walk around the town and look into the faces of the family whose lives *my* dad destroyed. I see their hatred, the way they wish I'd been the one who died. I've spent five years trapped in a town where I'm utterly unwanted and waiting for the day I can get out. And now you come along and everything is..." His words stopped sharply, his arms lifting in a despondent shrug.

"What? Everything is what?" I forced myself back into his line of sight as he spun on the spot, trying to avoid my scrutiny.

"Different," he sighed. "Wrong. Topsy turvy."

"Wrong," I repeated, unable to keep the wounded tone from my voice.

He shook his head violently, his curls lifting and falling haphazardly over his forehead in his apparent attempt to make sense of the turmoil inside his mind. "I knew what to expect before. Every day was predictable. It might have sucked but at least I was safe in the knowledge of what to expect. But now..."

"Now... you don't feel safe anymore?" It hurt to say, even more to believe.

He coughed out a humourless laugh, eyes a little manic as they finally consented to meet mine. "Safe isn't the first word I'd use to describe how I feel when I'm around you, no."

"What is? Irritated? Homicidal? Enr—"

"Dizzy," he cut in. "Like the world has spun entirely out of my control. You talk and I forget whether the sky is blue and the grass is green, or whether colours are even real. Maybe the sky is actually orange and the grass is purple, and dragons are real."

"Maybe they are," I agreed, lips twitching a little in spite of myself.

"You open your mouth, and they might be. Loneliness and guilt have been my magnetic north for so long, I don't know what to do with... this." He wafted his hand between the two of us, his face wrought with the discomfort of not knowing.

"You could start by trusting it."

His head dipped again, his hands cupping the back of

his neck as his elbows flapped back and forth in tortured uncertainty. "I don't know how."

"Nothing easier," I said with a tender smile, reaching out and tugging on his elbow until he reluctantly dropped his arms to his sides. "Just stand on top of that wall, close your eyes, and make the jump."

"Make the jump being a euphemism for 'go to the party' by any chance?" There was a tiny hint of amusement in his voice that ignited the tiniest spark of hope behind my sternum.

"It wouldn't hurt..."

He snorted, the sound half bitter, half amused.

And there we stood, locked in a battle of wills, the boy who loved his town and the boy who couldn't wait to leave. The boy who wanted to be friends with everybody and the boy convinced nobody wanted to be friends with him. The boy who lived for the sunrise and the boy who lived his life determined to hide away in the shadows.

"Please?" I hedged, cocking my head to the side and giving him my best puppy dog eyes.

"Tom..."

"Trust me," I pleaded. "Trust me to have your back. Make the jump."

He sighed heavily, and my eyes fluttered closed as I braced myself for disappointment. Perhaps a party with most of our year was a jump too far. Perhaps I was asking a little too much, too soon.

"If I burst into the flames the moment I enter the room, as my wingman, you better be carrying a fire extinguisher."

"Did you know the inventor of the frisbee was cremated and made into one after he died?" I questioned curiously, scrolling through another random page I hadn't been able to resist opening while scrolling through Facebook.

"That's disgusting." Trix turned with a mascara wand held perilously close to her eye, her face scrunched up in disgust.

"I dunno," Jake threw out. "I think it'd be kinda cool to live on as something that gave others pleasure after you died. If you ignore the creepy factor, it's kinda cool."

We were congregated in my bedroom, getting ready for the party all together. This consisted of Jake and I sneaking a bottle of Vodka from my parents' drinks cabinet and alternating sips from it while Trix moved through about a billion outfits, asking our opinions on every single one. One she'd settled on a green plaid dress that was just shy of being indecently short, she'd moved onto the painstaking process of making her face look like somebody else's while Jake and I watched on, fascinated.

He had been a little cautious in joining us at first, perhaps worried I'd continue my assault on his painful memories. But once the jokes and insults had begun to fly between Trix and I, he had quickly mellowed and relaxed into my ludicrously comfortable bean bag chair, occasionally piping up with a funny one-liner of his own and catching both Trix and I by surprise.

I had to admit the vodka was doing a great job of sending the herd of butterflies in my stomach into an alcohol induced coma. It was ridiculous that they were even there in the first place. I'd been to enough of these parties over the years that those kinds of nerves made no sense. But when the heart got involved, logic went out of the window and the only thing that felt right was proximity. Self-preservation was a foreign concept to me now, but the alcohol coursing through my system made me care a lot less.

"Thank you!" I exclaimed, holding up my fist up to Jake for a bump. "Finally somebody who appreciates my random facts for the awesome anecdotes they are."

His expression was mildly amused as he lifted his fist to mine and bumped it.

"I wouldn't get too excited, bud. I'm a social pariah. I'm not sure my approval should be something you celebrate."

My hand shot to my chest in mock emotion. "He's making jokes about his social status. I'm so proud right now." I pretended to delicately wipe away a tear from under my eye, dabbing at it dramatically.

Shaking her head, Trix turned back to the mirror and pulled the weirdest face I'd ever seen in order to apply the mascara. Part of me wondered what would happen if I made her jump while she was doing it, but I decided I wanted my intestines to remain *inside* my body and thought better of it. Still, it was an intriguing process, and by the time she was done, it was well past time for us to leave, and the vodka buzzing around my system had me loose, limber and ready to party. Even Jake appeared more relaxed than I'd believed possible considering he seemed to think I was leading him into the lion's den wearing a suit of steaks. In reality, he looked good dressed in a simple jeans and black t-shirt combination, shedding his usual hoodie for a smart wool coat with pockets deep enough to thrust his hands deeply into.

He didn't falter, laughing and joking along with Trix and me as we walked through the town to the outskirts where Luke's enormous house sat. It wasn't until we hit his gravel driveway that I could see any signs of discomfort from him, but his attempts to cover them up were so valiant there was no way I was going to draw attention to it.

His jokes dried up when I pushed open the front door I'd never had to knock on in my life, and by the time we reached the first revellers, I could see the death grip he had on the insides of his pockets, his white knuckles practically glowing through the fabric.

"Relax," I whispered, nudging his shoulder with mine and winking. "Fun, remember? Make the jump."

"Not so much a jump as a flying leap into the abyss. With rocks at the bottom. Really, really pointy rocks."

"That's the spirit." I laughed and linked my arm with his, dragging him alongside me on my quest to find Luke while Trix followed along behind us, stealing a drink out of the hand of the first person stupid enough to let her and draining it in one go.

Slamming down the empty cup onto a kitchen counter when we made it there, she smacked her lips and gasped out, "Christ, I hope somebody has a fire extinguisher on standby because whatever that is, I'm pretty sure it's flammable."

"'Bout time you showed up, bro," Luke's voice called

out as he entered the kitchen flamboyantly, Annika under one arm and a brunette I didn't recognise under the other.

I waited for the usual pang of painful longing at seeing him so obviously enamoured with various members of the opposite sex, but I found that when it came, it was duller than usual. Perhaps the sharpness had been exhausted by repetition. Or perhaps my heart was finally catching up to what my head had known all along: that I could dream all I wanted, but some things could never be, no matter how much I wanted them to be.

Forcing myself to contort and bend into the role I knew I was expected to play here, I squeezed a grin onto my face and punched his shoulder. "Had to wait for Trixibelle to put her face on," I slurred slightly. "You know how it is."

"Mate, tell me about it," he griped, raising his arms from around the girls and draping one of them over my shoulder to steer me in the direction of the gigantic punch bowl he'd been filling the previous day along with a plethora of other drinks. My spirits soared at the contact, no matter how hard I tried to tamp them down, repeating the same two words over and over inside my head.

He's straight.

My shoulder tingled with every single millimetre he touched, goosebumps rising right down my arms.

He's straight.

My neck stiffened and my heart raced as his already drunken breath tickled my cheek and he leaned in to make himself heard above the din of the music to ask what I was drinking.

He's straight.

He's straight.

He. Is. Straight.

I was acutely aware of Trix and Jake standing only feet away, watching Luke and me with interest as we performed the same old dance all over again.

For a few minutes he would give my moronic heart hope, and then just as quickly he would crush it to dust at his feet, never realising the torture he was doling out.

'And whose fault is that?' a little voice that sounded eerily like Abbi's questioned inside my head

Whose fault is it that you've drifted so far apart that you don't even know who he is any more?

Whose fault is it that you turn into a jabbering mess whenever you're near him?

And whose fault is it that he has no idea how you feel?

"Tchin tchin!" I cried out in an attempt to drown out that bothersome voice, passing cups of punch to Trix and Jake before lifting my cup in a salute.

Luke turned and cocked his head at my guests before eyeing me speculatively. "Going well with the little lady then, is it?" he questioned through the side of his mouth, as though that would somehow shield the words from Trix's hearing.

I could practically see steam emitting from Trix's ears at being called 'little lady' and stood back with amusement to watch her tear into him.

"Dude, did it hurt?" she asked, hand on her hip as it jutted out, her ruby painted lips pursed in a blatant display of attitude.

"Did what hurt?" he replied, clearly puzzled.

"When you were dropped on your head as a child... Y'know, back in the nineteen-fifties when people last used the words 'little' and 'lady' in the same sentence?"

Bubbling with laughter, I almost missed the amused snort that came from an unexpected source behind Trix. I glanced over at Jake who looked as though he was trying to hide behind her. His hand was covering his mouth like he could somehow shove the snort back inside before anybody heard it. It was clear that drawing attention to himself hadn't been part of his master plan for the evening. It was hardly surprising, knowing him as I did now, but Luke's responding glower definitely was.

"The hell are you doing here, Cooper?"

"He's with me," I interrupted, seeing the discomfort in Jake's awkward foot shuffle. "I invited him."

"Why?" Luke sneered in my direction, brow creased and eyes screwed tight in bewilderment.

"Because it's a party and sometimes people like to go to those."

Glancing between the two of them, it was clear there was some animosity there. What I didn't understand was why. As far as I knew, they barely knew one another. They had no classes together, and certainly didn't move in the same circles. From what I could tell, I was the only thing they had in common.

Luke sniffed dismissively, turning back to Trix and wiggling his eyebrows at her suggestively, as though that short exchange had never happened. "So, how are you finding my man, Thomas? Is he keeping you... satisfied?"

Meeting him stare for stare, her lips pursed into a thin,

judgemental line. "The twenty-first century really was just something that happened to other people for you, wasn't it?"

"Now, now, Beatrix, don't hate." He flung an arm over her shoulder in spite of her protests, and began walking from the kitchen with her, asking several more intrusive questions about our non-existent sex life before they moved out of earshot.

"And *that* is your best friend?" Jake questioned incredulously, keeping his voice low.

"Yeah. Well... I mean... Kinda. Yeah. Ish."

Huffing a humourless laugh, he leaned against the kitchen island and took a sip of his glass of punch. "Wow, Tom. When I grow up, I want a friendship with enough conviction to use the word 'ish' to describe it."

"Am I not worthy of an ish?" I asked with a cheeky grin.

"Everybody needs something to aspire to." He patted my cheek with his hand and winked before surprising me and sauntering off after Trix.

An hour later, after a thrilling game of beer pong during which only one table and a few of Luke's parents ornaments were harmed, I was buzzing from the punch, the steady beat of the music and the electric atmosphere. Even Jake appeared to be enjoying himself, having come up against no more opposition to his attendance since Luke had shrugged it off earlier. It turned out he was remarkably good at hurling ping pong balls into solo cups, so found himself in demand on every team to play.

I, on the other hand, sucked so badly that after the second priceless vase was sacrificed to my skill, I was relegated to the sidelines where I watched Jake's triumphs, growing slowly more drunk.

My eyes followed Luke's every move, my body acutely aware of his proximity, like metal filings drawn to a magnet. He circulated the room, charming where he felt the urge, and insulting and cajoling where he could. He was never short of a female companion, and I watched with increasing interest as they never appeared to be bothered by the others. Never mind the twenty first century—self respect was clearly just something that other girls had. I may not have had any romantic feelings for Trix, but the thought of her being so blatantly disrespected made my blood boil and my head spin.

Or maybe that was the punch.

Either way, by the time Luke had worked a full circuit of the room and made his way back to where I was standing listening to a conversation between a bunch of the lads I was supposedly friends with about whether or not Man City were going to win the Premier League that season, both my coordination and my verbal filter were shot to hell.

Standing beside me, he looked over the room that was bursting with life with a smug grin, king of all he surveyed. Only a few feet away, Trix was writhing and grinding on the makeshift dance floor to the mind-numbing trance music, totally lost to the moment, her eyes serenely closed to the room in what I assumed was either happiness or concentration.

"Your girl's got moves," he commented loudly over the cacophony.

"Mmm," I hummed non-commitaly in response. There was no doubt about that. She had the attention of every guy in the room with her seductively swinging hips. Even Luke, who had the most popular, beautiful girls in the school hanging on his every word and sitting on his speed dial just waiting for him to notice them, was watching her with a hungry look in his eyes. Had she really been my girl, I'd likely have been growling at him and marking my territory. As it was, I found myself more envious of his lustful expression, knowing there was no way it would ever be directed at me.

Perhaps sensing his gaze, her eyes flickered open and landed instantly on his, locking in place and refusing to budge. If looks could kill, he'd have shrivelled into dust at the arrows of dislike shooting in his direction.

"I'd hold on to anything you don't want to lose, bud," Andrew Jackson shouted, Trix's dancing having distracted even him from the football conversation. "She looks like she's about to show you a totally different set of moves."

He was right. She was moving towards us with purpose, all seductive movement gone in favour of speed. Her eyes sparkled with the single-minded determination of a lioness protecting her cubs from a dangerous predator.

"You two love birds not gonna dance together?" Luke piped up the moment she was within hearing distance, electing the adoption of the 'attack is the best form of defence' method of pacifying her.

Sparing him from her death glare for a moment in order

to turn it on me, she glowered at my failure to set the record straight.

"I'm not his type," she practically spat in his direction, her eyes still trained on me, half accusing, half threatening.

Luke's eyebrows shot up high into his meticulously messed up hair as his eyes drifted between the two of us in confusion. "Wait. What?"

"I'm. Not. His. Type," she repeated, over pronouncing every word as though either speaking to somebody very slow or somebody who didn't speak English. "No love birds. Tom is my friend."

"Was," I grumbled under my breath.

"Not your type, eh?" Luke questioned, apparently unfazed, eyebrows wiggling suggestively once again. "Even after that little display?"

"Even then," she insisted, eyeing him as though she couldn't quite believe it was possible for somebody to be that stupid.

"Then who is?" he asked, finally dragging his eyes from the girl he apparently now found highly interesting, in spite of the fact he'd once described her as 'the one with the hair'.

"Yeah, Tom," she snapped out, rapidly losing patience with this conversation. "Who is?"

The acrid taste of bile rose up into my throat as my panicked eyes darted between the two of them, my stomach sinking into my knees as I pleaded with the universe for that elusive hole to open up in the ground and swallow me whole. I could hear my heart thudding in my ears over the beat of the music, proving to me that although I felt like it, I hadn't actually died on the spot.

Misreading my silence completely, Luke leaned in and laid his arm over my shoulder with no clue what that simple gesture did to my already churning insides. "Don't worry, pal. I'll get you laid tonight or die trying."

The protest in my chest died the moment it hit my lips as he moved my robotic form in the direction of another pretty girl I recognised from my physics class.

"Hey, Mill, you know Tom, right?"

She nodded, looking up at us from her chair through hooded eyes, sucking her drink through a straw that seemed to be more sparkly flamingo than actual drinking tool.

"Good, well he's dying for a dance and you're just his type. What say you?"

Shrugging, she took another pull from her drink before setting it aside and stumbling drunkenly to her feet. Laughing triumphantly, Luke gave her a gentle but degrading slap on the backside that sent her careering forwards into my arms.

His voice in my ear as he sent us to the dance floor made my stomach revolt, threatening to bring all the punch I'd imbibed right back up again. "Millie's gagging for it, mate. All these girls are. They're dying to give it up before uni. You're well in."

Stunned into compliance by the soulless way he appeared to deem appropriate to treat a girl, I did nothing to stop what was happening as Millie latched onto me with her arms clamped around my neck. It was hard to tell whether her grip was on account of actually wanting to be there or simply to help her to remain upright. Either way, my skin burned like acid was searing through it with every awkward, uncoordinated step we took together.

My body felt as though it was made of lead, my limbs refusing to cooperate with any of the movements to flee I was making inside my head. I was a puppet on a string, helpless to do anything but allow Luke to control my every move in the hope that it would somehow switch up this nightmarish situation I'd found myself in.

Her body was warm as it gradually leaned further and further into mine, yet my skin had turned cold, my spine a block of ice as unwanted hands fumbled over parts of my body I had no intention of ever exposing to female eyes.

And then lips were on mine, heavy and reeking of a full night's drinking, and the entire world spiralled out of my control, leaving me drowning in a sea of panic and self hatred but unable to move a muscle to stop it. A million moments swam in my head—all the times I'd longed for this, longed to desire this, to be just like the others, one of the lads. I fought madly against the desperate desire in my head to pull away and scream at the top of my lungs that this wasn't what I wanted. What I needed. Because there was a part of me that still hoped, in spite of everything, that maybe I could make it work. Maybe I could kiss a girl and feel that popping in my stomach that happened every time Luke walked into a room. Maybe it was simply a question of persistence, of waiting and trying harder to be what almost everybody in my life wanted me to be.

But it all felt wrong, so wrong, my body on fire, not with desire but with revulsion and a searing pain at the knowledge that no matter how hard I tried, this was one act

I couldn't keep up, one box I couldn't force myself into, no matter how much I and others wanted it.

Ears ringing and heart hammering, I finally found the use of my hands and lifted them to Millie's shoulders, pushing gently just as an all too familiar voice cried out behind me, "What the hell is he doing?"

CHAPTER THIRTEEN

At first, I was convinced I was hearing things. I'd heard wishful thinking could do that to you, make you hear people you desperately missed or wanted to see. The thought that I was actually delusional wasn't exactly comforting, but was perhaps marginally preferable to the idea that Abigail Costa was here, in this room, watching me kissing a girl she knew full well I had zero interest in.

Closing my eyes tightly shut in one of Abbi's signature childish moves—because if you can't see them, they can't see you—I took a pained step back, my hands still pushing lightly against Millie's shoulders while my mind revolted against the entire evening's events.

"I'm sorry," I said softly, not at all sure Millie could even hear me but needing to say it nonetheless. "You're beautiful, and you deserve so much better than a drunken hookup at a crappy college party."

I leaned in, dropped an apologetic kiss to her shocked cheek, and then turned to face my fate with my chin up and my heart clogging up my throat.

There she was, Abigail Costa, staring at me as though she didn't know who I was, Italian temper flashing in her vivid green eyes. Elliot stood to her left, her hand in his and his gaze fixed on her, love emanating from his eyes with every blink.

"Surprise!" she said sardonically, her free hand lifting in a mock imitation of jazz hands.

My heart swelled in my chest as I stared at the friend I'd missed so much. The urge to dash forwards and throw my arms around her, cling to her and prove to myself that she wasn't thousands of miles away as I'd believed. But the way she was looking at me, disappointment etched across her face, kept my feet glued firmly to the ground beneath me and my tongue paralysed in my mouth.

See, she credited me with helping to keep her afloat when her world was caving in on itself. We'd spent so much time together in those final weeks of Nonna's life that we'd become almost as inseparable as she and Elliot. But what she hadn't realised was that while I was helping her to tread water, she was doing just the same for me. She had, in those few weeks we'd spent growing in understanding of one another, become one of the most cherished people in my life. So now, seeing the disappointment colouring her cheeks, I wanted to crawl under a rock and hide away from everything I'd failed to do in her absence.

"Can I have a word?" The words formed a question but her tone told everybody quite clearly that she wasn't asking permission so much as making a demand. So when she spun on her heel, pecked an affectionate kiss on Elliot's cheek then stalked from the room in the direction of the back door, I could do nothing but follow, legs like lead and heart thudding feebly somewhere around my ankles.

Standing in the frame of the back door that led into a garden that had played host to one of the most terrifying and exhilarating moments of my life, ironically with this very girl, I froze and watched her as she paced around the space, her sharp edges illuminated by the moonlight.

Eventually, she stopped her pacing and stopped dead in almost the exact spot we'd stood on the night I'd allowed my insides to bleed out to her.

"I didn't imagine it, right? I mean, sometimes my dreams are a bit kooky but I vividly remember standing here and hearing you tell me you liked boys. *One* boy in particular."

"You didn't imagine it," I confirmed, hating the lump in my throat that made my voice brittle and unsubstantial.

"Then what the hell did I just walk in on?"

I couldn't look at her as I pulled my sleeves down over my hands and swiped at my eyes as moisture gathered there unbidden. This night was meant to be perfect, and everything had crashed into dust at my feet because I was so damn afraid of what would happen when I let the mask fall. I'd spent so many years hiding behind the persona I'd unwittingly created for myself that I wasn't even sure whether *I* would like the me left behind once it was stripped away. And I was confident others wouldn't.

I couldn't answer. I had no words to offer, nothing to

give that could possibly explain. All I could do was stand there and wait for everything to burn up around me, leaving me alone like I deserved to be.

"Who even is she?" Abbi pushed with her usual tenacity.

My head moved minutely from side to side as my shoulders lifted in the smallest of shrugs.

"What's going on, Tom?" Her voice was different now, softer, kinder, as she took a step towards me, her feet shuffling into range of my eyes, which were determinedly downcast, unable to lift to meet eyes that I knew would radiate with confusion and accusation. "Why are you here kissing girls? Why do I feel like you're not remotely pleased to see me? And why, for the love of God, do you look so damn unhappy?"

My chest throbbed as I struggled to pull air into my lungs, my eyes stinging with droplets I absolutely couldn't allow to fall and expose to her just how right she was.

"I *am* pleased to see you," I whispered. "I... God, I missed you."

The single hand that landed on my shoulder was my undoing.

Letting out a feral cry that ripped free from my throat, I spun away from her, my fingers curling into a tight fist that collided agonisingly with the wall as the weight of every moment of uncertainty, every moment of self-loathing, every moment of pretence, of putting on an act to preserve the friendships I had, crashed down on me. The load crushed me until I couldn't breathe, couldn't think, couldn't do anything but pound that fist relentlessly into the solid brick, feeling the skin tear and bones splinter. But the physical pain didn't matter. Focusing on every millimetre of my body that hurt kept my mind away from the desolation of knowing that the real me couldn't stay hidden forever. Or that I wasn't even sure who or what that was.

"Stop!" Abbi's anguished cry registered somewhere in the periphery of my mind, but the motion was too soothing, the pain too cleansing for me to do as she asked.

"The hell?" Another voice curled into the bedlam inside my mind, sending my stomach flip-flopping and my hands flailing as an unexpectedly strong grip closed around my chest and upper arms, dragging me forcefully away from the brickwork now stained with my blood. "What is going on?"

I fought against the unrelenting grip for only a few seconds before sagging and hanging there limply as the smooth voice I knew so well talked around me to Abbi, whose distraught tone in response began to drag me forcefully back to myself. I couldn't make out the words they were saying over the rushing of blood in my ears, but even in my distress, my body registered the strange comfort the arms restraining me offered.

I would have been content to stay there, soothed by the low rumble of conversation. There was comfort in the familiarity of the voices and the way the arms around me slowly morphed from restraining to simply holding. Holding and warming from the inside out. There was no judgement here, only support and friendship.

"Cooper, what the hell do you think you're doing to him?" The low rumble of gentle voices was pierced by the harshness of another, not comforting but coarse and accusing.

The arms around me dropped away in a flash, the cold instantly beginning to suffuse its way through me again as I stared around me at the faces of the people I cared about, all looking back at me with unfathomable expressions.

"Tom? You okay, bud?" Luke called out, stalking towards me.

"Does he look okay to you?" Jake snapped back at him unexpectedly from beside me.

"Oh go home, freak boy. Nobody wants you here." The pure venom in Luke's voice startled me into action. It had been clear from the moment they'd locked eyes earlier that there was no chance of a friendship between the two of them, but I hadn't expected so much hatred to be packed into a few short words.

"I do," I said, my voice tremulous and uncertain as I lifted my eyes to see a small crowd had gathered at the door, through which Trix was trying to fight her way to get to us.

"You hit your head or something?" Luke questioned, his lips curling into a disgusted sneer. "Or are you two bumming each other now?"

Icy cold fingers of hurt moved down my spine as I lifted my chin to lock my wounded gaze with his contemptuous one. "What if we were?" I barked out through a throat that wanted to close right over and teeth that wanted to bite off my tongue rather than say the words

"Oh my god, you are!" he exclaimed, hands lifting to his

forehead as an ironically amused huff burst from him. "I knew something was weird with you."

"I never said that," I said, curling my fingers into a fist and relishing the searing pain that coursed through my damaged knuckles. "I said *what if* we were? What if I didn't want Millie or Beatrix or any other girls you might be thinking of trying next in your never ending quest to fix me?"

"Fix you?" he questioned, not even attempting to keep the scorn from his tone. "I wasn't even aware that you were broken."

"He isn't broken, you absolute twot," Trix blurted out breathlessly as she slid into the conversation like she'd been there all along. "Millie and I just aren't his 'type'."

"And *he* is?" Luke asked, pressing a finger firmly into Jake's chest like he was talking about a table or a cupboard and not a human being.

A feral growl raked out of Abbi's throat as she knocked his hand away with her own and thudded a fist into his shoulder. "No, you imbecile. For some God unknown reason, *you* are."

You know in films, sometimes after an explosion there's this moment of pure silence, when the earth has shaken and everything is broken and flying through the air. You know there's carnage coming. You're braced for it, every muscle tense and ready, but just for that tiny moment, there is peace while your ears ring from the blast.

The bombshell Abbi had just dropped left the five of us

suspended in a moment just like that. For several seconds, no one spoke. No one even moved. My breath was lodged high in my throat, refusing to move either in or out, and the world seemed to shimmer with an almost dreamlike quality. Or maybe that was wishful thinking. Maybe I merely wished I was dreaming, and that when the sound returned, I'd wake up and this would all have been just a horrific nightmare.

And then the first drops of rain began to fall, tiny droplets obliterating the peace and taking away any hope of waking.

The sound of shuffling feet followed by the crunch of gravel rang in my ears, but I couldn't turn. I only had eyes for one person—the person whose gaze was fixed incredulously on me, disbelief seeping from every single pore. The person everybody had told me wasn't worthy of my heart, but who I'd seen fit to hand it over to regardless. The person who, I could already tell, would discard it like an unwanted toiletry set at Christmas.

"You're sick," he barked at Abbi as the rain grew steadily heavier around us.

"Am I?" She showed no sign of being cowed by the fury radiating from him in waves, all headed in her direction.

"Why the hell would you make up crap like that?" he seethed, advancing towards her, earning himself a growl from the general direction of the crowd gathered by the door, all bearing witness to my humiliation.

Following close on the heels of the growl, Elliot moved forwards, his mile long protective streak engaging and yanking Luke's shoulder back and away from his girl.

"That's enough, man. Leave her be." His authoritative tone would have had far greater men than me cowed, but not Luke.

Unmoved, he turned on Elliot with fire blazing in his eyes. "Can you believe this crap she's spouting?" Air raged between his clenched teeth for several seconds before he turned again, this time picking me out from where I stood, trying and failing to blend into the background. "Can *you?*"

Frozen in place, I felt the world melting away around us with the forceful fire of his gaze. It was just us—just him and I—and nothing else mattered. We were ice and fire, he and I—oil and water. We could be near, but never mix. The rage emanating from his every pore told me that he could never accept me for all that I was, let alone embrace it. And the pain of knowing, after half heartedly keeping my dreams alive with silence for so long, ripped my insides to shreds as I stood there mutely, not confirming or denying, because I didn't need to. My silence told him everything he needed to know.

"I don't believe this," he hollered. "And you all knew? Every one of you?" He spun around, pointing to the small group of the most important people in my life, jabbing his finger at each person in turn. Abbi. Trix. Elliot... And the empty space where Jake had been stood. "You've all been laughing at me behind my back? Poor oblivious Luke. Doesn't know his 'best friend' secretly wants to..." He trailed off, his fingers lingering above his shoulders still forming his sardonic air quotes, apparently too disgusted to finish the thought, but in that moment, his anger and disgust didn't matter. They were predictable, expected.

But that empty spot beside me that one of my tribe had left vacant felt monumental somehow, and the earlier crunching of feet on gravel suddenly made sense.

CHAPTER FOURTEEN

"*Stay the hell away from me, all of you. Especially you. You disgust me.*"

The fractured words intruded on every one of my thoughts as I tossed and turned the night away, my bed suddenly made of rocks and my pillow spiked with acid. The ice in Luke's usually warm brown eyes and the flush of anger on his perfect honey skin as he spoke the words that broke me and then left would haunt me forever.

All was lost. Any fragments of hope I might have been holding on to had been shattered, the friendship was dead and buried, and Jake... Jake had left. Just walked away in the middle of one of the very worst moments of my life, and I couldn't fathom why that could be.

My thoughts were disjointed, like flies buzzing around my head—irritating and impossible to grab hold of. I couldn't settle on any one emotion. I was thinking too much, feeling too much, drowning in an endless night that I couldn't switch off to no matter how hard I tried.

The urge to watch the sunrise and be filled with the hope of a new day was like an itch buried deep under my skin, too deep to scratch, but my nails tore at my skin anyway, searching for something—I wasn't sure what. There would be no redemption with this sunrise, no coming back from the night's events.

I'd always found that silent screams were the loudest, fragments of your soul erupting from your chest with nowhere to go. They were so violent, so brutally soul destroying that it was impossible to understand how the world could continue to turn around you, oblivious to your pain. And so my family slept on, dreaming their dreams while my insides burned and my mind howled out, though for what, I wasn't sure. There would be no going back, no do-overs or time refunds. The damage was done—damage caused by simply allowing the real me to peek out from behind the mask. A few seconds was all it had taken to shake my world to its foundations. I was the epicentre to everybody's problems: Luke's hurt and disgust, Abbi and Elliot's ruined homecoming, and whatever it was that had caused Jake to turn tail and run. It was all on me.

Rolling over, I buried my head into my pillow and allowed myself five seconds of vocalised agony that was swallowed up by the material before pushing myself free of the bed, dragging on some clothes and making my way outside into the pouring rain.

By the time I made it to the jetty, I was soaked to my skin, and with my head down and eyes shielded against the driving rain, I was almost on top of her before I spotted the hunched form of somebody already there.

"Abbi?" I called out, instantly recognising the vivid red hair hanging in wet tendrils down her back.

She was sitting on the end of the jetty, her knees pulled up tightly to her chest, and chin resting on them, staring out over the lake. Startled, she yelled and jumped a little at my voice, toppling over sideways and almost falling off into the water. Reaching out, I clutched at her hand and pulled her back to sitting, shocked to see her red rimmed eyes.

"What happened?" I questioned softly, crouching down beside her and watching her with concern as she swiped fresh tears from beneath her eyes.

"Tom," she gasped. "What are you doing here?" Her voice was thick from crying and her expression sorrowful as she examined me right back.

Shrugging, I manoeuvred my body from the crouching position to sit beside her, our shoulders just touching. "Couldn't sleep."

She let out a soft sob before her arms flew out and landed around my neck, pulling tightly as her face buried itself into my neck. "I'm so sorry."

Pulling her in, I rubbed soothing circles over her sodden back as she cried. "None of this is on you, Costa. You gotta know that."

"It wasn't my place to spill your secrets, Tom. It wasn't fair. I wanted coming home to be a good surprise for you, not to mess up your life on my first night."

"Mate, my life was a mess long before you came home. He would have found out eventually. Pretending was becoming exhausting anyway. Don't worry about it."

"You shouldn't have to pretend," she asserted with

conviction, pulling back a little and levelling me with that bright green stare of hers that could bring whole civilisations crumbling down. "Nobody should have to pretend. Why does coming out even have to be a thing anyway? It should just be one of those things you do when you're growing up. You bring somebody home because you like-like them, and it shouldn't matter whether they're the same or opposite. Falling in love shouldn't be something to be afraid of for fear of being rejected by people who should love you regardless. It should be beautiful, magical. It should make your stomach dance with butterflies and your head spin with that dizzying combination of elation and need. The only fear involved should be 'does my bum look big in this?' or 'oh God, what if I walk around all night on my date with spinach in my teeth or garlic on my breath?'. It's not fair."

Unaccountably, a smile had drifted over my face, lifting my cheeks and crinkling my eyes at her vehement indignation on my behalf. God, it was good to have her back, even if the reunion hadn't exactly gone to plan.

"As it turns out, life isn't fair, Costa. But there are plenty of things I'm thankful for."

"Gobby friends, for example?"

Chuckling, I released her and moved to sit on the edge of the jetty, ignoring the water as it soaked through my clothes. "Friends who go to bat for you that vehemently are worth their weight in gold."

"Even when they drag you kicking and screaming out of the closet before you're ready."

"Even then." I smiled as she sat down beside me and

leaned her head onto my shoulder. "If Harry Potter taught us anything it's that living in closets isn't healthy for anybody."

I felt laughter rumble through her as she twisted her head in an attempt to look at me. "I thought we learned that love always wins?"

Tugging on a lock of her always scruffy red hair, I laughed softly with her. "If you think hard enough, I think you'll find they amount to the same thing."

We drifted into a silence that seemed to buzz with something, some words left unspoken, and I waited on tenterhooks for whatever it was she had left to say.

"Say it, Costa," I finally said, surrendering to the unremitting silence as the battle for words inside her head became practically audible.

"Say what?"

"Whatever it is you're not saying. Just spit it out. This is me."

She sighed, nuzzling into my shoulder a little deeper. "I just... How long have you been so... not okay?"

"Ah, Costa," I said, forcing cheerfulness I didn't feel into my voice. "I'm absolutely fine. You know me."

"Tom..." she warned, a knowing edge to her tone that told me she saw right through me. "You can't kid a kidder. I know what not okay looks like. I saw it in the mirror every day for nigh on a year. Tell me to butt out if you like, but for God's sake, don't lie to me."

I smiled in spite of myself, rubbing my hand up and down her arm as she shivered in the pervasive cold. "Hearing that makes me happy."

"Hearing what?"

"You, talking about being unhappy in the past tense. Seeing you smiling is everything. Remind me to shake Elliot's hand when I see him next."

"Come back with me and you can do it this morning," she suggested. "Last night wasn't exactly the homecoming we'd planned. He's kinda mad at me."

I chuckled, bouncing her head against my shoulder. "That boy couldn't stay mad at you if his life depended on it."

She turned her head to look up at me, flashing me a sly smile. "That's what I'm counting on. Figured if I stayed out here getting wet through and then went back looking suitably repentant, he'd forgive me."

"Good solid plan," I agreed. "Why's he mad?"

She shrugged. "Said it was none of my business and I had no right to do the thing... at the party."

"Well, who knows? Maybe if I'd done the same to you with Elliot, you two crazy kids would have got together sooner and saved yourselves a whole load of heartache. In your defence, you weren't to know how he'd react. If Luke had leapt into my arms and swept me off my feet, I'd have been kissing your feet right now."

"But he didn't."

I sighed. "No. No, he didn't."

"And how do you feel about that?" she asked, affecting her most convincing therapist voice with a small smile, but with her eyes full of concern and genuine interest.

How *did* I feel about that?

I didn't even know. All I'd done since the moment he

turned his back and walked away was try not to think about it. In fact, if I was being honest, that was all I'd done since the moment lightning struck and I realised that my life wasn't going to be the way I'd always assumed it would.

I'd avoided it, buried my head in the sand and lost myself in the safety of a crush that was always going to be unrequited. Because nothing was more scary than the thought of taking the leap into possibility and the unknown. A part of me was desperate for Luke to turn around in that moment and admit that he felt the same way, but another, much larger part would have been terrified. It was one thing to feel, but another thing entirely to *do*.

How did I admit to Abbi that while Luke was busy trying to dispose of my virginity, I was still afraid of what my first real kiss would bring? What if I liked it? What if I didn't? What if I'd immersed myself in trying to navigate an identity that didn't turn out to even be the real me? I didn't know which thought scared me the most.

"Empty," I finally responded, my voice soft and pained. "Just... empty."

"Yeah," she agreed. "Empty is a good word for it."

I knew she understood perhaps more than anybody else in my life. So many times I'd looked into her eyes during those awful months of Elliot's so-called relationship with Annika and seen nothing of the Abbi I knew looking back at me. She'd been a husk, an empty shell of the feisty girl I'd always admired for her tenacity and 'if they don't like it then tough' attitude. Because while it might have been easy to act like none of it mattered, ultimately, the one person you could never truly deceive was yourself, and the pain of heartbreak would come relentlessly no matter how good an actor you were for the rest of the world.

"But hey, look at you now—all loved up and travelling the world. You're living your happily ever after. And if that doesn't give me hope for my own then I don't know what will."

She huffed a laugh, nudging her elbow into my ribs. "There's no such thing as happily ever after, Tom. The world doesn't work like that. But I'll take a happy for now, because there was a time I didn't think I'd ever smile again."

"And you are?" I asked. "Happy, I mean."

Her eyes took on a faraway look as they drifted to the far shore of the lake where the sky was still dark and weeping. "I am... and I'm not. It feels wrong sometimes, to be so happy, to feel like I finally got everything I ever dreamed of, because when I dreamed of these things, *she* was still there beside me. She was my biggest cheerleader, my rock... my everything. So how can I possibly be happy now that she's gone? I can be in the middle of one of the most beautiful places on the planet, hand in hand with the only boy I'll ever love, and I'll feel this deep euphoria filling me up from the inside out. I'll be so lost in the moment that just for a few seconds, I'll forget that she's gone. And then when I remember, it all drains away and all I'm left with is guilt. Because how can I possibly experience pure happiness without her?"

It wasn't easy to see with the raindrops still wending their way down her face, but I knew Abbi well enough now to know that those once so elusive tears were joining them, and my heart silently ached for her. Yes, she'd got her heart's desire, but it was hardly a fairytale, was it? She'd lost so much along the way that sometimes I found it hard to understand how she was able to keep getting out of bed in the morning.

"I can't pretend to have known Nonna anywhere near as well as you did, but there's no way the woman responsible for raising one of the best people I know would ever want you to be anything but happy. She'd want you out there living your dreams and wringing them dry of every single droplet of joy you could possibly experience. She lived her life with the sole purpose of finding ecstasy in every situation and sharing it with the ones she loved. What better legacy could you ever give her than to do the same?"

Dragging in a shaky breath, she nodded as tears and raindrops dropped from her chin into her lap where her hand shifted to wrap around my waist and cling on tightly. "I know you're right. I do. But then sometimes there's just this guilt that I can't seem to shake."

"I understand. Grief is like that, I guess—love and memories with nowhere to go but back inside you where they slice through each moment of happiness without that person. But when they do that, just picture her face and how happy she would have been to see you finding beauty in every moment. Find the joy, Costa, and hold it tight. It's more precious than any of us will ever know."

She didn't reply, but she didn't need to. Her small nod was enough to know that she'd heard. The rest wasn't so easy, but I knew she'd get there. We sat in silence after that, watching as the furious sky began to calm, lightening with every minute that passed, the deluge slowing along with my racing thoughts.

The sun didn't really rise so much as apologetically brighten the sky a few degrees while hiding behind the thick clouds that seemed to echo exactly how I felt about the day and week ahead. With my friend by my side, though, it didn't feel so bad.

She sighed heavily once neither of us could kid ourselves that it wasn't as light as it was going to get, and squeezed my side once before pulling her hand away. "Time to face the music," she muttered. "If he wakes up to the smell of lemon cake in the oven, he might be more amenable to the idea of forgiveness."

My responding laugh caught in my throat at the thought of returning home and somehow acting as though last night had never happened. I was a professional at pretending everything was normal by then, but today I just wanted to hide under the covers and let the world go on without me for a while.

"He's a lucky guy," I said with a laugh. "I'd forgive anybody for a slice of lemon cake."

"That so?" She crooked her head at me hopefully. "You better come back with me then. If you forgive me, he has to, right?"

"That is the rule, yes," I agreed enthusiastically, selfishly keen to avoid going home even if it did mean being party to a lover's tiff.

On the short walk from the lake to the home that would always be known as Nonna's cottage, Abbi lightened the mood describing some of their adventures in Australia, including Elliot screaming like a girl when he found a completely harmless house spider in the shower and assumed it was venomous. I'd been to the cottage so many times while they'd been gone, lovingly tending the garden, but the place instantly felt different—more alive and vibrant—with Abbi by my side as we made our way through the gate that still creaked.

"Thank you, by the way," she said as she slotted the key into the lock. "The garden looks amazing. You didn't have to do that."

"How do you—"

"Lucy." She grinned, gesturing to the garden of her neighbour that was slowly taking on the beauty I'd envisioned in my mind.

"I wanted to." I smiled, following her as she pushed the door open and a flood of memories washed over me.

How did she do it? I'd spent comparatively little time there, yet my stomach instantly knotted and my chest contracted at the assault on my senses. The scent of Nonna's oil-thick coffee still lingered in the air, and the furniture sat untouched. I half expected to look up and see Nonna sitting in her chair or hear her confused cries from the top of the stairs. Did Abbi suffer the same way each and every time she pushed that door open? Did she feel the crippling grief that had to come with losing somebody so important with every inhale? The short pause she allowed on entering told me that maybe she did.

Reaching out, I squeezed her shoulder in a silent show of comfort, and she smiled gratefully before pushing through to the kitchen where the scent of coffee only grew stronger.

"Is it hard?" I asked. "Being here?"

"Yes... and no," she replied, busying herself grabbing ingredients from the sparsely stocked cupboards. It figured that of all things, she'd have picked up cake ingredients the moment she landed back in the UK. "I half expect to see her walking through the door or hear her voice telling me tales of her adventures. But I wouldn't want to be anywhere else. She might be gone, but her spirit is here. The only place I've ever felt closer to her was in Garda, standing by her lake."

I let the memories I had of Nonna fill me up as we worked together in companionable silence, and I was sure she was doing the same. Sometimes, her lips would tip up into a wistful smile and I knew she was remembering good times spent together. By the time the cake was in the oven, creating mouthwatering smells that wafted through the air, the kitchen looked a little like something had exploded in it. There was batter, flour and equipment littering every surface, including us. We were both laughing and whipping one another with tea towels when the sleepy, bedraggled figure of Elliot Peterson appeared in the doorway. His messy blond curls had grown exponentially in the months they'd been away, and he looked the very epitome of the Aussie surfer with his ridiculous tan. He was watching us with an expression caught somewhere between amusement and affectionate irritation.

"Sorry, did we wake you?" I questioned, cutting my tea towel off mid thwack and letting it dangle.

"No," he croaked with an early morning rasp. "Pretty sure that was the herd of baby elephants I didn't know we had."

"We made cake," Abbi hedged hopefully. "Lemon. Your favourite."

He chuckled, reaching out a hand for hers and pulling her to him when she accepted it. "The doghouse is fully stocked with baking ingredients, huh?"

"Yeah, well with this mouth, you never know when you might need an apology cake." She shrugged and melted into his chest as he enclosed her in his arms.

"Is lemon your favourite, too, buddy?" Elliot asked, one eyebrow raised, his meaning clear: I was the one she'd wronged, not him.

"Never met a cake I didn't like," I replied with a grin. "And I've heard apology cake has no calories so it's even better."

"That so?" He smiled, dropping a kiss to the end of Abbi's nose with a reverence that made my heart ache. "Do we have coffee?"

I watched on, still holding my tea towel, as they moved around the kitchen in what seemed like a long perfected routine.

It was like the two of them were a solar system with their very own gravitational field. They just drifted around one another effortlessly, almost like a dance. They couldn't have looked more perfect had every move they made been choreographed in advance. This was them, who they were together. They were like puzzle pieces that had always been destined to interlock. They just had to realise it, and the moment they had, the world had righted on its axis and all the planets had aligned to fit their new normal.

They were like yin and yang—her fiery impulsiveness and his level headedness—but the fun they both loved so much was the glue that made all the other stuff work. Their pranks had been legendary right through high school, and I'd lost count of the number of times I'd longed for what they had. Even now, I couldn't deny the tightness in my chest and the uncomfortable stirring deep in my stomach at the closeness they shared. I wanted what they had, no matter how much I tried to convince myself otherwise. I wanted somebody who knew me inside and out, and still wanted to spend every waking moment with me. I wanted that deep-seated sense of belonging, of being home anywhere in the world as long as that person was by your side. I wanted that *thing,* that feeling I'd never been able to pin down, of safety in handing your heart over to another person and knowing it would be taken care of no matter what. I wanted somebody in my life I could trust completely to take that leap of faith with.

When the cake was finally done, we moved to the sitting room, all of us avoiding sitting in Nonna's chair, with a silent agreement that it was a sacred space. With Abbi's head resting in his lap and his fingers twisting casually around locks of her hair while the other hand stuffed lemon cake into his mouth, Elliot recited tales of their adventures while she lay there looking blissfully happy, more content than I'd ever seen her. I listened to tales of their crazy escapades—pranks in the jungle, dancing in the desert and even one anecdote involving kangaroo excrement that I'd have quite happily lived without hearing—without a single ounce of jealousy. Their adventures were their own. Life in Colwich was enough of an adventure for me, and it amazed me that they wanted to hear all about it, in spite of all they'd experienced between them. It seemed so trivial compared with travelling to the other side of the world, but I dutifully recounted what I could. I omitted anything involving Luke, certain the mere mention of his name would rip off the plaster I'd stuck over the gaping wound he'd left behind the previous night. Thankfully, they took their cue from me and kept him out of their questions and memories of high school.

They bickered and laughed and filled every silence left by my preoccupied mind with their lively chatter, and I felt, for the first time in so long, like a normal college student hanging out with his mates. They even argued over who was going to empty the washing machine like an old married couple. Elliot won, but went with her anyway, standing pouring drinks for the three of us as though he couldn't bear to be too far from her for too long.

Leaning against their fridge with a broad grin, I watched him watching her hanging clothes on the airer.

"She seems happy," I observed, sinking a mouthful of Pepsi and twisting my eyes to Elliot who had a look on his face I could only describe as pure contentment. "She looks different."

"Yeah," he agreed. "There was a time when I never thought we'd get to this point."

"I gotta admit I didn't either. You have no idea how badly I want to punch you for going off with the shiny blonde chick when you had solid gold in the palm of your hand the entire time without realising it."

"Why didn't you?" he asked, one eyebrow lifting on an irritatingly perfect tanned forehead.

I shrugged. "I'm a lover, not a fighter. Not my place to get involved in other people's love lives. Hell, who would take my advice anyway? I'm hardly the poster child for healthy relationships, am I?"

He looked at me for a long, drawn out moment with those unflappable blue eyes Abbi had always said could see through skin and bone, cutting right to the soul beneath. It wasn't an uncomfortable sort of scrutiny. It was just a part of who Elliot was. In some ways, he and I were a lot alike. We both watched and saw far more than we ever let on. It was one of the many reasons I knew he'd make an amazing doctor one day.

"You will be," he finally asserted with no doubt whatsoever obscuring his tone. "Have faith."

"In what?"

He huffed a little, as though the answer should have been obvious. "In the fact that you're one of the most intensely likeable people on the planet and one day somebody worthy of you is going to see it."

I grinned in an attempt to cover up the warm wave of emotion that had swelled up inside me at his words. Self doubt was such a vital part of my makeup these days that it had slowly but surely chipped away at my childish belief that there was somebody out there for everybody. When people who mattered to you didn't or couldn't accept one of the most integral parts of who you were, it tended to leave a mark that couldn't easily be erased.

"Are you flirting with me, Peterson?" I quipped, wriggling my eyebrows suggestively.

"Only on weekends, buddy. Only on weekends."

"I'll take it." I snickered, planting my glass on the counter and bouncing forwards to where Abbi was wrestling with the washing. "Want some help Costa?"

"Quit making me look bad, dude," Elliot called out with a grin, joining us and lifting Abbi's hand to his lips. I felt my insides melting for a moment, thinking he was going to kiss it like something out of an old fashioned romance film. I should have known better. This was Elliot after all. Instead, he blew a series of raspberries against her fingers while she protested and fought feebly against his grip.

Having been on the receiving end of Costa sponsored physical violence on more than one occasion, I could easily tell that neither her heart not her strength were in it. She loved every second with him, and that dormant part of me I tried hard to suppress began to ache just a little more with longing. Would anybody ever look at me the way they looked at each other, like the sun rose and set in the other's eyes?

"Hey, don't hate, Peterson. It's the role of the gay best friend to make the boyfriend look bad. It's just the way it is."

"Knob," he muttered, rolling his eyes and dropping her hand to flick his out of control hair from his face.

"Whatever. You know you want me."

"In your dreams, buddy."

"Every single night." I winked and leaned in, pressing a sloppy kiss to his lips while he squirmed and the sound of Abbi's laughter filled the air.

"Do you two want to be alone?" she demanded with a long suffering huff.

I cast a speculative glance over Elliot as he laughed. "Hmm... He'll do until Niall Horan realises he can't live without me, I guess."

They both groaned together. "You still not over your One Direction phase, Williams?" Abbi asked.

I gasped. "Wash your mouth out! You can hate all you want. I know that deep down in that black soul of yours you secretly love them."

Releasing a sound that could only be described as disdain with a hint of actual real life disgust, she crossed herself like the good little Catholic she wasn't. "If I ever admit to a crime that heinous, shoot me. I'm already dead."

"Haters gonna hate," I mumbled, folding damp washing over the airer. "What do you think of—"

My words were roughly cut off by the Imperial March calling out from my pocket, and I plucked my phone out, confused. The only people who ever called me were either in the room with me or emphatically not speaking to me.

'The Ice Palace' flashed up on the screen and my stomach twisted just a little tighter.

"Wow, look at you remembering to carry your phone with you," Abbi said, impressed.

"It's my parents." I stared at the screen warily, unwilling to swipe it and answer.

"It's easier to speak into it if you answer it first," Abbi said with a laugh.

"They're probably wondering where I am," I guessed.

"They don't know?" Elliot questioned, looking genuinely confused. He came from the sort of family who always knew where the others were. He probably checked in with his mum even from the other side of the world.

"Uh... no."

The phone was plucked unceremoniously from my hand and before I knew it, Abbi was answering it using her best 'speaking to the parents' voice. "Hello, this is Tom's phone."

A pause, then, "Yes, Mrs. Williams. He's right here. I'll pass you to him."

Covering the mouthpiece with her finger, she growled at me, "You haven't told them what happened last night, have you?"

"Of course not. I'm not crazy," I hissed, scowling at her for selling me out, and reluctantly taking the phone. "Hello?"

There was a pause on the other end before my mum's voice filled my ears, vanquishing the calm that had overtaken me at being with my friends. "Where are you, Thomas? It's almost lunchtime and your girlfriend has just arrived. We raised you to have better manners than this."

Shit.

Trix.

In the emotional storm I'd been lost in after the party, I'd completely forgotten I'd invited her for Sunday lunch on Mum's orders. Everybody would be there—the entire family, including my perfect brother who had never let our parents down a single day in his life.

"I'm sorry," I mumbled.

"She seems a nice girl," my mum went on as though I hadn't opened my mouth. "Her hair is... interesting."

"I'll be there in ten minutes." I hung up before she went on any further, not even sure whether she'd heard me over her attempts to convince herself and me that she liked Trix's rainbow hair.

CHAPTER FIFTEEN

Silence was my biggest enemy.

It was during those long, awkward pauses that I found it the hardest to contain my need to fill the gaps with pointless facts and inappropriate jokes. Today, though, I had no trouble keeping my mouth shut. I had no desire to speak, and nothing at all to say that could possibly be of any use in the stifling room.

Mum had pulled out all the stops, probably thinking she was entertaining her future daughter-in-law. The crystal glasses that usually only saw the light of day when one of my dad's politician friends came over had been polished to a high shine and 'the good plates' had been pulled out of hibernation almost two months before Christmas.

All the polishing in the world, though, couldn't change the fact that I was lost inside my own head, thinking of everything in the world I possibly could to keep from tormenting myself with thoughts of the previous night. Trix was clearly out of her element, her usually sharp and unfettered tongue bizarrely curbed as she stared down at her plate as though the secrets to the universe were printed there. My dad was stewing quietly over my earlier rudeness, presumably waiting to get me alone to give me a lecture on how to treat a lady. Laurence, my older brother, was tucking into the roast lamb dinner as though he hadn't eaten in months, which in all likelihood he probably hadn't. He might have been the golden boy with his important job nobody but him understood, his studio apartment in London, and his long term girlfriend I was sure would be my sister-in-law within the year, but his skills in the kitchen were woeful at best. And my mum, after several aborted attempts to stir conversation in her unwilling subjects, had lapsed into silence, but for the occasional check-in to make sure that Trix was still enjoying her dinner or find out whether she needed another drink in her already full glass.

Look up the word awkward in the dictionary and you'd find this scene printed out in vivid detail, down to the last bead of sweat on my brow.

In between mouthfuls of the admittedly delicious food, Trix occasionally spared me concerned glances that she rounded off with uncertain smiles when I caught her looking at me. In all honesty, I wasn't sure which of my dinner mates I was more nervous about being alone with once the food ran out.

Finally losing patience with the taciturn silence, my dad slammed his knife and fork down on the mahogany table with a clatter, barking out, "For goodness sake, Tom. You invite this poor girl to dinner with us and then can't even have the decency to speak to her. What in heaven's name is wrong with you?"

Staring at him, a little dazed at his sudden outburst in the midst of my internal monologue, I opened my mouth to speak, not having a clue what would come out, but by the grace of God, Trix got there first.

"It's okay, Mr. Williams. Tom had a really rough night. I'd expect him to be a bit quiet, wouldn't you?"

Dad's brow creased, totally perplexed, while my stomach filled silently with acid, and fear churned it around.

"What rough night? What happened? Tom?"

"Nothing important," I mumbled, staring down at my plate to avoid seeing every eye in the room fixed on me.

"You didn't tell them?" Trix asked, sounding, if possible, even more confused than my dad.

My heart thudded loudly in my ears, the blood rushing to my face and painting it bright red surely audible to the entire room as I muttered, "May I please be excused?"

I was already on my feet when my dad's voice cut through me, low and dangerous. "Sit down!"

My knees locked and I froze in place, eyes wide and staring at a small blemish on the golden line circling my almost untouched plate of food. I was stuck, caught in limbo between getting out of there as fast as my feet would carry me, and following my dad's order to sit back down. From the corner of my eye, I could see Trix shifting uncomfortably and I was hit by a momentary pang of regret for never telling her anything about how my parents felt about my sexuality.

Nobody spoke as I hung there, but I could feel all eyes on me, questioning, curious, irritated. Eventually, Trix pushed to her feet beside me, clearing her throat before speaking as her hand closed over mine and squeezed. "I, uh... think it's time for me to go home. Thank you for having me, Mr. and Mrs. Williams. It was... delicious."

"I'll see you out," I agreed robotically, numbly turning my hand and linking it with hers.

My parents showered her with the usual platitudes about what a pleasure it was to meet her, even though it clearly wasn't, and how she was welcome any time, and I pulled her from the room. She didn't need to voice her apologies as she mutely pulled on her coat at the door. They screamed from her posture, her expression and her uncharacteristic silence. When she turned to go, I reached for her hand and pulled her back towards me, wrapping her up in a hug. I wasn't sure which of us needed it more, but she clung back just as tight as I whispered in her ear, "I know. It's okay."

I heard her breath turn shaky as she squeezed me a little tighter before releasing me and turning, and before I knew it, she was gone, leaving me alone to face the firing squad in the dining room.

Stalling for time, I stepped out into the perfectly manicured garden as rain still fell steadily from the dull grey sky. Every blade of grass was perfectly trimmed, every flower bed evenly spaced and containing an impeccable balance of colour.

No sunflowers.

When I was a child, my mum and I had spent hours every weekend working in the garden, getting messy and creating a wild space with an explosion of colour and light. I'd grown my very own sunflowers all along the south facing wall because even then, I'd associated the brightly coloured flowers with sunshine and happiness. And then my dad had decided to leave his job to take a foray into politics, and the garden was taken over by a gardener who had to keep it neat and tidy. No more wild flowerbeds filled with crazy mixes of colour. No more giant bushes with places to create dens with my friends. And no more sunflowers.

For a moment, as I walked stiffly around the space, I could see it how it once was, and a small smile tugged at my lips, but fell sharply at the sound of footsteps approaching rapidly from behind.

Digging my hands into my pockets, I rounded my shoulders and waited, knowing I couldn't put the conversation off anymore.

"Where are you going, son?" His voice wasn't irritated or angry anymore. It was more resigned, as defeated as I felt.

"I was just... thinking. Remembering."

It didn't take long for him to fall into step with me, his pose mirroring mine—hands in pockets and shoulders curling—and it occurred to me for the first time just how much I looked like him. We might have been polar opposites in many ways, but there was no denying whose son I was.

"Remembering," he repeated, not exactly a question

but it was clear he was curious. He was curious about lots of things, it seemed.

"Do you remember when mum and I used to do the garden?" I glanced over at him to see his lips tipping up slightly in a smile almost as wistful as mine had been.

"You loved it," he said. "You'd spend entire weekends out here, doing whatever it was you did."

"I was never very creative. I couldn't draw and make up stories, and the less said about my musical abilities, the better. But this... this I could make beautiful."

"I used to take photographs of everything you did out here and then take them into work to show the guys how good you were," he murmured.

"I always figured you hated it."

"It made me proud. The other guys would bring in stick drawings their kids had fashioned where you couldn't make out what they'd intended to draw, or show videos of little girls running around the stage in a dance recital. But you... You were making things grow, creating life even at such a young age."

"And then I grew up."

"And then you grew up," he agreed. "And I wished I hadn't taken for granted all the times you'd come running into the house, excited to show me something new you'd created or tell me about your day." Sadness suffused his tone as he spoke wistfully about times gone by, but I found it hard to be sympathetic.

"You ripped it all up," I stated simply, trying to keep the accusation out of my voice. It was rare for us to talk these days without awkwardness and walls between us, and the little boy in me didn't want it to stop.

He sighed, rippling his hand through his hair as he turned on the spot to survey his kingdom of neat lines and organised rows. "You'd grown out of dens made out of bushes, and the sunflowers I'd spent years standing at the window listening to you talking to were dying. You grew up and discovered life outside of your small garden. You spread your wings, wanted to play football in the park every weekend instead of hanging out with your mother here. When her back started to give her trouble, we had to make the decision."

"I... It wasn't because you hated it?" Years of resentment began to coagulate in my mind at his explanation.

"Of course not. Why would you think that?"

I shrugged. "I dunno. I just thought..."

A frown creased his forehead as he met my eyes for the first time since the fiasco that was dinner. "I was as proud of your garden as I am of all your achievements."

I tried hard to hold on to the words threatening to spill out into the air, but they forced their way out regardless. "Just not of who I am, huh?"

His frown deepened, his eyes narrowing on mine as hurt flitted briefly through them. "What?"

Sighing heavily, I dragged my gaze from his and turned, knowing the pleasant reminiscence portion of the conversation was over and not ready to enter into recriminations and having my character torn to shreds because of something I had no control over.

For a moment, the image of Jake's face flashed in my

mind—the nice guy who had suffered years of people casting aspersions over his character because of something he hadn't even done. Perhaps we weren't so different, he and I.

"Doesn't matter, Dad. It's cold. I'm going in."

I made it a few steps before he called out again. "What happened last night, Tom?"

I snorted. "Nothing you want to hear about, trust me."

Frustration coloured his heavy exhale as he pursued me up the garden path. "I wish you'd *talk* to me."

I froze, a bitter snort bursting free as I spun on the spot and glared at him. "Well, with all due respect, *Dad*, that didn't exactly go well for me last time, did it?"

I felt his eyes on me all the way back into the house, but he didn't say anything. What else was there to say?

The sunrise held no magic for me the next morning. The *world* held little of interest. As another sleepless night morphed into a listless morning, nothing short of an earthquake could have forced me from my bed. The prospect of going to college and facing the crowd of people who had witnessed my humiliation had me burrowing deeper under the covers and burying my head beneath my pillow when my mum rapped repeatedly on my door.

Was it cowardly? Probably. But eyes open or closed, all I could see in my mind's eye was the look on Luke's face as he'd barked those words, those final nails in the coffin of my hope.

"Stay the hell away from me, all of you. Especially you. You disgust me."

"You disgust me."

"You disgust me."

Three words, repeating over and over in my head until it span with nausea and my stomach churned. Anxiety at the thought of seeing that expression and hearing those words all over again kept me pinned in place and calling out that I was too ill to go in.

So there I stayed all day, wallowing in what could have been self-pity or self-hatred. I wasn't sure which. I was lost in a sort of trance, hearing the world going on around me but unwilling or unable to bring myself to be a part of it. The sounds of life in the house slowly dwindled as my parents left for work, leaving only the rain battering against the window and the occasional chirping of my phone beside me, which I studiously ignored.

I wanted to be alone, yet craved company, wanted to see the sunrise yet feared that it couldn't help. I wanted to hide away forever, yet felt the need to scream out loud for everybody to hear that I didn't ask for this, didn't choose to be any different to anybody else. But instead, all I did was lie there, cocooned in the safety of my bed covers, ignoring the world and letting it ignore me.

I dozed on and off, catching up on some of the sleep I'd missed the last two nights, but the rest didn't refresh me so much as make me feel more sluggish than before. A headache borne of overthinking and worrying about what the future held began to throb at my temples. Trying not to think about the future and live in the now hadn't got me very far up to now, but trying to picture where I'd be in five, ten, fifteen years time made my head ache so acutely I wound up buried back under my pillow.

What if I never had the courage to live my own truth instead of the one the world seemed to want of me? Would I die alone, unable to truly love anybody for fear of rejection? I wasn't sure what scared me the most—the prospect of living my life completely alone or putting myself out there to be judged by the people who couldn't accept me for who I was.

I couldn't spend the rest of my life hiding in this bed. Sooner or later I'd have to go through the front door and face the world. But not today. Not today.

Two more days of lying in my own bubble, hiding away from the world passed by. I spoke to nobody. Not one person broke through the solid wall I'd erected around myself until hammering on the front door woke me from a fitful sleep on Wednesday afternoon, and I childishly held my breath as though that would somehow stop me from being detected. Whoever it was, though, they had a fist of iron and, apparently, no intention of letting being ignored deter them from their mission.

Rubbing the sleep from my eyes, I cringed as I sniffed my t-shirt but decided if they wanted in that badly, they'd have to deal with the stench.

"I know you're in there, Williams."

My forehead fell against the door with a small thud at the sound of Trix's accusation filled voice.

"Don't think I'm above picking this lock, buddy. I don't

want to be arrested for breaking into the mayor's house, but I'll do what needs to be done."

There was no hiding the fact I was in now. She'd be able to clearly see me through the glass panels in the door.

"I might even strip naked and shout loudly that the prostitute you ordered has arrived. Imagine the scandal."

"Jesus," I muttered, pulling back and reaching for the latch.

The moment the door swung open, a hurricane of rainbow coloured hair flew at me. Grabbing my hand, she turned it palm up in hers, and not-so-gently tugged on each of my fingers, huffing with each one.

"Yup, they're all still attached," she barked, dropping my hand and stepping back, hands on hips and death glare radiant. "I can't wait to hear your excuse for ignoring me for *three damn days.*"

"I..." I had nothing. How did I explain that I just couldn't?

"Oh that's right. You don't have one. You're just *rude.*"

She punctuated her accusation with a finger harshly stabbed into my chest.

"Christ, Beatrix, steady on," I cried out, wincing and rubbing the spot she'd attacked.

"Steady on nothing," she spat in reply. "I've been trying to contact you *all week*. Me. Your friend. Did it ever occur to you that we might be worried?"

"I..."

"No, it didn't," she went on, apparently not requiring any active participation from me in this conversation. "Because you were too busy here blowing up balloons and hanging banners for your pity party. Well, I have news for you. Parties with only one person are just lame, but if you keep pushing those of us who love you away, that's exactly what you're going to wind up with."

Gaping at her now that she seemed to have finally run out of steam, I couldn't find anything at all to say. Apologies danced like fireflies over my tongue, but none of them settled long enough for me to give them voice.

Her nose twitched for a moment before her face split into a disgusted frown. "You stink, Williams. Did you forget how to shower as well as how to friend?"

"I'm ill," I lied.

"Yeah, and I'm on a sugar free diet. Pull the other one. It's got bells on it. We can continue this conversation once you've showered. Honestly, my nose is kind of insulted." Gripping my shoulder, she forced me into an about turn and added a kick up the backside to reiterate her point.

Freshly scrubbed and smelling a little less like a rubbish dump, I hesitated behind the bathroom door like the coward I hadn't realised I was. The fact was I knew she was right. I'd been utterly inconsiderate, so lost in my own head that I hadn't given any thought to the fact that people might be worried about me. What that said about what sort of person I was when I wasn't forcing myself into boxes I chose not to think too hard about. Was this my real self when I wasn't busting a gut to please everybody around me? If it was, I wasn't sure even *I* liked me, let alone anybody else.

When I finally manned up and made it down the stairs, I had to hunt to find Trix, who I eventually caught making herself at home in the kitchen, making drinks and stealing chocolate biscuits from the tin. And she wasn't alone.

My stomach flipped over at the sight of Jake sitting at the kitchen island, hands clasped tightly on the counter and eyes focused intently on Trix's every move.

"Help yourselves," I muttered dryly as Trix went in for another biscuit and passed one to Jake.

"Oh please," she threw back sardonically. "Staging interventions is exhausting. We need fuel."

"I don't need an intervention."

Her withering stare instantly cut me down as she forced me into the stool next to Jake and shoved a can of Pepsi in front of me along with one of my own chocolate biscuits.

"All addicts need interventions. Drink."

Dutifully, I took a sip, and the moment it hit my tongue, I realised just how parched I was and drained the can in a single drink then slammed it down on the counter. "I'm not an addict."

Choking sounds erupted from Jake's chest as he coughed through a sip of his own drink. His fist pounded against his ribs as he stared at me incredulously.

"What?" I snapped defensively.

I felt cornered, their intense scrutiny shrouding me in an uncomfortable, claustrophobia.

"That was Jake's subtle way of disagreeing with you, bud," Trix explained. "You are absolutely, one hundred and ten percent an addict."

"The hell are you talking about, Beatrix?" I practically growled out, losing patience. "What am I addicted to?"

"Approval," Trix asserted.

"Being liked," Jake added.

"Being needed, wanted, loved," she finished up, as though she were revealing some great secret.

"Those aren't addictions," I scoffed. "Everybody wants those things."

"Not everybody is willing to sacrifice their own happiness quite as completely as you were in order to have them," Jake said softly, his eyes finally meeting mine, their expression almost apologetic, but determination burned right through the apology with the effort it took him to be so verbose.

"I mean, Christ, Tom, you were willing to date girls, to kiss girls, just to keep Luke... To keep him what? Happy?" Trix went on, the constant barrage of words in stereo from my friends sending me into some sort of sensory overload, where all I could do was sit numbly and listen without protesting. "You're gay, Tom. Sooner or later you're going to have to realise that there's nothing wrong with that. And maybe then, you'll stop spending so much time worrying about the people who have rejected you for being yourself."

Traitorous tears stung my eyes as I blinked rapidly in an attempt to bat them away. But then... did I really need to? Of all the people in the world, hadn't these two proven that appearances didn't matter to them. They were here, weren't they? Fighting for me when I'd fallen into the trap of refusing to fight for myself.

Ducking my head, I stared down at a small splash of

Pepsi on the counter and watched as small salty droplets began to join it there.

I wasn't much of a crier. Never had been. I'd always considered it something of a waste of time and energy. If the problem could be fixed then crying was surely not the way to do it, and if it couldn't, well, what was the point in shedding tears over something you could do nothing about?

But in that moment, my mind was like a pressure cooker, ready to burst open and bleed out every ounce of uncertainty, rejection and hurt right there on the kitchen counter.

"I just want to be like everybody else." The words were out there before I'd even given them thought, catching even me by surprise. But there it was, the secret longing that plagued my every thought. The truth that had been buried so deeply I hadn't even realised it myself.

What they'd said might have been true. I had willingly compromised myself repeatedly in an attempt to make people like me, but it wasn't approval I sought so much as that elusive feeling of belonging, of fitting in, of having a place where I fitted completely. But instead of searching for puzzle pieces that fit with mine, I'd expended all my efforts into forcing my pieces to contort to fit where they had no business being.

"Isn't that what we all want, Tom?" Jake questioned, his voice impossibly soft and his eyes more intense than I'd ever seen them.

Trix raised her hand as though wanting to answer a question in class. "I'm the freak with the rainbow coloured hair who lives with her auntie because her mum killed herself. I'm prime friendship real estate."

I stared at her, aghast, not a single usable word coming to me that could do justice to her bombshell.

"Yeah, I know," she said. "You're sorry, and you don't know what to say. Trust me, if I wanted platitudes I'd have done the crying thing. That always brings all the clichés right out. I'm just making a point. And hey, look at Jakey boy here. He's got the killer dad thing *and* the gay thing to contend with."

This time, it wasn't just *my* head that shot up in surprise. Jake's whipped up so quickly I wondered he didn't get whiplash. He stared at her, eyes wide and disbelieving, earning himself a good natured laugh in response.

"Oh come on. You boys think I'm stupid or something. Give me some credit. Just remember: Trix. Sees. Everything." She tapped the side of her nose with a wink and a smile that did nothing to ease the disquieted expression on Jake's face.

"The point we're trying to make, young Thomas, is that the feeling you have—that ache in your chest and yearning in your soul—is completely normal. Everybody feels it. Probably even that knobhead you fell for for whatever reason. Boys don't go through that many girls that quickly unless they're searching for something."

"Sadly not searching for me," I threw back sarcastically, trying and failing not to glance Jake's way several times a second.

"I can't pretend to be sad about that," she said with a smile. "He's not good enough for you."

"He's not good enough for you, either," I added with a smirk, remembering the strange way they'd eyed one another at the party before it all exploded.

"What?"

"I'm just saying." I held my hands up but continued to grin.

"Damn right, Williams. He couldn't afford me." Flicking her hair in an affected manner, she spun on the spot and dropped into a mock curtsy before levelling a finger at Jake. "And just to complete the trifecta of awesome, he's not good enough for you, either."

"Trust me," Jake mumbled. "That is not going to be an issue." There was disgust in his voice, a bitter edge that held something more than general dislike that made me curious to know more, but before I had the chance to let my nosiness out, he jumped down from his stool. "Anyway, I'm glad you're okay, Tom, but I have to go. If I don't get home soon, Deefer will have trashed the house in protest at how late his walk will be."

"Deefer," I repeated.

"I believe you've met."

"The Dalmation?"

He nodded. "Deefer. D for dog. D for Dalmation. Deefer."

He turned to leave then paused in the doorway, appearing to fight some sort of internal battle for the longest time while Trix and I watched on curiously before turning back. Expression apprehensive, he cast his eyes between the two of us a couple of times before speaking far less confidently. "You guys are welcome to come along. I mean, it's apparently monsoon season so it'll be gross and I can promise you Deef *will* jump up and get his muddy paws all over your clothes, but..."

"Count me in." I jumped up with a grin. "I'm not afraid of a little mud."

Trix, however, hesitated for a moment, eyeing me with an appraising look as though weighing something up. "Actually, my aunt is expecting me. Wednesday night is enforced family time night and I said I'd bake cookies."

There was something to be said for the rapturous welcome home Jake received from Deefer the moment he pushed open the front door to the terraced house I'd never known was on the street where Trix lived. The dog was a blur of black and white kisses and a whippy wagging tail as he loved on his owner like he'd never seen him before. I couldn't remember ever being so cheerfully received anywhere in my life before, but once he was done with Jake, he moved on to me.

Apparently, he operated on the basis that familiarity bred understanding, as when Jake chastised him for jumping up at me a little too enthusiastically, he looked to me to back him up.

Shrugging, I backed up a step and laughed. "Sorry, buddy, he's the boss, not me."

He was right about the mud. By the time we'd done a single circuit of the park where I'd played football my entire life, my clothes were covered in paw prints and I couldn't have cared less. It was so good to be out after hiding away for three days. The wind felt like the breath of life against my skin and I felt my spirits beginning to lift with every step. We'd been walking for at least half an hour before either of us spoke except to the dog. There was a strange sort of companionship to the peace, though. It felt right, natural, almost as though we'd spoken a thousand words in every beat of silence.

Was that true friendship—the ability to spend time together in silence yet still come away feeling like you'd had the best conversation? There was no pressure, no urgency to fill the peace with mindless chatter or endless jokes. He seemed perfectly content to just be, to just walk, and it surprised me how refreshing that was.

"Are you coming in tomorrow?" he finally asked as we rounded the path out of the park and on towards the canal.

"You ask that as though I have a choice." I snorted, imagining Trix's wrath if I opted for another duvet day.

He chuckled, plucking a dog treat from a bag in his pocket and tossing it in the air for Deefer to catch. "Not sure I'd want to take my chances making Beatrix mad, but it's totally your call."

Grimacing, I nodded, stooping down to ruffle Deefer's fur as he nudged my thigh with his nose. "I'll be there. Sacrificing my education because of one person isn't exactly the most intelligent thing I've ever done anyway. I need these A levels."

"You keen to get out of Colwich, too?" he asked with interest.

Was I?

I never had been before. In fact, my plan had always been to go to university as nearby as possible and then come back and try to get a job in one of the local high schools. Now, though... did I want to come back to a town where I'd experienced so much rejection? Where heartache had taken root and blossomed inside me? Where my dreams had not only been broken but utterly obliterated into dust at the feet of the boy I'd once called best friend?

"I don't know anymore," I admitted. "Half of me loves it here and never wants to leave. The other half wants to run as far and fast as possible and get away from all of... this."

"Understandable," he said with a smile.

"And you? You want out?"

Jake didn't talk about himself much. He was a master at turning conversations away from himself when he was uncomfortable, but today, he seemed different, relaxed almost.

"Yeah..." he agreed. "Yeah, as far as possible."

"University?"

His shoulders tensed just a little as his lips drew into a slight frown. "If I pass my A levels, which is a big if right now."

"You'll pass," I asserted confidently. "We'll make sure you do. You want to study art?"

"You'd think, wouldn't you?" he laughed. "Wouldn't have any trouble getting onto a fine art course, but no. I may be crazy to even try, but I've always wanted to work with animals, and Plymouth university offers a degree in animal behaviour and welfare."

"Plymouth," I said, my eyes widening and my heart sinking a little. "That's... far."

An unfathomable sadness welled up inside of me at the thought of him running so very far—practically to the other end of the country—to get away from the town that held the very worst of his memories. I mean, sure, I'd had some hard moments here recently, but I'd also been happy here. I'd had moments of ecstacy, of joy and friendship that had somehow formed a tether that kept me bound to the place. I couldn't imagine being so far away from the place that had, for better or worse, always been home.

"You have your sunrises, I have the sea," he said enigmatically as the dog danced around us, tail wagging and tongue lolling out excitedly at the stick in Jake's hand, waiting for it to be thrown along the towpath ahead of us.

"I've never been down there," I said with a laugh as Jake flung the stick into the distance and Deefer went bounding after it, his bum wiggling madly as his tail swished all over. "Always wanted to."

"It's beautiful. We used to go down there every year when I was a kid. There's this beach along the coast in Cornwall where we'd go on every trip. My dad would build a campfire as the sun went down, and we'd roast marshmallows. The we'd take it in turns to tell our problems to the sea, because the waves would carry them far away." He laughed bitterly, kicking at the stones beneath our feet as we moved further along the path past the brightly coloured longboats moving gently on the water in the quickly fading light. "Back then, of course, my problems were stupid things like the fact that my pocket money wasn't enough to buy the new toy I wanted, or that this kid or that from school didn't like my new trainers."

"And now?"

"Now?"

"What would you tell the waves now?"

He scoffed. "I'm not that naive little kid anymore. Telling your problems to the waves doesn't make them go away. I'm not stupid enough to think that I can outrun them by moving to the other end of the country, either. But at least there I won't be *that kid*."

We walked on for several minutes in silence as I weighed his words. He wanted to run to escape his demons. I wanted to stay in order to silence mine.

"What about you?" he finally asked when our feet turned onto a rickety looking wooden bridge to take us back towards the town. My confused eyebrow quirk had him going on, "University? Jobs? Setting up your own gardening business? Bright, shining future with that big brain of yours?"

I grinned. "I want to teach."

"Yeah." He nodded, lips lifting into a smile. "You'd be good at that."

CHAPTER SIXTEEN

Life went on, as it tended to do, the wet autumn trundling relentlessly towards a frosty winter. By the time December came around, everybody was far too busy going crazy over Christmas to even remember that something had happened with Luke Chang and Tom Williams. The curious stares and pitying looks began to dry up over time, and with the armour of my friends by my side, and Abbi and Elliot announcing they were sticking around until after Christmas, I began to move from getting through each day to something that vaguely resembled happiness.

I had something I hadn't really had before—a tribe who knew, understood and accepted me. It was a revelation what a difference that made.

Much of our free time was spent together, the five of us. I'd recruited them all into helping me to transform Lucy's garden, and it was getting more and more beautiful every day. She was over the moon with the changes we'd made, and I suspected with the company our constant presence gifted her. She was an amazing lady with a wicked sense of humour and an endless supply of funny stories about her grandchildren. I couldn't wait for the spring when all the bulbs and seeds I'd planted would begin to come to life, painting the flowerbeds in an array of colour.

It was hard to think of spring, though, when there was snow on the ground and everybody was so focused on thoughts of Christmas.

My suggestion of a fun group swim in the depths of December when the remnants of the feeble snowfall had closed the college for the day hadn't initially gone down well. Apparently, swimming was 'a summer activity', but I had just enough residual post-unintentional-outing pity to guilt them into going.

The pool was, unsurprisingly, almost empty, giving Trix, Jake, Abbi, Elliot and I almost the run of the place. After Trix used her boobs inside her tiny bikini to convince the lifeguard to open up the store filled with ridiculous floating toys meant for kids' fun sessions, we spent a happy hour splashing, ducking, screaming and laughing. This was a me I recognised—a me who remembered how to have fun, to laugh and enjoy being with friends without allowing my overactive mind to throw barrier after barrier in the way of my happiness. I didn't have to pretend here with them. There were no masks, no expectations, nothing to prove and nobody to force myself into painful boxes for.

I was in the middle of a very serious fight to the death with Jake—or at the very least serious splashing injury—using a pool noodle, when the air in the room shifted. What had been light and carefree suddenly cloyed and thickened with a stifling atmosphere as echoes of mocking laughter and voices that were all too familiar rent the carefree sounds of our group in two.

I stiffened, pool noodle held aloft as my eyes locked with Jake's in dismay. The very last person I wanted to see was here with his entourage, and in an instant, the fun was over.

I watched without looking as they made their way down the side of the pool, my eyes still locked with Jake's. It wasn't hard to track their movements, though. They were shouting, laughing, and pushing one another all the way down to the deep end. All movement around me had stopped sharply, the lighthearted sounds of my friends drying up as they all froze, apparently waiting on me to see what to do.

They weren't far from us now, the cacophony of their voices growing. And it was only a matter of time before they spotted us.

The decision was made in an instant. Call me a coward but I had no desire to stay where they were—where he was—and once I made the decision, I didn't hesitate to make the move to get out.

Droplets rained from my skin as I pulled myself up on the side of the pool, hearing the sounds of the others following my lead behind me. We would get out, leave—that way they could enjoy their swim and we wouldn't have to be party to it. It was almost impossible to believe that once upon a time I would have been one of their number, and now I couldn't even look at them. Overnight, I'd gone from one of them to persona non grata, all because of something I had no control over.

"Well, would you look who's here."

My heart dropped like a stone into the soles of my wet feet as I kept my eyes focused firmly downwards. Hurt, pain and sadness all bubbled around the empty space where my heart had been, and I had to curl my lips inwards and bite down hard to keep from speaking out.

"Come to perve on me in my swimming gear, have you, Williams?"

His voice was like sandpaper on an already gaping wound, searing my healing soul and wrenching the day's happiness away from me in a moment.

"We're leaving. Back off." Trix's voice was strong while mine was too weak to even utter a single syllable, and her firm directness kept my body moving where it wanted to roll over in submission.

I might have been healing, but there were some wounds I doubted would ever truly close. The loss of a friendship I'd valued above all others was something that would likely haunt me forever, but borrowed strength from the friends around me could at least get me from the room and away from his taunting.

"And Cooper, too. Well this is priceless."

My stomach revolted, threatening to regurgitate my breakfast as I felt rather than saw Jake pulling himself from the pool beside me.

"All the rejects in one place. How cute."

I could hear his entourage snickering nastily and my hands fisted at my sides as I slowly rose to my feet, only barely hearing Jake's softly muttered, "Ignore him," over the rushing of blood in my ears.

I'd felt hurt by his dismissal, even guilt at not being honest with him right from the start and making him feel as though he was the butt of some ridiculous joke. But now all I felt was anger—stone cold fury at the icy cold way he spoke not just about me, his former best friend, but also Jake, the guy who deserved none of this.

I was mid-turn, ready to throw some bile right back at him, when a solid hand landed on my shoulder, pulling me back.

"Let's go, buddy." Elliot's voice was as calm and unflappable as ever, and his grip on my shoulder never loosened as he steered me towards the changing rooms.

"Need your little posse of freaks with you now, Williams? Too much of a princess to face me alone?" Luke's acerbic voice called out, the words echoing around off the tiles and battering the insides of my head.

"Or perhaps he doesn't need to."

I froze, my body only vaguely registering the cold as the droplets from the pool evaporated from my skin, leaving goosebumps in their wake. Or perhaps it was the sound of Jake speaking out where he was so often silent that had all the breath leaving me in a whoosh and my skin pebbling. He was uncomfortable with the conflict; it was plain to hear in his voice, yet there he was, moving to my side as I turned back to face the hostile sneers of the gang I had once been a part of.

"Nobody was speaking to *you,* Cooper." Luke stepped forward, away from the group, and prodded Jake sharply in the shoulder, not hard enough to hurt, but a clear attempt to rile him. "How's your dad?"

"What the hell happened to you, Luke?" I blurted, glowering at the boy I didn't recognise at all anymore. I could understand him being shocked and hurt, but I'd never known him to be so intentionally cruel.

A little voice inside my head murmured at me that I'd always been on the right side of him in the past. I'd certainly heard him speak disparagingly about others before, and to my shame I'd never spoken up, preferring instead to remain a part of the crowd. Over and again, I'd chosen fitting in in favour of standing up for those who couldn't do it for themselves, and now it was me he was gunning for—me, and somebody I had come to care about more deeply than I'd realised until I found myself standing shoulder to shoulder with him, facing down my former best friend.

"Nothing happened to me," he spat. "I just have a low tolerance for murderers and liars. Now, why don't you two just get on with whatever it is you people do, and let the decent people here enjoy the pool."

The following seconds were a blur. One second, we were all standing there, sparks flying from our eyes and acid floating from our lips. The next, I felt a rough hand yanking on my shoulder and forcing my body inwards towards Jake, who appeared to be in the same position. The grip on my shoulder held bruising force as I resisted, my neck cracking in my attempts to pull away.

For a moment, I was grateful when the hand fell

sharply away and I stumbled several feet backwards before finding my feet.

A blink.

And when I opened my eyes, all I could see was red.

It stained the tiles, running in rivulets along the dips between them and melting into the water. My insides twisted painfully as I followed the line of crimson to a prone form lying precariously on the edge of the pool with blood leaking from a wound that marred the otherwise perfect honey coloured skin of his temple.

For a beat, nobody moved. Shock held us all in place, the silence thick with fear and tension before panic set in and everybody began to move all at once.

Ignoring the painful crack as my knees hit the solid tile floor, dread filled me to the brim as I watched Andrew Jackson attempt to rouse Luke without any luck. The lifeguard was with us in seconds, taking control of the situation with ease and leaving me floating in an endless space of uncertainty, not knowing how Luke had wound up injured or what was going to happen next.

All I knew was that this was my fault. If I'd just had the strength to walk away, to ignore Luke like Jake had told me in the first place, this wouldn't have happened.

"You're finished, Cooper." Andrew's voice cut through the fog in my mind, abruptly forcing me to abandon my 'what if' wishful thinking and rejoin the real world where Luke was unconscious and bleeding, and Jake and I were somehow responsible for it. "You'll be joining your precious daddy behind those bars soon enough after this."

On the instructions of the pool manager, we numbly changed back into our clothes, none of us speaking a single word, but for once, I was grateful for the silence. Speaking would have made all of this real. The time would come when we'd have to work through all of this and figure out how the confrontation had got so out of hand, but none of us were ready just yet.

Minutes later, we found ourselves sat in a stupefied line —us and them—faces pale and jaws set with fear and confusion. Even Luke's friends, so vocal only a short while ago, were silent now. We were all lost in thought, and hope that, in spite of everything, Luke would be okay after being loaded onto a stretcher and carried away in an ambulance.

By the time the police arrived, I'd lost all possibility of coherent thought. I'd been over and over the moments before red had blighted the pure white tile and everything had changed, and nothing was any clearer. In a daze, I sat as they asked me question after question I couldn't answer with any clarity then waited alone in a small office for my dad to collect me.

The moment we got into his car, doors slammed closed on the outside world, he turned in his seat, his keys spinnning round and round his finger as he assessed me from head to toe with enquiring eyes. "Are you hurt?"

My gaze shifted in surprise from the movement of his keys to grey eyes that were mirrors of mine, narrowed not in anger but concern.

"No," I replied softly, hands twisting in my lap as I waited for concern to morph into interrogation. Instead, he simply nodded once before turning and starting the car without saying another word.

Scanning the car park to see whether my friends were leaving, too, the direct line from my eyes to my chest throbbed with agony at the sight of Jake being led from the building by a single officer and loaded into the back of the police car like some sort of criminal.

CHAPTER SEVENTEEN

It was hard to believe that only a month ago, I'd deliberately hidden away, isolating myself from the people I loved. Now, all I wanted was to see them, to speak to them, or even to hear some news. The house had turned into a prison, the four walls of the living room mocking me with their cold civility and impersonal artwork that nobody actually liked but everybody pretended to. The phone was maddeningly out of reach in the kitchen while I sat stiffly in an armchair and my dad tried to extract some sort of sense out of me. I wanted to cooperate, if only so I could get out of there and try to find out what was going on, but I had no sense to give. All I could think of were the images of Luke's lifeless form and Jake's empty eyes as he was loaded into the car.

"Tom." My dad sighed heavily, pinching the bridge of his nose in frustration at my lack of useful information. "I need you to be honest with me. This is serious."

"You think I don't know that?" I shouted, jumping from

the armchair as though it had bitten me, my hands behind my neck in irritation.

"Sit down, son," he said with a deep, eerie calm that assured obedience much more readily than shouting. "I'm not the enemy here. It would be nice if you would at least try to remember that. Now tell me. What happened?"

"I don't know," I barked out for what felt like the millionth time. "It was a mess. One minute we were talking —arguing—and the next..." I shrugged helplessly, vocalising what I'd opened my eyes to just a step too far.

"Right. Now we're getting somewhere. You said arguing. Arguing about what?"

"About..." I slapped my hands down on the arms on the chair, my head falling back as my eyes searched the impeccable ceiling for divine inspiration. "Does it really matter what it was about?"

"Yes," he asserted simply. "It will matter to the police so it matters to this, here, now."

"Fine," I snapped. "We were arguing because Luke didn't like it when he found out that I'm gay and decided to make an issue of it right there in the swimming baths."

He flinched, his eyes closing against the single word that seemed to cause him so much difficulty to process as he pushed out of the seat, perhaps to shake of the thought that he clearly found so unsavoury.

"That's right, Dad. I *am* gay. I've got used to the idea. Now it's your turn."

When he replied, his voice was strained, as though every single word caused him intense physical pain. "Your sexuality is not the issue here."

"Isn't it?"

His hands dropped to his hips, and it was his turn to search the ceiling, perhaps hoping that a hole would open up and beam him away so he didn't have to have this conversation.

"You're never going to be okay with it—with *me*—are you?" The thought was oddly freeing. Letting go of the need to fight for approval or acceptance might just prove to be liberating if I let it.

"You're my son."

"That's not an answer."

His hands dropped to his sides in defeat, and he turned his eyes on me, looking less like the dignified politician I was used to and more like a lost little boy—a little like I felt. "One day, you might understand just how much of an answer it is." Raking his hands through his hair, leaving it sitting in disarray atop his head, he moved to the liquor cabinet and pulled two glasses out, pouring himself a large whiskey from the crystal decanter and hesitating for a moment before pouring another and offering it to me.

He'd never given me alcohol before, never acknowledged the fact that I was growing up beyond allowing me more freedom to roam. I took a sip and grimaced as the burning liquid cut its way down my throat, waiting for him to say whatever it was that was gathering inside his mind.

Finally, he sat, perching right on the edge of his seat and taking a long swig of his drink that would likely have had me choking.

"I wasn't there when your brother was born. It was snowing, much heavier than it is now, and I was stuck in

Manchester when I got the call. By the time I arrived, he was already here. He was the most perfect thing I'd ever seen. I never knew I could be so happy. And then we found out she was pregnant with you, and I was determined... This time I would be there. I held you when you were only seconds old. Your mother was fast asleep, exhausted, and I stood at the window of that room, showing you the stars and wishing upon every single one that you'd be safe and happy. I wanted to take on the entire world for you, to make sure that nothing could ever hurt you.

"You were so tiny, and I've never felt so big, so powerful. It felt like I'd be able to protect you from everything for the rest of your life—like I could pave an easy path for you to walk. But the reality is that as a parent you can't protect your child from the jagged edges life throws at them. You can't stop the world from sometimes being a cruel and difficult place. And then one day you told me this thing that I knew instantly would make your path even harder to tread."

"This thing..." I repeated softly, sadness tinging my tone because although this story was filled with the love I'd been convinced had gone, he still couldn't say the words.

"It's never mattered to me who you fell in love with." I scoffed but he shot me a look and went on talking. "I believe that love is love, and that's all there is to it, but ever since I held you in my arms that night, I've conjured up a thousand dreams of how your life would be. Fighting off ignorance and bigotry never factored into my plans for you."

I wanted to melt into the words he'd spoken, to lie back

and let them wash over me for a little while. I wanted to bask in the words 'love is love and that's all there is to it' coming from the mouth of the first person to reject me for being gay. But there was too much that hurt, too much residual pain from his rejection to just accept his explanation.

"So, what? You thought you could magically cure me, or scare the gay out of me by threatening to kick me out on the streets?"

"I thought..." He groaned, dropping his head into his hands, his body diminishing right before my eyes—my once imposing and intimidating father now seeming impossibly smaller by the second. "I don't know what I thought, son. I reacted, and not well. I sat there in that moment and all I could see was all my hopes for you burning to ash, and I reacted. We like to pretend, as parents, that every decision we make is the right one—that every word we speak is measured and weighed before ever being given voice, so we can ensure that we only ever say the things that will truly reflect what's in our hearts. But sometimes, we just... react. We react out of fear, blind terrifying panic... or sometimes just love."

I stared at him, my heart beating so fast inside my rib cage that I was sure it was beginning to hum. My head was swimming, trying to process so many things all at once and failing miserably.

"W-which one was it that time? Fear? Panic? Love?"

"All of them," he admitted quietly, lifting his head from his hands to meet my gaze head on. "Fear of a future littered with scenes just like the one you had to endure today. Panic because I was never a Boy Scout and just wasn't prepared for those words to come out of your mouth. The panic didn't last long, but by then the damage was already done. I'd spoken words aloud that I never should have said. When you were a boy, I used to always remind you to think before you spoke, because on—"

"Once the words are spoken, you can't take them back," I finished for him with a small smile that took even me by surprise. "I remember."

His lips twitched into a reluctant smile that was belied by the sadness still colouring his eyes. "It'll never be enough, but for what it's worth, I am sorry."

I waited a beat, weighing his words and the honesty radiating from his every pore before giving him a single nod of acknowledgement. I wasn't ready to tell him what he'd done was okay. Maybe it would come, but for now, it was enough that he'd said the words, and that he had, I believed, acted out of some misguided sense of love and not disgust as I'd originally assumed.

"You're sorry..." I stated faintly as my mind turned over both his words and the events of the day.

"More than you know."

"Then... help me. Please."

He held his hands out to his sides, his tense smile melting into pure relief with a smile I remembered from happier times in my childhood. "Just tell me how."

* * *

Waiting was pure agony. He'd been on the phone for what

felt like hours, and my nerves were scratched raw with worry. Was Jake sitting in a cell somewhere, alone and terrified, feeling again as though the whole world was against him? Did the police believe he'd hurt Luke on purpose? And if they did, would his dad's record stand against him? Already, in the hearts and minds of certain people in the town, he was nothing more than a chip off the old block—son of the man who killed an innocent child.

It wasn't fair, but in a town like Colwich these things tended to stack up against you regardless of whether or not it was right that they did.

"Yes, I understand that, officer, but I have my son here telling me that—" He growled slightly as somebody down the line cut him off. He hated being spoken over. You'd have thought he'd have been used to it working in politics. I only hoped that he would somehow use his position in the town to influence things in Jake's favour, or at least find out what was going on and where he was. "Yes, he has already given a statement. Yes, I understand that, but..." His fingers pinched the bridge of his nose as irritation had his tone degenerating from his usual diplomatic lilt.

I couldn't listen anymore. I'd been eavesdropping the entire time and all I'd learned was that my dad's fuse was way longer than mine. My mobile phone was infuriatingly silent. I'd had no word from any of my friends, and wondered if similar scenes of interrogation were happening in all of their houses, too. Up in my bedroom, away from the exasperatingly fruitless conversation downstairs, I threw myself onto my bed dramatically, and allowed myself a moment of self-indulgent wallowing.

Things had been going so well—too well. I should have known it was only a matter of time before they came crashing down around us. I could imagine all too well the thoughts that would likely be crashing through Jake's mind as he went through whatever he was going through at the police station. He'd be thinking some messed up thoughts about how he deserved this based on his own inaccurate perception of himself and his role in his dad's mistakes. He'd be thinking that the odds were stacked against anybody giving him the benefit of the doubt. And... worst of all, was he thinking that we'd all left him to rot, running off and letting him take the flak for something that was in no way his fault. When the chips had been down, he'd stood by my side and gone to bat for me. It was my turn to do the same for him.

Idle uselessness was beginning to make me irritable and edgy. I needed action, needed to be doing *something* to change a situation of which I wasn't even sure of the details. I felt itchy, like my insides were trying to burn their way through my skin, and no amount of scratching could ever ease it.

I all but flew down the stairs, fumbling with my coat on the way, and burst into the study just as my dad hung up the phone.

"That's the trouble with these new cordless phones," he grunted. "You don't get the satisfaction you used to get from slamming the phone down on people."

"Not very seemly for the town mayor, is it?" I said with a laugh that physically hurt my chest. This was hardly the time for cracking jokes, but it seemed some habits died harder than others.

His unenthusiastic chuckle, indulging my poor timing, told me just how hard he was trying to make things right. "I'm going to go down there."

I blinked, stunned for a moment before nodding and striding to his side. "I'm coming with you."

He wanted to argue. I could see it in his eyes as he appraised me for a moment that felt like a lifetime. There was a time when I would have withered under his scrutiny, but not now. I stood firm, determination rippling through me, my need to help Jake like a fire inside me, spurring me on.

Eventually, he nodded, stalking to retrieve his coat before ushering me out to the car.

"This boy," he said, laying an arm across the back of my seat and craning his head back to reverse the car out of the driveaway. "This Jacob Cooper they have in custody—the boy you want me to help... Is he...?"

"He's important," I replied, letting him off the hook of asking the question that he still had trouble voicing.

Baby steps, Tom.

CHAPTER EIGHTEEN

I'd never been inside the police station before. It was one of those places in the town—like the fire station or the hospital—that you knew were there but ignored in the hope that you'd never have to use them. It was a drab, elderly building with a heady odour of a vile combination of damp and urine, with a charming side helping of stale alcohol. It was the sort of place that sucked the life and hope out of you the moment you walked through the door. I suspected it had been deliberately designed that way, ready to demoralise any lawbreakers brought in through the doors.

As we approached the desk, though, my own hope soared at the sight that greeted me. Abbi was already there, armed with her solicitor father, apparently arguing with the terrifying looking woman behind the desk. I would have shrunk clean away at the withering look she was shooting at him, but he appeared completely undeterred.

Legal jargon spewed forth from his lips, bouncing off the woman's thick skin like ping-pong balls.

"Mr. Costa," she barked over his tirade, "as I have already told you, if you would just, *please,* take a seat, I will have somebody come out and speak to you shortly."

"And as I have already told *you,* this is a seventeen-year-old boy who doesn't realise he has representation. If I find out that he's been interrogated without even so much as an appropriate adult present, I'll be ensuring every single officer involved is investigated for misconduct."

He was an impressive sight, all dark hair and fiery Italian temper. The absolute confidence he carried just made him even more so. I left him to continue his fight, certain that he'd win over eventually. He was one of the most successful solicitors in the area, and the fact he was there to fight Jake's corner gave me more hope than I'd believed possible.

Tapping Abbi lightly on the shoulder, I rebounded at the sudden attack on my person as she let out a short sob and threw herself into my arms. "Tom, you're here. I knew you'd come. Have you heard—" Her words cut off sharply the moment she looked over my shoulder to see my dad joining Mr. Costa in his mission at the desk. "Is that...?"

"My dad. Yeah." I smiled, taking her hand in mine and giving it a squeeze. "It's okay. He's here to help."

Time passed by painfully slowly as I alternated between sitting in an unforgiving plastic chair beside Abbi and pacing the floor. Mr. Costa and my dad were eventually allowed to go through to 'the back', whatever that even meant, but that had been two hours ago and we'd still heard nothing. It was probably childish, but I'd secretly thought that Mr. Costa going back there would somehow magically fix everything, and I'd scanned the door they'd disappeared through solidly for the first hour, expecting them to walk out with Jake in tow, everybody smiling and laughing, and agreeing over what a silly misunderstanding this had all been.

But reality wasn't like the films I'd watched or the hopes I'd dreamed. Reality was a freezing cold waiting area with seats that made my back ache and hunger gnawing at my insides. Abbi was paler than I'd seen her since the day Nonna had died, and worry had her brow furrowed and her foot bouncing rhythmically against the squeaky parquet floor. Her usual propensity to talk a mile a minute when she was nervous seemed to have abandoned her, leaving her oddly mute, her eyes constantly flicking between the clock and the door, waiting and hoping.

How had a fun, lighthearted snow day turned so easily to this? How had we gone from splashing and laughter to police stations and ambulances—to silent pacing and clock watching with hearts that wouldn't stop hammering?

I was sitting staring blankly at the clock with Abbi's tired head resting on my shoulder when the door finally opened. My head shot up in hope, the thought that maybe Jake would be there stalling every single function in my body for just a second, but only my dad and Mr. Costa came through it.

Crouching down in front of me like I was seven and not seventeen, Mr. Costa cleared his throat before speaking.

"Tom, we need to ask you some questions, and we need you to be absolutely honest with us."

I nodded slowly, unable to stop questions from firing out of me like bullets. "Have you seen him? Is he okay?"

"He's as well as can be expected, yes. We're here now, don't you worry about that. But I need you to think. Have you ever had any reason to believe that the injured young man—Luke Chang—was capable of assault?"

"Uh..." I stalled, blinking at him in surprise as I felt Abbi stiffening beside me, her head lifting from my shoulder. "I'm sorry?"

"Think carefully, son," my dad said from behind Mr. Costa. "Have you ever seen Luke behave aggressively towards another young person?"

"I..." Baffled, I scrubbed my face with my hands, trying to reason out the question. "Before today?"

"Yes," both men confirmed.

"I don't think so. I mean..." Rubbing my temples with my fingers as a headache that had been threatening for hours began to overpower my thought process. "He could be a bit cutting sometimes—thoughtless, you know? But I never saw him hurt anybody."

Mr. Costa sighed, looking even more tired than I felt. "How about Jacob? Have you ever seen him behave aggressively towards anybody before?"

This question was much easier to answer. "No. No, I've seen him provoked almost beyond endurance, and he's always kept his cool. Always." I looked up at my dad beseechingly. "He didn't do this, Dad. I don't know how

Luke ended up getting hurt, but Jake didn't put him there. He wouldn't."

"It was all a mess." Abbi's low voice from beside me drew everybody's attention. It was strange to hear her speaking up after holding her silence for so long. "Luke was being a twat. Sorry but he was," she went on when her dad shot her a look of amused disapproval. "He was..." She hesitated, turning to me with a brow raised in question. At my nod, she went on. "He was giving Tom grief over his, uh, sexuality." Despite my permission, she still shot me a look of apology before going on. "Jake stood up for Tom, then Luke wound up pushing them together, trying to force them to—I dunno—kiss, I guess. It was inevitable somebody was going to get hurt. Jake lifted his arm to get free and Luke wound up falling. It was self defence. No question."

"Listen," my dad said, dropping into the chair next to me and leaning forwards with his arms rested across his thighs. "Jacob is making some pretty serious allegations against Luke, which rightly or wrongly, the police are sceptical of."

"What kind of allegations?" I questioned in alarm.

His hands wrung between his legs as his head dipped to his chest. "He's claiming that Luke and his friends have been bullying him on and off for months, including several quite serious assaults."

My whole world bowed in on me as I stared at him in horror. Only one word had stuck of all the ones he'd thrown at me—*bullying*.

Was it possible? In my experience, Jake wasn't a liar. He may have been cagey with the truth at times—little wonder after what he'd been through—but as far as I knew, he'd never outright lied to me.

But bullied... all this time? And he never said a word, never told me anything? Surely it was impossible...

And then images started to flow through my mind, slowly like treacle to begin with, each one lingering and turning my stomach just a little more by the second.

Jake's face when I'd told him who I was going to meet that afternoon in the garden.

The uncomfortable, slightly afraid way he'd held himself that day in the common room with Luke crowding him from behind.

The way he'd been so very reluctant to come to Luke's party, and the apprehension I'd put down to pre-party nerves when I'd finally coaxed him into going.

The not only dismissive but actively cruel way that Luke had spoken to him on ever single occasion I'd seen them interact.

And...

"Oh god," I let out on a gasp. "He had a black eye this one time. I thought somebody at home was hurting him for a while, and then he told me about his dad being in prison and..." Ashamed, I ducked my head. "And then I forgot all about it."

"Do you remember when this was?" Mr. Costa asked, his voice as dark as his eyes that bored into me with frightening intensity.

"I'm not s— No, wait." I smiled, the memory assaulting me with fortuitous timing. "It was a Friday. The third Friday in September."

The mystery of Jake's absences on the third Tuesday of the month had plagued me until I found out about his prison visiting. There was no way I would forget that week. It seemed like a different world now—the maths classroom and Mrs. Bright's poor treatment of Jake. Gardening in the rain, then leaving the boy who never hurt anybody and running to the one who did.

"You're sure?" Mr. Costa asked seriously.

"Positive."

He stood, the sound of his knees cracking as he rose echoing through the room as Abbi and I stared at the grown men we were relying on to fix this.

"The dates match."

My dad nodded and turned to me. "You two, go home. We won't leave until this is sorted, but you two need to get out of here."

"But—"

"No buts, son," my dad said, cutting off my protest. "You can't do any more here, and we will work better knowing you're not sitting out here for every criminal in Colwich to be dragged past.

I didn't have the energy to protest that not one single other person had come through the whole time we'd been there. So with promises that they'd call us as soon as there was anything to know, we slouched out of the police station tiredly, knowing that somewhere in the building, Jake had to be feeling even more exhausted and terrified.

Deciding to use my father's use of the word 'home' creatively, I went back to Nonna's place with Abbi where Elliot was pacing a hole in the carpet waiting for her. Their reunion as we walked through the door destroyed me. She melted into him as he cupped her cheek in his hand and stared at her as though she was the part that had been missing from him for years and not just a few hours. That look in their eyes, the connection that spoke a million words without either of them even opening their mouths, made me ache for the same for myself. Now that the world knew what I wanted, it seemed like the need for it had grown more acute. It was an ache I tried to temper with thoughts of Jake and what he must have been going through, but that only seemed to make it hurt even more.

I should have been worried about Luke. After all, the last time I'd seen him, he'd been bleeding from the head and drifting in and out of consciousness as he was loaded into the back of an ambulance. But today's confrontation coupled with the bombshell about what he'd been doing to Jake had tempered my ability to feel anything but dislike for the boy who had made my stomach flutter and my heart stall for the past year.

By the time the pizza we'd ordered arrived, Trix had joined us, and we'd all been over and over what had happened a million times. It was like we couldn't stop going over it, maybe hoping to find some reason in the whole thing, some meaning that would give what poor Jake was going through a purpose. But there was none to be found. One minute, we'd been having fun, just a small group of friends enjoying an extra day off together. The next, we'd found ourselves under a verbal assault I couldn't see we'd done anything to deserve.

What we were doing was less than useless. We couldn't fix anything, couldn't do anything more to help Jake, couldn't change what had happened by rehashing it, but at least we were together. The voices of my friends gave me hope that somehow, in spite of the gap in our five piece puzzle, we would get the missing piece back eventually.

The pizza was still sitting going cold in its boxes, none of us as interested in food as we'd imagined when faced with the prospect of eating junk while our friend was being interrogated. A knock at the door had us all stiffening, but before any of us had moved, the door latch had lifted and two extremely weary men walked in.

"Dad!" Abbi leaped from her position on the floor and rushed to the door, dragging her father further inside the cottage, followed somewhat warily by my own dad.

He looked uncertain, as though he wasn't sure whether he was welcome. I guess our relationship had been so strained for so long by then that in spite of his efforts in the police station, he wasn't sure of the welcome he'd receive.

Smiling reassuringly at him, I gestured to the pizza. "There's food if you're hungry."

It took every ounce of self control I had not to immediately start questioning them. It was only the worn look in both of their eyes and the exhausted slopes of their shoulders that kept me quiet as they both took slices of pizza and sat, holding them rather than eating.

"How's—"

"He's fine," my dad interjected with a small smile.

"He's tired and shaken up, and probably pretty angry with the world right now, but his mum was finally able to get away from work to be with him, and she's taken him home now."

I jumped up from the couch at his words. "He's out? He's home? I should—"

"Leave him be for tonight, son."

"But..."

"But nothing. He's had the day from hell. He's shattered, emotionally and physically, and he needs to rest and be with his mum tonight."

"And tomorrow? Is it over?" I asked hopefully, feeling Trix sidling up beside me and linking her arm through mine to listen in.

"They have one witness who has said he clearly saw Jacob *push* Luke with the intention of hurting him, but another four witness statements contradicting that. With no real hard evidence, they are putting the incident down to a spat and nothing more. Luke is going to be absolutely fine, though the sixth form college will be informed about the allegations of bullying. As to whether it's over..." His hands moved to scrub at his face. "Legally, for now it's done. For Jacob, though, I suspect 'over' may take a little longer."

"He's not okay, is he?"

The thought made me physically hurt in that cavity behind my sternum I'd believed empty. How had he gone from being the silent boy in maths whose dragon sketches I was so curious about to somebody whose happiness was so intricately interwoven with my own? I imagined the dragons he would draw tonight—the fire they would wreak as he soothed his soul the only way he seemed to know how.

Tomorrow... tomorrow I would go to him. Maybe I could help him. Maybe I couldn't. But if I'd learned anything in all of this, it was that sometimes you just needed somebody to be there by your side. Not saying anything. Not doing anything. Just there.

CHAPTER NINETEEN

The sunrise was the last thing on my mind the following morning after a fitful night's sleep, though my mind dimly registered the stunning array of colour painting the sky as I marched my way through the snow that had thickened through the night, in the direction of Jake's side of town. Colwich wasn't exactly a large place, but when I spent a good half of the time falling on my backside because my shoes had no grip, it took a frustratingly long time to get to his front door.

Leaning against the door with my eyes to the sky, I took a moment to compose myself and brush the latest offering of snow from my backside before a furious barking and scrabbling at the door gave me away.

"Cheers, Deef," I muttered, shaking the snow from my hair before knocking.

I was about ready to give up on anybody answering and plant myself on the doorstep to stage a sit in until somebody let me in, when the door opened a crack, tethered by a chain, and a tired looking female face peered through the gap.

Unmistakably familiar eyes narrowed the moment they latched onto me while Deefer desperately pawed at the wooden door. "Why can't you lot just leave him alone? He's done nothing, you hear me? Nothing. Just get out of it or I'll call the police."

"No, wait," I called out too late as the door slammed home in my face and a sad little canine whimper echoed through to me. "Mrs. Cooper, please." I knocked again, hammering on the door as anger tinged sadness rocked through me at the thought that he'd been home less than eighteen hours and he'd already been harassed.

When that failed, I ducked down to the letterbox, pushing it open and hollering through. "Please listen to me. I'm not one of them."

It was hopeless. The simple wooden door might as well have been a stone fortress complete with drawbridge and a shark infested moat, as Jake had once joked, and the only sounds from beyond it were the snufflings and whinings of the dog.

Twisting, I fell back and sat with my spine pressing into the barrier that kept me from Jake. My head dipped between my shoulders as my hands lifted to massage my neck.

What could I do? I couldn't leave—not until I'd seen Jake with my own two eyes and told him... Told him what? There were so many thoughts inside my head, desperate to come out. Half of them probably needed to stay there, but I'd never been much good at controlling my tongue in front of him. There was just something about him that made me want to be the truest me I could possibly be—an affliction I'd never been plagued with before.

With him, there were no masks, no pretences, no stupid jokes to cover up my shortcomings. There was just me, standing there with my heart in my outstretched hand, silently begging him not to toss it away.

Deefer wasn't giving up his quest on the other side of the door. I could hear the desperate scrabbling of his paws against it, and I sighed. "I know how you feel, buddy. But hey, do me a favour?"

I was sure his sudden silence on the other side of the door was a mere coincidence, but I still convinced myself that he was listening and waiting to carry out my orders.

"Go to him, Deef. Go to wherever he is, and tell him in your own special doggy way... Tell him that I'm here for him, and that if I have to die of hypothermia on his doorstep waiting for him then that's what I'll do. Tell him that he *matters*. Tell him that everything is better when he's around, that not even the sunrise is more beautiful than him when he smiles at me. And tell him that we're on his side now, all of us. I know he's stubborn and thinks he has to do everything alone, but I'm not scared of sharks or drawbridges or dragons. So unless he wants me losing body parts to frostbite on his conscience, he needs to open this door."

Nothing.

I wasn't sure what I was expecting Deefer to do. He was a dog after all. Perhaps his silence had convinced me he was listening and ready to leap into action, and not just slumping into sleep in the warmth on the other side of the door. I could feel tiny tendrils of it seeping through into my spine that was already beginning to ache with the cold. My nose was numb, my cheeks stinging and my eyes watering with a combination of cold and disappointment.

"Not scared of dragons, huh?"

The door peeled away from my back, sending a rush of blessed heat at me that I lapped up like a starving man.

"Some things are more important," I said earnestly, unfolding my protesting body from its spot on the doorstep and swinging around to face Jake, where he stood looking like he hadn't slept in a month with Deefer sitting at his feet looking proud of himself.

Dark circles were bedded in deeply beneath Jake's eyes, which were red raw and glistening in the sunlight. He was impossibly pale, the blue tinge of his veins standing stark against his translucent skin, and he stared at me as though he wasn't sure whether to invite me in or beg me to leave and never come back.

"You heard?" I asked with a small nervous laugh.

"Every word."

"Well, for your information, that was an extremely private conversation between me and your dog."

"Don't do that, Tom." The smile twitching up the corners of his mouth belied the single tear that had escaped from his eyes and was wending its way down his cheek.

"Do what?"

"Start cracking jokes just because you're embarrassed because you think you said something you shouldn't have."

Biting my lip, I looked down at my feet, stuffing my hands into my pockets to protect them from the biting cold that was cutting right down to my bones. "Did I?" I asked. "Say something I shouldn't have?"

"That depends really." He stood back and gestured for me to come inside, an invitation I didn't hesitate in accepting.

"On?"

"On whether it was the truth. The words were beautiful, but they only count if you meant them. I mean, it's easy to say that stuff to a door, right?"

"Not as easy as you might think," I mumbled. "I'm not used to speaking my mind. I tell jokes and make people laugh—at me or with me, it doesn't matter as long as they're laughing—but you... You make me feel utterly exposed, like a raw nerve. You strip all that stuff away and I have no idea what's left underneath."

"What's left underneath is *you*, Tom. The boy who enjoys digging in the rain and swimming at midnight. The boy who loves sunflowers because they make people happy, and underneath all the facades, that's who you are—the boy who wants everybody to be happy because he knows what it's like to be desperately lonely."

He was so close to me now I could feel the warmth of his breath whispering over my chilled cheeks as he lifted a hand to brush away the tears I hadn't even noticed I was shedding with a single finger.

"Why didn't you tell me?" I blurted out on a half sob as my eyes fell closed to relish in his touch. "About Luke. About everything. You never said a word."

His hand dropped and he stepped back, sliding down the wall until he was sitting with his knees to his chest and his head tilted back against the tired wallpaper. A short huff of a sigh broke from his chest as his eyes closed, shutting off my access to the emotions that were all so plain there. "You looked at him like he was everything to you. You talked about him with the same reverence as you do the sunrise."

"You thought I'd be okay with what he was doing to you?"

He shrugged. "For a while... At first I thought you had to know. I mean, you called him your best friend. You don't have to be a part of something to be complicit in it, do you?"

"You thought I knew—that I just let it keep happening to you and did nothing?"

"At first." He dragged in a deep breath that seemed to fortify him for the conversation, then lifted his head and stared right at me. "And then I got to know you and I knew that there was no way. You didn't have it in you to stand back while somebody you called a friend did... those things."

The shaky edge to his voice as he said those final two words told me clearly that I didn't know the half of what Luke had subjected him to. Perhaps there was a part of me that didn't want to know, couldn't bear to hear about all the times he'd been screaming out for somebody to help him and I'd sat back, lost in my idealistic bubble where Luke was everything I dreamed he was.

"But then you didn't trust me enough to tell me?"

He scoffed. "Tom, with all due respect, I jumped off a ten foot wall for you and broke into the swimming baths in the dead of night with you. Trust was hardly the issue."

"Then what was?"

"You were in love with him," he replied softly, his eyes squeezing tightly closed. "Knowing what he was, what he did, would have torn you in two. I didn't want to be the one responsible for breaking your heart."

Sighing, I crossed the space between us and slid down to sit beside him. Our shoulders were barely touching but the air around us seemed to settle into that peaceful calm that I'd begun to associate with being around him. "So instead you endured..." I swallowed, the weight of guilt settling onto my chest almost too heavy to bear. "The black eye that day wasn't the worst of it, was it?"

His low, humourless laugh sent frissions of sadness barrelling towards me as his little finger closed the gap between our hands on the floor and linked through mine. "I'm sorry I didn't meet you in the library. I was..."

Giving his little finger a squeeze, I rolled my head against the wall to face him and let the pain on his face wash over me in the hopes it would somehow diminish it. "I'm sorry I was mad."

And then, seized by madness, I jumped to my feet with way more grace than I would have thought myself capable of and held a hand out to him with a coaxing smile. "You said you trust me, right?"

He nodded, staring at my hand as though waiting for it to bite him as he placed his into it.

"Come on. I have an idea."

CHAPTER TWENTY

"Where are we going?" Jake asked for the millionth time that hour.

The blindfold may have been slightly overkill, but frankly, he was quite lucky he didn't have to see how close Trix drove to the car in front. As the only one of us with a license, though, I'd used my not inconsiderable begging skills to convince her that she was up for a road trip in the snow.

So, with no luggage—except my dad's battered old suitcase that had been bound for the tip, filled with the supplies I'd decided we needed—we'd been to drag Abbi and Elliot protesting from their beds and set off. It was a long drive, but I was sure it would be worth it.

Jake was in the back with the sleeping forms of Abbi and Elliot beside him, and I was testing my inadequate map reading skills to find the way to where I was adamant we needed to go. Deefer was snoring in the boot of the car, letting out the occasional yap of protest when we hit a particularly savage pothole.

Trix was of the opinion that any beach would do, but I knew differently. We had to find the right place. It had to be perfect. After everything he'd been through, Jake deserved that much at least.

"Relax, would you?" I chastised, twisting from the front seat to glare into the back despite the fact he couldn't see me. "And don't you dare touch that blindfold."

"So bossy," he grumbled.

"You better believe it. Take a nap. You clearly didn't sleep *at all* last night."

Trix chuckled beside me as I flopped back into place and studied the map some more, turning it upside down to see if that would help it to make some sense.

"What?" I questioned curiously.

"Oh, nothing." She grinned, fiddling with the heater until it blasted hot air at us. "Just... you know, you two."

"What about us?"

Making no effort to hide her eye roll, she opted to ignore the question and concentrated back on the road, hitting the volume button on the stereo until an Imagine Dragons song blasted through the car and I couldn't help but chuckle at the irony.

Dragons...

We were on our way to slay some of them, all of us, together. Because we were a team now, the five of us—a team of misfits, maybe, but a team nonetheless.

Guiding Jake through the unknown town, still blindfolded with my arm hooked through one of his and Elliot's through the other, earned us a fair few odd looks—some simply curious and others edging towards concern. I half expected the police to turn up asking questions after one elderly woman hurried past us, plucking an ancient looking mobile phone from her handbag and fumbling to use it, but we made it unchecked to patch of grass marked on the map with Deefer dancing around our feet excitedly.

The air was rich with that seaside smell of salt and seaweed, and overhead seagulls wheeled in the sky, calling out to one another with the sound that always transported me right back to childhood holidays by the sea.

And there it was, the ocean stretching out in front of us towards infinity. The late afternoon sunlight glimmered and danced off the rippling waves, painting the scene in a carpet of diamonds. We stopped walking just short of a tall red and white lighthouse that overlooked the coast like a sentinel.

It was still cold here, but the ground was blessedly free of snow and ice, both of which had marred the early parts of the journey.

Under the blindfold, Jake's nose twitched, his body stiffening and his muscles melting into relaxation at the familiar seaside sounds and smells. "Can I take this off yet?" he questioned impatiently, his fingers hooking beneath the fabric of my scarf eagerly.

I skipped forward with a happy grin, certain I was about to see the most radiant of all his smiles so far, and waited until the sun hit the waves just right to pull the covering away.

He blinked rapidly at the sudden influx of sunlight, taking a moment for his eyes to adjust before he rotated slowly on the spot, scanning his surroundings with mounting recognition that widened his eyes and had his mouth falling open in a more and more pronounced 'O' as he went.

"I... You... This..."

"Use your words, Jacob," Trix teased with a grin, moving to his side and linking her arm with his as her head rested on his shoulder. The desire to mirror her pose on his other side was maddeningly strong, but I just about managed to resist, instead squeezing his shoulder—an utterly inadequate display of the affection I felt for him in that moment.

"Plymouth," he said, his voice so shaky it managed to fragment even the single word. "We're in Plymouth?"

"I have my sunrises, and you have the sea."

He lifted trembling fingers to his lips as he stared out over the sun dappled ocean with tears glistening in his eyes. His lips shook as so many memories of happier times worked their way through his mind, almost visible to all of us with the changing of the seasons in his eyes.

Finally, he turned to me with summer in his expression, an emotion filled smile lighting up his face. "I can't believe you did this. This is crazy."

I grinned and threw caution to the wind, reaching for his hand and curling my fingers around his, watching his face carefully for a reaction that never came. Holding hands with him was as easy and natural as breathing in and out. Just like everything with him, there was peace in the action. "We're not done yet. We have your cove to find."

We ran back to the car. After being cooped up for so long and with the weight of the last forty-eight hours to shed, the five of us seemed to fly along that coastline with the winter wind in our hair and the enthusiastic Dalmatian leading the way.

By the time we found the beach from Jake's memories, the sun was starting its inevitable descent over the water, painting it in stunning hues of pink, orange and purple, but I only had eyes for Jake as we worked hard to build a small campfire before we lost the light.

The driftwood crackled and burned bright blue as we huddled around it for warmth, toasting marshmallows and fighting one another over the burned ones. We laughed, chattered and allowed happiness to cloud us in a bubble. Just for a while, it was easy to forget all that had happened, but I knew that unless we laid all our hopes and fears out there, the things that plagued us would only fester and grow until they tore us apart all over again.

"What on earth are you doing with that old relic?" Abbi questioned as I dragged my dad's old suitcase over the sand and dumped it right beside the fire.

"Baggage," I stated simply, sitting back on the rock beside Jake who was staring at the case just like everybody else. "Every single one of us here has it. I doubt there's a person alive who doesn't."

"Okay. And the relevance of the actual suitcase?" Trix

pressed, her lips pursed into an expression of amused curiosity.

"We're going to burn it."

Silence.

"We're going to tell our troubles to the sea—" I grinned at Jake "—and then we're going to burn them. I don't know about you guys but I'm tired of living in fear of the things that haunt me. After we've burned them, it's time to let them go—all those things that stop us from truly living. No more letting them rule us."

More silence.

Demoralised, I was ready to give up the idea entirely when Jake laced his arm through mine and took my hand in his. "It's a great idea."

"I'll go first," announced Trix unexpectedly, her face set with a rare determination I'd only ever seen connected with her Freddo habit before.

Grabbing a handful of sand, she sat with it cupped there in front of her, staring intently at the flames for several seconds before speaking. "I wasn't enough. In spite of everything I did to make my mum happy, I wasn't enough to keep her here, to make her want to live. She chose to die rather than stay with me." Her hand shook as she angrily thrust the sand it held into the open suitcase in front of her. "I'm pretty terrified that every relationship I ever have will end the same way."

Abbi, who was sitting on the blanket beside her, tugged her into her side and rubbed her shoulder in comfort. Nobody spoke, because that wasn't what this was about. It was all about exorcising demons, not chasing them.

"I miss Nonna every single day," Abbi said softly, picking up her own handful of sand. "I love my dad, and Elliot owns every single piece of my heart from the inside out, but nothing can ever replace the way she made me feel. Nobody can share the memories I have of her or fill in the missing bits I was too young to remember. So many stories died with her that I wish I'd taken the time to write down before she died. There will never be another like her."

Tossing her sand into the suitcase, she kept one arm around Trix while accepting Elliot's offered appendage from her other side. Tears leaked from her eyes as she buried her face in his neck. He was her rock, her comfort, her everything. And for the first time in my life I was starting to believe I might be able to have that myself one day.

Elliot raked his hands through the sand for a moment before lifting his own handful and staring at it dolefully.

"I'm afraid I'll never stop feeling guilty for not being there for Abbi when she needed me so badly last year." She looked up at him and offered him a watery smile that he returned with a shaky one of his own. "She's forgiven me over and over again, but all the moments when I should have seen her pain still haunt me every night when I close my eyes. She was my best friend and, even then, the love of my life, and I should have been there. She tells me to forgive myself but I don't know how to forgive when I can't forget."

He dropped a soft kiss to her forehead as she mouthed 'elephant juice' to him, her eyes shining with pure love as he tossed his sand into the case.

And then it was my turn.

The sand was rough against my palm as I curled my fingers in tightly around it and stared at the way the pressure turned my fingernails pure white.

"Somebody I care about was being hurt by the boy I thought I loved for months and I never knew. And I honestly don't know whether I willfully ignored those traits in him because I wanted to believe he was better than that." I tossed my sand on top of theirs and watched as the grains rolled around in the light of the flames. "I'm afraid that I'm seventeen years old and I don't know who I am," I went on softly. "I've spent so long defining myself by what other people thought of me and adapting myself to fit their molds for me that now I don't have to do that anymore, I find myself second guessing every single decision I make without reference to what somebody else might think."

Slender fingers squeezed mine almost painfully tight, and I glanced down at where our hands were joined.

I'd always thought when I met the one, everything would shift. There'd be flashing lights and electrical currents. My heart would beat faster and my stomach would churn. I thought the Hallelujah Chorus would play inside my head and fireworks would light up the sky.

All I got with Jake was this stillness, this peace that settled inside me each and every time he was near. The world didn't erupt; it took on a placid hush that stilled my whirring thoughts and allowed my heart to feel at home inside my chest for the first time in as long as I could remember.

When Jake lifted his sand, I expected him to talk about

his dad, or the bullying he'd been subjected to. About his fear that he wouldn't get the grades he needed to move down here for university. There were so many facets of his life that had to hurt him, yet as he stared into the flames that danced in his eyes, the words that whispered from his lips caught me completely by surprise.

"I'm too afraid to tell the boy I like how much he means to me."

That was it. His sand was gone and the suitcase closed before I'd even had chance to process what he'd said.

The old suitcase was thrown unceremoniously onto the fire, burning up slowly along with our confessions as we watched on silently, minds and hearts full for one another and the secrets we'd heard.

CHAPTER TWENTY-ONE

By the time we'd found a bed and breakfast with enough rooms to fit all five of us and settled in, sleep came easily. My dreams were fragmented, flitting from place to place, person to person. Everyone I loved seemed to feature, their faces indistinct but the feelings they each elicited more than clear.

I was a melting pot of emotions after our night on the beach. The confessions of my friends ticked over and over in my mind, the hardships each one of them had experienced a physical pain in my chest. There was pain, but there was contentment, too. Because pain was so much more endurable when it was shared, problems so much more fixable when you had others on your side.

Jake's confession, though... The words had echoed through my mind, driving me to distraction on the drive through the city to find somewhere to stay. He'd been there right by my side, our hands not joined but touching, but doubt had stolen my tongue and kept me from asking the question I so badly wanted to know the answer to.

What if I asked and the answer wasn't what I wanted to hear? What if it was? Both scenarios scared me more than I cared to admit.

He was there, his face more distinct than any of the others as his voice called to me through the fog in my sleep addled mind.

"Tom..."

Somewhere between asleep and awake, I registered I was no longer dreaming, and then a hand shook my shoulder gently, the voice calling out again. "Tom, wake up."

"M'wake," I grumbled through a residual snore, my eyes struggling to open in the almost complete darkness of the room. The only light came from the torch on a phone that was shining upwards and lighting up Jake's face.

He was wide awake, still dressed, and his eyes were bright with excitement.

"Whadya want?" I grumbled through a yawn, stretching my body luxuriously under the warm covers.

"I have something to show you." I groaned as he tugged on my hand to force my protesting, still half asleep body upright. "I'm switching the light on," he said excitedly once I'd remembered how to sit up.

"No," I cried out in response, but I was too late. The bright light that may as well have been pure sunlight for all the mercy it showed to my retinas burned through the room instantly, revealing a Jake I'd never seen before. He wasn't just happy, he was positively bouncing, and it proved more than infectious.

From somewhere, I found the energy to drag myself out of bed and pull on some clothes on his orders while he waited awkwardly in the corner, bouncing on his heels and averting his eyes.

Fully clothed, I laughed when he grabbed my hand and bodily dragged me from the room, not even bothering to close the door quietly behind us. By the time it slammed closed, we were at the other end of the corridor.

The crisp night air cut into our skin the moment we broke through the threshold, but Jake went on, completely undeterred. I'd never seen him like this, so alive and animated. Something had lit a fire beneath him and nothing would stop him.

"Where are we going?" I called out through my laughter as he ran, pulling me along behind me. "And where's Deefer?"

"Relax, would you?" he threw back with a grin. "And be grateful you're not blindfolded."

"Touché."

"Deef is with Trix. He's fine. He understands."

It wasn't long before I found myself back where we'd started earlier that day. The lighthouse was lit up now, casting light and shadows over the grassy area. But I couldn't see the grass. It was scattered all over with small yellow scraps that took my breath away the moment my eyes adjusted and I worked out what they were.

"Sunflowers," I breathed, bending down into the stream of light from the tower and lifting one of the cardboard offerings into my hand. It was only small, just about filling the palm of my hand... and there must have been at least a hundred of them. "How did you...?"

Grinning, he plucked the flower from my hand and towed me to stand right in the centre of them. "You gave me so much today. I wanted you to have sunflowers. So many sunflowers. But after an hour of being laughed out of all the florists in Plymouth, I finally worked out that it's not exactly the right time of year for real ones." He shrugged, turning slowly on the spot with his arms outstretched. "So I improvised."

"You improvised," I repeated, staring at him in wonder. "You... made these?"

"Hey, let's face it. We always knew I belonged at the back of the class with the safety scissors and glue. This was just good practice for when we go back to college."

"You did this for me?" A lump the size of China had risen up in my throat, almost but not quite choking off my words as I gazed around at the sea of little sunflowers handmade just for me. "Jake, have you slept at all?"

"Nope." He beamed. "I had to do this while we were here."

"But..."

"Because the sea gives me courage," he went on, ignoring my protests. "*You* give me courage."

"Courage to do what?"

"To make the jump!" He was radiant, his wide grin infectious, and I found myself smiling widely right back at him as he bounced with a sort of nervous energy. "To tell you how I feel."

"And how is that?"

"Absolutely terrified," he said with a laugh. "But also exhilarated, excited, and hopeful for the first time in so long."

A bubble of laughter so strong it hurt my throat burst its way free of me as I looked down at our hands where he'd chosen to join them. "You're not making any sense."

"I've been hiding for so long, Tom. I was so afraid to be seen, to be noticed, sure that people would hate me the moment they realised whose son I was. But then you came along, and you didn't care about any of that. You're like this whirlwind of sunshine, barrelling through every one of my defences. My life was beige, and you made it brightest yellow with your dreadful jokes and your inability to accept anything less than everything. You forced me out of my hiding place and thrust me into light I didn't even know I wanted. It's terrifying, but I love it. I love you, and it's... Oh."

He froze, realisation of what he'd said written clearly across his features as he stared at me—not terrified like I expected, not regretful. There was only hope there as he levelled his eyes with mine and held them tightly, waiting for me to say something.

"You love me." I grinned, my eyebrows lifting with amusement at his flustered declaration.

"Yeah... You know, a bit."

"A bit? Hard for a guy to fight that kind of intensity," I teased.

He groaned, lifting his eyes to the sky where the first

faint strains of the colours of sunrise were starting to fight their way past the stars.

"You have no intentions of making this easy for me, do you?" he asked good naturedly.

"None whatsoever. But please, do go on. I've never had somebody love me a bit before."

"I mean, it's a big bit, you know. Like—"

"Jake?" I interrupted before he had the chance to tie himself in more knots with his words.

"Yeah?"

"It's a big bit for me, too."

"You..." His panicked expression melted into relief, and his lips lifted once again in that heart stopping, life altering smile that I vowed to myself in that moment to ensure I saw every single day from then on.

"I..." I laughed. "You know, if we keep on practicing, one day we might even work out how to speak in full sentences."

"I'd like that," he said hurriedly. "With you. I'd like all of it with you, everything."

"It won't be easy, you know? We're gonna come up against that stuff with Luke time and time again."

"If we're a *we*, it doesn't matter. None of that matters. Only you."

"Not even *a bit?*" Smiling slyly, I shot him a wink and squeezed his hands tightly in my own.

"Never going to let me forget that, are you?" he groaned.

"Maybe one day, when we're old and grey and surrounded by Deefer's grandpups."

"He's neutered," he said drily.

"You ruined it again." I tried to keep a straight face but failed at the miserable ecstacy on his.

"Make the jump with me, Tom. I'm terrified and clueless, and I have absolutely no idea what I'm doing, but—"

He drew beautiful dragons and I was good with numbers, but we were both dreadful with words. I'd had enough of them now, so I did the only thing I felt in my gut was right.

I didn't hear music, birds didn't take flight around us, and fireworks didn't explode in the heavens. But with my lips pressed tenderly against his, surrounded by the sunflowers he'd made for me, my hand cupping his cheek and his clutching my waist like a drowning man holding onto a lifebuoy, something inside of me shifted into place. A puzzle piece that had been missing for so long finally slotted home. We didn't need cannons or parades. We just needed each other.

I'd been chasing the sunrise for so long, searching for something that was missing, foolishly hoping to find it in the early morning light, when home had been sitting right behind me silently drawing dragons the whole time.

"A bit," I said softly when our lips finally parted, our foreheads joined and my nose nudging against his.

"A bit," he agreed, his arms encircling me as he drew me in tightly for another kiss.

The world wouldn't make life easy for us. That much we already knew. We'd already had a taste of what we were up against, but side by side and hand in hand, we would face every single challenge head on. I was his courage, he was my hope, and together, we could take on the entire world and win.

The sun rose slowly, as it always did, but today it was behind me. The only vision I needed was right in front of me, in my arms, right where he would stay.

The End

ACKNOWLEDGMENTS

This book has been a true labour of love. Tom became so special to me during the writing process of The Pebble Jar that when various people asked for his story, I didn't take much convincing at all. Cue: twelve months of agonising over his tale, complete with meltdowns and tantrums, because I wanted so badly to get his story right.

I can honestly say that without the support and input of the following people, this book would never have happened.

To my parents, Mama and Papa Ross, my twin pillars and the very best people I know. Thank you for everything—from keeping Luna occupied while I desperately scrambled to get this book finished in time, to Dad spending an entire day at the computer proof reading in order to get it done in less than twelve hours. Thank you for being there every single step of the way, cheering me on and keeping me afloat when I was determined to sink. For freely given dinners and even more freely given love, thank you. I love you both more than I have the words to tell you.

To Eleanor Lloyd-Jones, who sat with me in a pub in Nantwich one afternoon in summer and helped me to plot this story out. Who then proceeded to alpha read throughout the writing process and give me amazing feedback. Who held my hand and told me to snap out of it when I doubted. Who kept me on task when the deadline was looming and I was convinced I'd never be ready. Who designed a beautiful cover for this book, and then two months later, designed another one that we loved so much more. Who has been on her own writing deadline recently but still found the time to help me out with Chasing the Sunrise. Who not only prettified the outside of the book, but also helped me to dot the I's and cross the T's inside. What would I do without you?? Thank you, a million times over!

To Sarah, who has championed this book right from its inception and selflessly offered to alpha read for me in spite of her busy life. Thank you for holding this basket case's hands through this process and for sending me dog pics when I was freaking out. For sending me all your favourite quotes while I was sleeping so that I would wake up smiling and motivated to keep going the next morning.

To Suzie, who read Tom in a single evening then left me stewing all night waiting to hear what you thought! Thank you for being there through everything. For putting up with me sitting at my laptop on holiday, and for being the very first person to tell me that Tom needed his own story. Thank you for cake and laughter and a million goofy moments. Love you KBMIMAWBH!

To Katy, who has held my hand through the writing process, championed my words all over social media, made beautiful necklaces filled with pebbles, read when your health allowed and supported when it didn't. You've been one of the best things about 2018 in spite of the name-calling. Thank you for taking me into your heart, and your squad, and trying to make this past-it grandma cool again!

And finally, to everybody in the Hobbinson House, for your constant support, cheerleading, sharing of posts, for making me giggle constantly and for not judging my Harry Potter obsession, thank you! Thank you to KA Hobbs, my partner in Protectors of Light crime for not slapping me for hijacking the house for Chasing the Sunrise for the last few months. You are all remarkable people. Every single ounce of love you give has kept me going when I've wanted to stall.

ABOUT THE AUTHOR

H. A. Robinson is a jet-setting billionaire with a home on each continent, who spends her free time saving kittens from trees and babies from burning buildings. A graduate of Hogwarts and a frequent visitor to Narnia, she drinks coffee in Central Perk and tames dragons on Westeros.

In her dreams...

In reality, she's a support worker living in a small town in Cheshire, who would almost always choose fantasy over reality. She's been an obsessive reader from the moment she picked up her first Enid Blyton book, more years ago than she cares to admit, and enjoys nothing more than getting lost in new worlds and adventures from the minds of all the amazing authors out there.

She's had the voices of characters in her head for as long as she can remember, and puts them down on paper in order to convince herself and the men in white coats that she isn't crazy.

Printed in Poland
by Amazon Fulfillment
Poland Sp. z o.o., Wrocław